Pap nodded like he leaned his chair back o.. ... . and seemed to be taking stock of the night. After a long time he said, "What you boys got penned up out there is the Velvet brand. The reason they're runnin' wild and unclaimed is because Velvet left Texas some years ago."

"I don't recall ever hearin' about a rancher named Velvet," Wayne said. "Where'd he light out to? And why didn't he take his cattle?"

Pap let the night sky go for a while and looked at me and Wayne like he was considering something important. He rubbed his hand over his chin, but I was pretty sure he wasn't thinking about shaving cause he hardly ever did think about that. After what seemed a long time, he said, "Velvet was a beautiful young woman."

Something happened to his eyes, something that made them soft, the way my own eyes felt when I thought too much about Jessie and started missing her real bad.

"Don't that beat all?" Wayne said. "A woman rancher ain't a likely thing."

"Well," Pap said. "She didn't start out to be a rancher. It just kind of happened."

"I wish something like that would kind of happen to me," I said, but I doubt anyone heard me. Wayne was studying his Pap kind of close-like and Pap had that faraway look old men get when they start remembering down the years.

"Tell us about her, Pap," Wayne said. "I'm takin' it that you knew her."

"I knew her," Pap said. He studied the lit end of the cigarillo for a minute. "Yeah, I knew her."

Erv Bobo

The Velvet Brand

Echelon Press

Echelon Press Publishing
56 Sawyer Circle #354
Memphis, TN 38103
www.echelonpress.com

First Echelon Press paperback printing: April 2005

Cover Art © Nathalie Moore 2005 Arianna Award Winner
www.GraphicsMuse.com

Printed in Lavergne, TN, USA

Dedication

To Mike and Kelly
for the good times past and
for those ahead

Dear Readers,

We would like to invite you to join us in a time and place that offers action, adventure, and more laughs than should be legal. With the release of Erv Bobo's debut novel, *The Velvet Brand*, we step into a new era of the wild west.

Erv Bobo has a gift for humor and has made Roy Lee and Wayne irresistible in their characters. With an outstanding supporting cast, readers are sure to put this book on their keeper shelves and rush out to tell their friends.

And don't miss our other exciting western novels, *Redemption* by Morgan J. Blake and *Trails of the Dime Novel* by Terry Burns.

Echelon Press is always pleased to hear your thoughts and suggestions for how we can make our publishing house, your publishing house! Please send your comments to suggestions@echelonpress.com.

Happy Reading!

Karen L. Syed, President
Echelon Press

Prologue

Seven deadly men lined themselves out across the dusty street of Dodge City. Six of them wore black frock coats and the seventh wore a long tan saddle coat. All of them wore guns and all of them shared a single purpose: to shoot Wayne Denton.

Me and the Cheyenne Kid and Rambler were siding Wayne in the fight, though good sense told me we ought to be elsewhere, especially since Wayne was still up in the hotel with his woman. The Cheyenne Kid was about ten years old that summer and Rambler was a bull with only one horn.

The only edge we might have would be if the men facing us were drunk or hung over from the day before.

The man in the saddle coat was Shanghai Pierce and he was the one I couldn't figure out. I knew him for a cattleman, not a gunfighter, but he'd been drinking with the others when Wayne got us into this mess so I guess he was where he thought he should be.

Mysterious Dave Mather was another hard one to figure, but that was doubtless because he was mysterious.

The five others I knew had all been in gunfights, and since they were still alive it figured that they'd done well in them. They were Wild Bill Hickok, Wyatt and Virgil Earp, Doc Holliday, and Bat Masterson.

"Well, Kid," I said. "I guess it's just us against them."

The Kid looked up at me and grinned. "We go, Roy Lee."

We started slow toward the seven men and the only thought in my head was that it wasn't supposed to be like this.

Chapter One

The Roundup

Wayne and me had been friends for years and each of us had the scars to prove it. Of course, if he ever found out about me and Rose Reilly, my next set of scars was likely to be bullet holes.

Since we'd come back down the cattle trail last fall–dead broke as usual–it seemed the only thing he talked about was Rose. I couldn't let him do too much talking about her, for fear I'd slip and let him know I'd been with her the night before he met her. Besides, I was getting more than a little tired of it because I had woman troubles of my own. And though I didn't know it at the time, we were about to have a lot more.

The only way out of the troubles we knew about was to earn some money, and to do that we had to work the brush country from sunup to sundown to gather some cattle.

The way it was supposed to work out was this. Me and Wayne Denton was to spend the early part of spring popping the brush around Waco. The plan was that we'd get a herd of maverick cattle together and have them ready for when my Uncle Earl McAllister came up from San Antonio with his own herd. Uncle Earl would combine our cows with his and then take them on to Dodge City up in Kansas while me and Wayne just sat back and waited for Earl to come back down the trail with our share of the money.

It was a good-enough plan, but Wayne wasn't too patient

about it.

"You reckon your Uncle Earl would let me hire on?"

"I told you before, Wayne, you're just gonna have to wait and ask Uncle Earl."

I knew why he was fretting and I knew if he had ten dollars in his pocket he'd already be on his way to Kansas. The year before, when we'd made our first drive up the trail with John Winslow's herd, Wayne had met this girl in Abilene and he couldn't hardly stand to be away from her.

"Well, I got to get back up there this year, one way or the other," Wayne said. "Me and Rose made promises."

That's the way Wayne was, smart about a lot of things but ignorant about women. I knew Rose was a whore and I'd tried to drop a hint a time or two, but the hints just slid right by him. If I came right out and told him, his hat would hit the floor and he'd tear into me like a Texas cyclone. I didn't mind fighting with Wayne, for I'd whipped him as often as he whipped me, but I did like to have a better reason.

He never did say what kind of promises him and Rose had made, but I thought they must have been pretty powerful to still be calling to him over six hundred miles of rough country.

"Can we just not talk about Rose all day?" I knew she did more than cooking and cleaning at that sporting house, but last time I'd tried to talk to Wayne about it, he'd busted my lip.

"I guess you'd rather talk about that gap-toothed schoolteacher."

Talkin' wasn't what I wanted to do about her, but Wayne already knew that so I didn't tell him again. "That ain't so much a gap as it is an endearin' quality," I said. "Besides, you know as well as I do how she lost that tooth."

It happened at a church picnic when we were all twelve years old. I'd flung a cow chip at Jessie Meacham to show I cared about her and when she ducked out of the way, she mashed her face against an elderberry tree.

She came running after me and I let her catch me and knock me down. She sat on my chest, flailing at me with both open hands but not hitting me anywhere except on my arms, and me laughing at her until her Ma came and grabbed her by the arms and lifted her up.

"Now, chirren, you know this ain't seemly at a church social."

When her Ma led her away, Jessie had looked back over her shoulder and said, "I like you, too, Roy Lee."

Later on, we got older and got to where we was stealin' kisses now and then, but when her Pa found out about it he started telling her I'd never be anything but a worthless hardscrabble farmer and I had to admit he had the right of it. Which was why, a few years back, I'd talked Wayne into coming with me to be a cowboy.

I still had dreams about Jessie now and then, the good kind of dreams that made me wake up quivering, but at least they wasn't the kind of dreams I'd had about her when I was twelve. Then I'd wake up with my drawers damp and wonder what the hell had happened. Since then, I'd been up the trail a few times, spending my wages the way cowboys do, and now I knew what the hell happened.

"Reckon it's about quittin' time?" Wayne asked, looking at the sun.

"Yep."

On this particular day, we'd flushed about thirty head of cattle out of the brush and had them in what we called our holding pen. It wasn't much, just a long draw with high steep sides. We'd barricaded one end of the draw with about ten feet of brush and the other, the one we used for a gate, with about four feet of brush.

Thirty head was what we considered a fair day's work, so now we were just hoping to scare up a few more critters that would lend themselves to busting, which was the main game Wayne and me played when we was in camp. In busting, you ride up hard behind a cow and grab its tail. You can do it the easy way, which is to ride alongside the cow while holding the tail, which generally will cause him to swap ends. Or you can drag the tail up over his back and try to make the cow go ass-over-teakettle.

Wayne was riding ahead of me and I was swatting at the brush with my coiled lariat, when suddenly the brush seemed to explode and a big bull went running up alongside Wayne.

"Another one of them damned Upside-Down-A-Without-a-Crossbar brand," Wayne said.

"I'll bust him anyway." I hooked my lariat over the saddle horn and leaned way over to my right so I could grab the bull's tail when I went past.

Before I could spur my horse, Wayne yelled, "Wait! Don't do it!"

"Dammit, Wayne! What now?"

"You'd better quit cussin' and come look, Roy Lee. You ain't seen nothin' like this."

I straightened up and cantered up alongside Wayne, and be damned if he wasn't right. I hadn't ever seen anything like that old bull.

He had only one horn, though it was clear he'd once had another that had got broke off somehow. The one he did have only came out the side of his head for about six inches, then it kind of corkscrewed back in to the middle of his face, where it started straight again and kept going until it stuck out about three feet beyond the bull's snout.

"That ain't no horn," Wayne said. "That's a damned harpoon."

About that time, the bull looked back over his shoulder. Wayne danced his horse out of the way of that horn and was going for his six-gun when the bull bellered as loud as any I'd ever heard. That patch of brush came alive and in no time at all there was about twenty more mavericks out in the open and following that one-horned bull.

"Looks like he's got his own herd," I said.

"Reckon we can head 'em and get 'em over to the holding pen?" Wayne said.

"Reckon we can try." I rode up alongside the bull and then edged closer to him until he got the idea I wanted him to change direction, while Wayne rode on the other side to keep him from turning too far. The bull lined out in just the direction we wanted him to go and the rest of his herd followed behind.

"He's smart," Wayne said.

"Yep." I figured he was a trail bull, one that had a natural leaning for taking charge of a herd and making it to follow him.

"Uncle Earl would want this one for sure, wouldn't he?" Wayne said.

"If he ain't already got a good one like him."

I was watching the bull kind of close. With that horn running down the middle of his face he had a kind of cross-eyed look, but he wasn't bumping into trees or stepping into gopher holes the way my cousin Phil did, so I guessed it was all right.

"Reckon we could sell him to Earl for enough money to get me to Abilene?"

"Dammit, Wayne, wait and ask Uncle Earl." I had my doubts about it because cash money was still scarce in Texas, but I didn't say so to Wayne.

We were at the holding pen now. I lassoed the post at the end of the brush gate and backed my horse to pull it open. That bull led his herd inside just like he knew what we wanted him to do, and then I threw the rope to Wayne so he could pull the gate closed.

He hadn't no more than got the gate closed when that bull leaped over it and took off at a high trot into the brush. Now, I know a cow can leap a four-foot fence, but I also know they don't usually have the gumption to do it. I was kind of sorry to see that bull go, but it was too late in the day to go chasing after him so I decided to have some fun with Wayne instead.

"Well, Wayne, there goes your ticket to go see Rose," I said. "Fact is, he's headin' north. You might want to follow and see if Abilene is where he's goin'."

His ears got red and he snatched off his hat and threw it at the ground. "Dammit, Roy Lee! I told you I won't stand funnin' about Rose! You..."

I didn't hear the rest for I'd put the spurs to my horse and was racing back to our camp, trying to hold on and laugh at the same time. Wayne was gaining on me for he had the faster horse, but then he pulled up short and went back to get his hat.

By the time he did get back to camp, he was laughing as hard as I was, and after we'd both wiped down our horses and staked them in some grass he said, "You know, if we had that bull on a trail drive, he could take the place of three or four hands."

It ain't often Wayne is right about anything, but I thought that over and guessed it could be true. I'd heard stories about trail bulls so smart that their owners wouldn't take a hundred dollars cash money for them. "He probably could," I said, taking off my chaps. "Except that we ain't makin' no trail drive."

Now, I wanted to go up the trail again. It seemed those times on the trail and at the end of the trail were the best times I'd ever had, even the time me and Wayne had our gunfight. But I couldn't see any way we could take this herd up ourselves, even if we did manage to catch that one-horned bull again. We'd need money for a cook wagon and a remuda and food for half a dozen hands, and there probably wasn't more than five dollars between us.

So the way I saw it, I'd spend the year right here in Texas, riding by the schoolhouse now and then and hoping me and Jessie could have a few words or maybe something more. But at the same time I knew that wasn't ever going to happen and all I'd ever have of Jessie was my dreams about her. Being a cowboy was fun, but it wasn't making me any more money than farming would have done.

If Wayne got to go up the trail with Uncle Earl, my year was mostly going to be spent sitting on the porch with Wayne's Pap, drinking cheap whiskey and talking about the weather and waiting for some traveler to come by and tell us some news.

Our camp was near the Brazos River, under a big cottonwood tree, and even though there was no fire going we sat down where the morning fire had been and I leaned myself back against the tree, sliding my hat over my eyes to keep out the glare of the sun. We'd quit work early because our hearts weren't really in it, and unless one of us came up with some kind of devilment, it was going to be a long time until morning. I wondered if I'd have that dream about Jessie again.

"How many head you reckon we got in that draw, Roy Lee?"

"Six hundred and two, countin' today's take."

He picked up a blade of grass and started chewing on it.

"How many you figure got that brand?"

I didn't have to ask what brand he was talking about. There was only one that we'd found. Mavericks are unbranded cattle and Texas was full of them in those days, but we were having an awful run of bad luck in getting so many branded ones mixed in with our take. "About four hundred, I'd reckon."

"Reckon we ought to mark over those brands and let Uncle Earl take them along?"

"No, I don't reckon and you don't either. Not without knowing who they might belong to."

"Yeah, I know." He looked kind of mournful. "Reckon we'll have to start cuttin' 'em out in a day or two." He threw away the worn-out blade of grass and went to looking for a new one. "I was just thinkin' that if we did sell them, me and Rose might have enough money to set up housekeeping somewhere."

There she was again, but Wayne looked so mournful and hopeless that I didn't have the heart to talk sharp to him.

"That's what I figured you was figurin'." And right then I started thinking that I might not look so worthless to Jessie and her Pa if I had a pocket full of hard cash. I stood up and grabbed up my saddle. "Let's go see what your old man says about it. I bet he knows every brand that ever grazed this country."

We saddled up again and rode through the hot day to the Denton place.

Wayne and me had grown up together. Our folks was farmers, so we lived kind of close and if he wasn't over to my house then I was generally over to his. When my own kin died, I kind of moved in with Wayne and his Pap but I never was took for family by anybody.

Pap Denton and Wayne could have been cut from the

same chunk of wood. Both of them were handsome men with bright blue eyes, but Wayne's hair was still black and curly whereas Pap's had a lot of gray and was getting thin on top. Wayne stayed clean-shaved to impress any ladies he might happen on, but Pap was generally grizzled some. Pap had got a little stooped with age, too, so Wayne was the taller of them now, though he hadn't always been. And then Pap had that scar over one eye that he wouldn't talk about.

The reason I didn't fit in as family was 'cause my eyes were brown and my hair was kind of lion-colored and went off in a lot of directions. As far as tall was concerned, there was only half an inch of difference between me and Wayne and there'd been many a cut lip given and taken over exactly which one of us had that half inch. I figured it was enough that he was the oldest, so I had a talk about boot heels with the shoemaker in Waco. Wayne finally admitted he was shorter than me, though sometimes he still seemed puzzled about it.

By the time we got to the Denton place, it was early evening. When the sun went down, a breeze had come up and cooled the day. Pap was sitting out on the porch trying to roll a cigarette and swat flies at the same time, and I guess he'd been at it for a while because he had a lap full of tobacco.

"Has anybody here got a damned pipe?" he said. The cigarette paper was stuck to his lip so he wouldn't forget where it was and he was putting pinches of tobacco back into his sack.

I reached into my shirt pocket and gave him a cigarillo.

"Obliged," Pap said. He struck a match and lit the cigarillo, then swatted at a fly with the hand that held the match and I thought he was about to set hisself on fire. He took a couple of puffs and the flies left the county rather than buzz around in that foul smoke, and then Pap looked content. "What brings you boys back home? You got the law after you?"

Now, the law never had been after me and Wayne, though maybe sometimes they should have been, and Pap knew that. I guess asking that question every time we came home was his way of putting us at ease.

"They ain't after us yet," Wayne said, hitching his horse to the rail and stepping up on the porch. "But they might be if anyone takes a close look at the cattle we've rounded up."

Pap narrowed his eyes at us. "You're roundin' up something besides mavericks, then."

"We got some mavericks," Wayne said. "But we got a lot of old branded ones mixed in with 'em and we don't know who they might belong to."

"Old, huh?" Pap said. "What brand?"

"Upside-Down-A-Without-a-Crossbar."

Pap perked up and looked at me, his eyes kind of crinkling at the edges, and then he looked at Wayne and then back at me again. "Did you try to tell him, Roy Lee?"

I just kind of smiled. "Did you ever try to tell Wayne anything when his mind was made up?"

"All his damned life. Don't do a bit of good, does it?"

"What the hell are you two talking about?"

"Never has done me any good," I said, grinning. I thought Wayne's hat was going to hit the porch any minute now. "I expect it never will."

"No," Pap said. "It never done me any good, either. I guess I oughta be grateful his Ma ain't here to hear this."

"She was a fine woman and deserved a lot better," I said, taking off my hat and trying my best to sound reverent.

"I'm fixin' to whup somebody if I ain't told what's goin' on," Wayne said. His fingers were twitching and I knew his hat was as good as on the porch. I'd be on the porch next, because Wayne would never raise a hand against his Pa, no matter how much Pap might devil him.

"She was a fine woman," Pap said. He raised his voice. "I don't know how a woman of such fine stock ever whelped such a dumb pup as Wayne, here."

"Amen."

"By God, that tears it!" Wayne flung his hat down and came at me with fire in his eyes. I was backing away and laughing and Wayne was so mad he didn't see Pap stick his foot out. Wayne's feet got all tangled up with Pap's and he hit the porch with his face and then jumped up and noticed me and Pap was both laughing fit to kill.

Wayne looked surprised and then started in to laughing, and that's one thing I knew I could count on about him. He might get mad and fly into a rage, but he could also laugh at himself when he finally got the joke.

"All right," Wayne said. "If you two are through funnin' me, I guess I'm ready to hear why."

"Are we through funnin' him, Roy Lee?"

I scratched my head and tried to look serious. "Well, it's your house and we're your guests, so I reckon it's up to you to call the tune, Pap."

"What brand did you say that was, Wayne?"

Now Wayne began to get a hint about what was going on, for he looked at me and he looked at Pap and then he kind of put his head down and mumbled, "Upside-Down-A-Without-a-Crossbar."

Pap reached out and put his hand on Wayne's shoulder. "Wayne," he said, kindly, "that's a goddamn V." Then Pap looked at me. "Did you know that?"

"Well...I wasn't for sure, but I kind of guessed. Wayne's idea sounded real good, though."

Pap nodded like he'd got the answer he expected, then he

leaned his chair back on two legs and seemed to be taking stock of the night. After a long time he said, "What you boys got penned up out there is the Velvet brand. The reason they're runnin' wild and unclaimed is because Velvet left Texas some years ago."

"I don't recall ever hearin' about a rancher named Velvet," Wayne said. "Where'd he light out to? And why didn't he take his cattle?"

Pap let the night sky go for a while and looked at me and Wayne like he was considering something important. He rubbed his hand over his chin, but I was pretty sure he wasn't thinking about shaving cause he hardly ever did think about that. After what seemed a long time, he said, "Velvet was a beautiful young woman."

Something happened to his eyes, something that made them soft, the way my own eyes felt when I thought too much about Jessie and started missing her real bad.

"Don't that beat all?" Wayne said. "A woman rancher ain't a likely thing."

"Well," Pap said. "She didn't start out to be a rancher. It just kind of happened."

"I wish something like that would kind of happen to me," I said, but I doubt anyone heard me. Wayne was studying his Pap kind of close-like and Pap had that faraway look old men get when they start remembering down the years.

"Tell us about her, Pap," Wayne said. "I'm takin' it that you knew her."

"I knew her," Pap said. He studied the lit end of the cigarillo for a minute. "Yeah, I knew her."

"Well?" Wayne said. "What was she like, Pap?"

"I guess Velvet was just about the prettiest and finest woman I ever saw," Pap said. He was looking out at the night sky again like he could see her up there among the stars. "Golden hair, deep green eyes, a smile that made you know you was welcome, and a figure that didn't need no corsets or stays to make her look like a woman should."

"Damn, Pap," Wayne said, grinning and winking at me. "How come you to know all that much about her?"

"Huh? Oh. Ah...well, there was talk. You know how it is when men get together and get to talkin' about women." He kind of peered at Wayne. "You do know that, don't you?"

"Aww, Pap." Wayne shuffled his feet like he was looking for a cow chip to kick. "You know me and Roy Lee has been up the trail a few times."

"I know you been up the trail, but I don't know if you've seen the elephant."

"There was this one in Newton," I said, trying to be helpful. "Though she 'minded me more of a giraffe than..."

"We seen the elephant, Pap." The way Wayne said it was like he was going to say, "And now we're ready to take our licking."

"Well, good," Pap said. "That's a talk we won't have to have, then." He looked thoughtful and fretful for a minute and when he went on his voice kept starting and stopping. "Uh...You boys...you boys never hired out...Ah-hem...You all never hired out to herd any sheep, did you?"

"Why, hell no!" If Wayne had been wearing his hat, it would have hit the floor. "What do you take me for, Pap?"

"Good. That's another talk we won't have to have."

I wanted to get Pap to talking more about this Velvet woman, so I said, "If she's been gone for a time, that explains why those cattle are old and the brands most haired over."

"Yes," Pap said. "We branded 'em deep, not no road brands. I guess we thought she was here to stay."

"How'd you come to be brandin' her cattle, Pap? You never was a cowboy."

"Well...you know...I was just giving some of them other fellers a hand." He cleared his throat. "See, there wasn't much hard money in Texas in them days, so Velvet did a lot of her business in livestock. A man that wanted to visit with her would bring a calf or a pig or maybe a brace of chickens..."

"You mean she was a whore," Wayne said.

"She wasn't no whore!" Pap roared, his fists balling up just like Wayne's did when he was ready to tear into someone. Then he held up his hands and saw what had become of them and very slowly he relaxed until his fingers was splayed out straight. "Huh." He shook his head. "After all these years..."

I knew Wayne wasn't about to say anything, not after coming that close to a whaling, so I thought I'd take a chance. "Well, what kind of business was she in, Pap? I mean, men were giving her livestock for some reason or other. And from what we've rounded up so far, she had a hell of a lot of livestock."

"Well...she was an entertainer. Yes, by God, an entertainer. She could play the piano and sing like a bird, and her house had furniture a man could relax in and there was good whiskey for them that could afford it." His voice had gone soft while he was remembering. "She always wore pretty clothes and had her hair fixed nice. But most of all, she was fair. She wasn't sunburned and wind burned like other Texas women. Her skin was as soft..."

I could see her in my mind, looking just the way Pap told about her, moving slow and graceful.

"Pap..." Wayne kind of giggled.

"I said she was an entertainer, Wayne, and that's by God what I meant." His anger made him throw away the cigarillo and there was a shower of sparks where it lit in the dooryard. "I doubt there was more than three of us in the whole county ever made it into her bed."

Wayne nudged me and gave me a big wink.

Pap realized what he'd just said and studied on looking sheepish.

I gave him my biggest grin and said, "That kind of tears it, don't it, Pap?"

"Wayne, that was all long after your Ma died, you hear?"

"Sure, Pap. I ain't faultin' you. I know a man has got needs."

"Well...You keep your needs in your pants until after you're married to someone," Pap said.

"Uh, Pap...Me and Rose has already..."

"I don't believe I want to know what you and Rose have done or thought you did." Pap looked at me. "Did you ever meet this Rose girl he's forever talking about?"

"Well...I kind of did..."

"What's she really like?"

There it was. As Wayne's best friend, I could tell what I knew and save him from making a fool of himself, but as soon as I told how I knew, I'd probably be a dead man.

"Roy Lee thinks she's a whore," Wayne said, grinning big. "But that's just because she worked as a maid in a sportin' house. Wore one of them little maid outfits with short skirt and long black stockings, and..."

She'd worn that outfit the night Wayne met her, but the night before she'd been dressed like someone called Marie Antoinette and I'd spent the night with her, sneezing my way into a new kind of pleasure every time I got a big whiff of her powdered wig.

"Well, anyway," I said quickly, "Gettin' back to the main

question, what should we do about all those cattle with the Velvet brand?"

"They don't belong to you, do they?" Pap said.

"No, sir."

"Then who do they belong to?"

"Well...this Velvet woman, if she's still alive, but..."

Pap slapped his hand on his knee. "By God, boy, you got it right the first time. They're her cattle, so we'll take 'em to her."

"Pap," Wayne said, "What the hell are you talkin' about?"

"I mean we'll drive the cattle to Dodge City, or wherever they're goin' this year, and after we sell them we'll find Velvet and give her her part of the money."

I thought finding Velvet after all those years might be a taller order than he was thinking, but there was another problem on my mind. "Listen, my Uncle Earl is expectin' to pick up those cattle from us and..."

"Oh, to hell with your Uncle Earl. We're gonna do it my way. Should have thought of it years ago." Pap peered up at me. "Your Uncle Earl was a Yankee anyway, wasn't he?"

It was something no one in my family ever liked to admit, but I nodded my head.

"All right, then. You boys can spend the night here, but at first light, you get on back to camp and round up some more cattle. I'll find us a cook and a chuck wagon and throw together some kind of remuda."

"You're goin' with us, Pap?" Wayne asked.

"Hell, yes. I got nothin' to stay around here for and I always thought I might like to go see the elephant myself." He peered at Wayne. "Besides, you might need someone to read any brands you see along the way."

Well, I knew Wayne was excited about going up the trail,

excited about getting to see Rose again. Truth to tell, I was some excited myself, though I didn't know why until next morning. That's because my dreams about Velvet started that very night.

I'd seen the house many a time, going in to Waco and coming back from there, but I'd never paid it much mind. It sat out in the middle of nowhere, like most houses in Texas, with empty windows turning blue from the sun. The reason I didn't pay it any mind was because there were a lot of such places around us. Texas was a poor state in them days and there was always people going away and leaving behind what they couldn't put in a wagon or tie on a horse.

But I'd never seen the house like it was now, all lit up and gay with piano music coming out of the open windows where lace curtains blew in the spring breeze. And I'd never stepped on the porch before or knocked on the fresh-painted door with the big brass knocker.

The door opened and a young darky woman bid me come in, taking my hat and brushing at my shirt with a little whiskbroom. "You go on in the parlor, Mr. McAllister. Miss Velvet been waitin' on you."

I don't know how the parlor got to be bigger than the whole house, but it did. There were half a dozen easy chairs with footstools, and a sofa too, and they were all stuffed and covered with fancy cloth instead of horsehide. There must have been a dozen coal oil lamps in the room, and over at the upright piano sat Velvet.

She turned when I entered and smiled that smile at me. Her blonde hair was falling soft and loose about her shoulders and she was wearing some kind of white gown that seemed like it must have been made out of clouds. "Have a seat, Roy Lee." There was a kind of faint whistle in her words, kind of like the way Jessie sounded when she said a word that started with S. "Rest yourself a bit. Amanda, bring Mr. McAllister a bit of bourbon and branch water. You know how he takes it."

The maid was putting the drink in my hand as soon as Velvet said the word, and as I took a sip of it Velvet grinned and I could see she had one tooth missing near the front. Then I blinked my eyes and looked again and she had all her teeth just like she was supposed to have.

"You can leave us now, Amanda," Velvet said. That whistle was gone from her words.

Amanda backed out of the parlor and closed the big double doors, and now me and Velvet was all alone and it started to feel like it was summertime instead of spring.

"Aren't you kind of warm, Roy Lee?" Velvet asked. She stood up from the piano and came toward me, her white gown flowing out behind her in back and molding itself to the curves of her body in front. "Wouldn't you like to get out of some of those old range clothes?"

I kind of cleared my throat and tried to talk, for she was close enough now that I realized I could see right through that white gown and the only thing under it was her, but the frog was still there so I cleared my throat again.

"Yes, I thought so." Her voice was as soft and warm as the breeze that played at the lace curtains. "Why don't you stand up for a minute and let me help you?"

I was looking for a place to set my drink and then there was a table where there hadn't been one before, so I set it down and stood and Velvet reached her hands to my neckerchief. Then she stood back just a bit, her head cocked to one side and a fingernail painted bright red touching her soft lips.

"No. Let's leave the kerchief on this time." She chuckled way back in her throat. "I want to remember I'm with a real *cowboy and not some farmer."*

"I'm a cowboy, all right," I said.

"Oh, Roy Lee, I know you are." She giggled. "And I know you're a hard rider, too. Why, after last time I was so sore...Now look at you! You're all blushin', Roy Lee. I think that's so sweet in a man."

She leaned closer and kissed me and I felt her tongue try to slip between my lips and I kind of sputtered.

"Why, Roy Lee, don't you like to kiss the French way?" She kind of pouted for a minute and then she put her lips up next to my ear and whispered soft, "There's other French things I can do for you, too, Roy Lee." Her tongue touched my ear and I felt the tingle all the way down to my boots.

Somehow, while she was talking, she had got rid of my vest and shirt and boots and gun belt. Now her fingers were working at my other belt but then she stopped and looked right into my eyes. "I bet you got something for me, don't you, Roy Lee?"

"Yes, ma'am, I surely do."

"Let's just see about that." Now her voice was as husky as mine and she took one hand from my belt and slid it down the front of my jeans. When she got to where she was going she gave me a gentle squeeze. "Ummm. You do have something for me. Something I just know I'm going to like."

Velvet knelt before me, opening the fly of my jeans and sliding them down around my knees. My eyes were squinched tight shut while I tried to keep control, trying not to imagine what was about to happen.

"Roy Lee...?"

"Hmm?"

"Did you bring me a pig?"

"Damn, I forgot the pig!"

"I don't care whether you remember pigs or not," Pap said. "Get outa that bed. It's damned near daybreak and we got work to do."

Chapter Two

The Velvet Brand

I wasn't worth a whole lot to myself or anybody else that day. It got to where I didn't even have to close my eyes to see golden hair gleaming in the lamplight and the way Velvet's body had looked beneath that white gown.

Wayne and me rode back toward our camp, popping the brush on the way, and we had about twenty more head of cattle by the time we got to our holding pen.

"Well, will you look at that!" Wayne said.

I kind of raised my head and thumbed my hat back, but I didn't see anything.

"Dammit, Roy Lee, turn your fool head. What's got into you today?"

"Dreamin', I guess." I looked to where he was pointing and there was that one-horned bull standing in front of our gate while another thirty or so cattle milled around behind him.

"If I didn't know better, I'd say he's joined our crew," Wayne said.

"Maybe he has." This was something I could take an interest in. "Let's get these cattle behind the gate and see what he does."

As soon as the cattle were penned and the gate closed, that bull took off just like he had the day before, stepping high and proud like he knew what a good thing he'd done and was off to do it again.

The day was young and before it was over that bull had made three more trips into the brush. Each time, he came back with ten or twenty head of cattle and stood waiting at the gate until we came and locked them in.

Toward evening, Pap came out to camp. He was driving six horses before him, and trailing along in the dust they raised was a chuck wagon. I right off recognized the man driving the wagon. It was Harvey Nodder, a man just a bit younger than Pap who was said to be simple and said to be of a temper, but also said to be a good cook.

I'd never seen him in a temper, but I had a taste of his cooking one time at a church social. He'd brought along a rabbit stew and it was good eating until the lady sitting next to me spit out a mouthful of fur, so I guess we'd had a taste of simple, too.

"Don't be looking at me that way," Pap said. "'Less you want to be the one to put together a drive with no cash money." He smoothed out some dirt and took a seat at our campfire.

"I didn't say anything," Wayne said, grinning. He thumbed back his hat to show that curly hair. "I can see how you got Harvey and his wagon with jawbone. He ain't worth a lot more. But how'd you talk someone out of six horses?"

"In the mornin', you take a good look at them horses and you'll know. Don't be ridin' 'em too hard." He gave both of us a hard look, like he was expecting a challenge.

"Just tell Harvey he's got to skin everything before he puts it in the pot," I said. I looked around to see if Harvey had heard me, but then I heard him snoring. I didn't know whether he'd ever been up the trail before, but he surely knew it was a cook's right to sleep under the cook wagon. It was a handy place to be in case of rain or a hailstorm.

"Pap, I'm having doubts about this. It's shapin' up to be a

mighty ragtag drive and we haven't even hired any hands yet. And what makes you so all-fired sure we can even find this Velvet woman?"

All Wayne had to do was say her name, and instead of staring into our campfire I was back in that big parlor I'd dreamed about, thinking about her golden hair, thinking about the way her breasts pushed out against the front of that gown and how rosy her nipples were.

"What's wrong with Roy Lee, there?"

"Damned if I know, Pap. I been havin' trouble with him all day."

"Is there any loco weed hereabouts?"

"I don't know of any and Roy Lee don't graze much anyway." The voices seemed far away, but I could tell Wayne sounded disgusted.

"Don't get touchy. I was just askin'."

I kind of came back to myself, knowing they'd been speculating about me, so rather than tell them what was the matter, I just muttered something about working too hard that day.

"Hell's fire," Wayne said. "That one-horned bull did all the work. All you did was open the gate for him."

Pap perked right up. "A one-horned bull? With the horn sticking straight out over his nose?" He slapped his knee. "Old Rambler?"

"He didn't say his name," Wayne said, still disgusted. "Dammit, Roy Lee, are you here or are you somewhere else?"

"I'm here. You know about that bull, Pap?"

"Well, I'm surprised he's still alive. He's the best trail bull I ever heard about and if we got him we don't need any more hands."

"He does seem to have thrown in with us," I said.

"That's that, then," Pap said, slapping his knee again. "Them cattle with the Velvet brand are bound to be too old to be frisky, and we got Rambler to watch over 'em. We got ever'thing we need to hit the trail."

"Don't get goin' too fast, Pap," Wayne said. "High spirits or not, you still ain't said how we're goin' to find that Velvet woman."

I was ready for her name to be said that time, so I was able to keep my mind on the conversation.

"Why, that's simple, Wayne. She left Texas to go where there was hard money, and if the railroad is at Dodge, then that's where Velvet and the hard money will be."

Wayne was shaking his head. "No, Pap, it ain't that simple. In fact, that sounds pretty thin. What do you think, Roy Lee?"

"I got to agree with Wayne," I said.

Wayne looked surprised. He wasn't used to me agreeing with him.

Pap kind of squirmed himself around, looking uncomfortable. "Well, boys, I guess I'll out with it. Me and Velvet has kept in touch from time to time, sending word by travelers, mostly. I know for a fact she's planning to be in Dodge when the herds come up the trail this summer. In fact, she's already there and has got herself a house."

Wayne stared at his dad, his mouth open a bit and then he threw back his head and laughed long and loud. When he was just about done with laughing, he pointed at Pap and said, "What do you think, Roy Lee? Ain't he just full of secrets lately?"

"And all of 'em having to do with that Velvet woman, seems like." I found I was more than a mite jealous about that.

"Well, come on, Pap. Tell us some more secrets."

"I ain't sayin' a damned thing more to either of you two pups!"

"Aw, come on, Pap." Wayne nudged his dad. "Tell you what. You tell us another secret about Velvet and I'll get Roy Lee to tell you about the time me and him had a gunfight."

"You boys was never in no gunfight."

"Yes, we were." Wayne was looking smug and I figured he could tell the story his own damned self. "And we were fighting against each other."

Pap looked hard at Wayne and then hard at me, but with an eyebrow raised. I nodded.

"Well, it's a deal, then," Pap said. "Go on and tell it, Roy Lee."

"Go on, Roy Lee. Pap won't go back on his word."

I told it, but only because I wanted Pap to tell me more about Velvet.

Wayne and me had been fighting one another since we were seven or eight years old–fists, feet, and sometimes even chunking rocks or cow chips at one another. Maybe we'd have got to guns sooner, but it wasn't until we went up the trail to Abilene that we even had guns. We bought our first pistols when we signed on to drive cattle for John Winslow.

We'd spent the last bit of our money on them but didn't regret it at all. Fact is, we felt pretty good about it and maybe even strutted a bit when we reported to where Mr. Winslow had the herd bunched just outside of Waco.

"The first thing you two do," Mr. Winslow said, "is to take off them brand-new popguns, wrap 'em in oil cloth, and put 'em in the cook wagon. I got my last dollar tied up in these cows and I don't aim to have any of 'em shot should one of you fall off his horse."

"What if there's trouble on the trail?" I said.

"Roy Lee, if there's trouble of any kind then I'll just send for my grandmother and have her whup whoever's causing it." Mr. Winslow turned away, his hand to his mouth and his shoulders shaking, and I guessed he felt out of sorts. We put our guns in the cook wagon, but not because we wanted to. We did it because this was our first chance to be real cowboys and my first chance at making enough money to impress Jessie's Pa.

There wasn't any trouble on the trail, not the kind that could be handled with guns, though Wayne and me kept hoping we'd run into some Indians or some border roughnecks. We made the drive up to Abilene just itching for a chance to put our pistols to use, but we never saw them again until the day we got paid off and Mr. Winslow gave them back to us.

"You boys did good," Mr. Winslow told us. "I'm heading back down the trail tomorrow and if you want to go along I'd admire to have your company."

Wayne and me looked at one another and scuffed our toes in the dirt some, and as polite as can be we turned him down. Fact is, we'd done a lot of talking and planning on the trail and had about decided we wanted to be gunfighters.

So, naturally the first thing we did was to buy us a bunch of cartridges and ride far enough away from town that we could shoot them off without troubling the local marshal.

Wayne was faster on the draw than me, but I hit my mark more often. I figured that made us a pretty good pair for a gunfight, as Wayne could get the drop on them while I took my time about shooting their ears off.

We shot up every cartridge we had, and then Wayne started to practice fancy spins and border shifts and such while I just worked at getting my gun out of my holster a shade faster. I was making some progress, but not much, and by the time we quit Wayne was only dropping his gun one spin out of three.

"Be too dark to see pretty soon," Wayne said. "Reckon what we ought to do now?"

I was surprised he asked me. Being six months older, he usually tried to tell me what to do and that was what started most of our fights. I took a minute to think about it and then said, "We'd better save what money we got left. It could be a while before we get paid to shoot somebody."

"Roy Lee, you are a caution. You really figure we ought to be gunfighters?"

I did have my doubts about it. Fact is, I was pretty sure the original idea had come from Wayne. For my part, I had always been too big for my age and had spent the best part of my life just trying not to hurt people. But I wasn't about to admit my doubts and give Wayne a chance to say I'd backed off.

"What I figure is there's easier ways to live than farmin' or drivin' cattle up the trail."

"That's so," Wayne said. "We'll never make a stake doin' that." He gave his gun a fancy twirl, picked it up and twirled it again. "How do you figure gunfighters get a start?"

It was in my mind to say they just found somebody who needed shooting and somebody else to pay for having him shot, but I knew Wayne wasn't in no mood for funning. "I figure there's range wars and water wars and such, now and then. All we got to do is pick the side that's in the right and go to work for them." I was kind of simple in those days. I figured right was right and wrong was wrong and everybody knew which was what. "But what I think we ought to do right now is go back to town and have some supper, then have a drink or two just so we can say we did the town."

"That ain't much of a start for a couple of Texas hellbenders," Wayne grinned.

"No, it ain't." I hefted my gun, and then put it in my holster. "But right now, I don't think we're in any shape to tree the town."

"That's so."

And that's how we come to be in the Drover's Bar in Abilene the night they shot the piano player.

He wasn't such a good piano player, for he watched the door more than he did the keyboard, but Wayne and me didn't mind about that. Fact is, we felt too good to let anything bother us.

We'd done men's jobs getting that herd up to the railhead. Our bellies were full of food and getting full of beer, the smell of black powder smoke still hung around us, and our pistols—mine at least—was a heavy and comfortable weight against my leg. I fingered at it now and then and scratched my fingernails against the leather of my holster, trying to take some of the new shine off it. That's why I happened to have my hand on my gun when the door flew open and a man with a pistol in his hand stomped in.

He was about the biggest and ugliest man I'd ever seen and the little ratty man with him wasn't any prettier. The big man had a red beard and was wearing clothes that looked and smelled like he'd wallered with buffalo. He held the pistol out at arm's length and he yelled, "Stand up, Jack Fletcher, and take it like a man."

The music stopped and the piano player stood up and faced the door. Lord, I admired the look of that man. He had a little gambler's mustache with half a smile twitching beneath it, wavy black hair, and black eyes. He was dressed all in black, too, save for a white shirt that was stiff with starch. But it wasn't so much the dark good looks I admired, for I'm proud enough of my own lion-colored hair. What I admired was the way he stood full square to the big ugly man, his arms folded across his chest, and said, "Do your best, Moss."

The red-bearded man pulled the trigger, the room filled with black powder smoke, one of the fancy women screamed, and the piano player fell to the floor. My ears were ringing and I saw the look of surprise on the big man's face and then I turned and saw what he was surprised about. The man in black was pulling himself to his feet, his right hand gripping the piano, his left arm hanging at his side with blood dripping from his fingers.

"Damned thing ain't no show for accurate," Moss said, holding the pistol with both hands while he tried to get the hammer cocked back for another shot.

"You never was much show for accurate either, Moss," the ratty man said.

"Don't devil me, now!"

"Well, you did do better than last time," the ratty fellow said. "You want me to shoot him, Moss?"

"No!" Moss roared. "Now be quiet while I aim this damned thing."

Fletcher had got to his feet and made himself stand steady again, and now he said, "Before you shoot again, I want to make it clear that no harm has come to your daughter, Moss."

"By God, she's harmed just bein' with you, you four-flushing gambler. You've ruined my little girl." He had the revolver cocked and was taking careful aim. "No one bothers my kin."

Fletcher stood still, not trying to move or hide. I didn't know whether I was looking at a brave man or a simple one, but right then I knew I wasn't going to allow Moss another shot at a man who wouldn't defend himself.

My hand was still on the butt of my gun, where it had been most of the day. I surprised myself with how quickly I whipped it out of my holster. One step took me to Moss and I swung that heavy gun right at the center of his dirty face.

He went down to his knees, looking cross-eyed, tottered back and forth for a moment, then hit the floor with his face.

"Hold it right there, partner," Wayne yelled. I turned to see that he had his own gun out and was covering Moss' friend. The little ratty man slid his pistol into his holster, tried to smile, and then tried to find something else to do with his hands. He finally settled for shoving one hand into his coat pocket and wiping his upper lip with the other.

The barroom was awful quiet, with a lot of people looking at me, and I was having my own troubles in thinking about what to do next. I kind of tossed my gun in my hand, wishing now that I'd practiced some of those fancy spins with Wayne, then I took a long look at my gun, thought of what I'd done, and decided I was in enough trouble without dropping my gun on the floor. Real easy, I slid it back into my holster and rubbed my hands together to hide the trembling, some surprised to find they were slick with sweat.

"Roy Lee, what in hell did you think you were doing?"

I got surprised again. There was fire in Wayne's eyes, the kind of blue fire I always saw in them just before one of us whupped the other, and I wasn't ready for that. I was so nervous thinking of what had just happened and what could have happened, that all I could say was, "Huh?"

He shook his gun under my nose. "You know what you damned near got us into?"

"Don't yell," I whispered. "I know."

"Then what the hell did you do it for?"

"Why, I was keeping that smelly old man from killing the piano player."

"You don't like music that much."

My head was starting to feel like it was stuffed with cobwebs that were keeping me from hearing Wayne right. "Dammit, Wayne, you backed my play."

I felt good about saying that. It sounded like real gunfighter talk.

"Because I figured you didn't know what you was doing but would likely come to yourself."

"Now, by God, Wayne! That man was standing up there waiting to be shot and this old geezer would have done it. Hell, you saw the same thing I did."

Wayne pinched his mouth up and shook his head, the way he always did when he was about to call me seven kinds of a fool. "Yeah, I saw it. That's why I can't figure out what the hell you thought you were doing. If you was going to side somebody, you should have sided old Moss, there." He jerked his thumb toward Fletcher, who was coming toward us. "The piano player's the one did the old man's daughter wrong."

"But he said she was all right."

"You tarnal fool!" Wayne snatched his hat off his head and threw it at the floor and I knew we were going to fight for sure. "Naturally he'd lie about it! He don't want to get shot any more than he has to! He ain't worth siding, but old Moss here has a right to protect his daughter."

Now Wayne was making me mad and, just for spite, I kicked his damned hat across the room. "No one's got a right to shoot an unarmed man," I yelled. "Not when I'm here to do somethin' about it."

We were moving at one another, fists balled and ready to fly into a knockdown, drag-out fight when I felt a hand pull at my shoulder.

"I'm sorry to be the cause...of trouble between friends," Jack Fletcher said. His face was pale and he looked like he was about to pass out. "But I do thank you, Cowboy. Now you'd...best get out of here before Moss comes to himself."

"He don't scare me none," I said, patting the butt of my gun. Then I caught Wayne's disgusted look, but I knew I couldn't back down from what I'd said. "I reckon I can handle him again."

Fletcher shook his head. "Son, Moss is a buffalo skinner and he's lived out on the prairie so long he doesn't think like we do. If he'd seen you coming, he'd have whipped out his knife and cut off your ears before you ever cleared leather. And he could do it...even if you had a fast draw, which you sure as hell don't have."

Up to then, I'd been pretty proud of the way I'd shucked my gun when I pistol-whipped Moss, and Fletcher's criticism didn't go down easy. Still, I hadn't yet been tested in drawing against a man who was drawing against me, so I let it go by but not without giving him a look down my nose.

"Moss is a vengeful man," Fletcher said. "You and your friend had best go while you can."

"We ain't goin' nowhere together," Wayne said.

"Now, just what the hell do you mean by that, Wayne?"

"I mean that poor old man needs someone to pick him up and take care of him." He motioned the little ratty man over. "I figure it's up to me to do it."

"Don't take his side, son," Fletcher said. "He'll be back looking to kill your friend when he gets conscious."

Wayne gave me a long, hard look, his mouth kind of twisted, and then he looked back at Fletcher. "Mister, I don't have any friends in Abilene."

"Now listen, Wayne..." I started to say.

"You'd better...better...help me to a chair," Fletcher said. He was holding himself up on the bar, looking pale and weak. I grabbed hold of him and staggered him back into a chair, then went to get him some brandy.

When I got back with his drink, Wayne and the ratty man had picked up Moss and were carrying him out the door.

"Now listen, Fletcher..." But Fletcher wasn't listening to me either. His eyes rolled back into his head and he passed out cold.

"Anyone know where I can get help for this man?" I said. No one answered. The whole room had been watching Wayne and me, but now they all took a sudden interest in studying their drinks and cards and the fancy women. "Has he got a home anywhere?"

Still no one answered, and I started to get mad. I had to get Fletcher to a safe place before Moss came back and finished killing him and then killing me. So, I grabbed the nearest man by the collar of his shirt, lifted him half out of his chair, and shoved my face close to his. "Now, I figure you can give me an answer or point to someone who can."

"Cowboy, was I you I'd let Fletcher take care of hisself. He's plenty able to handle a gun and he didn't need you to get into his troubles."

"Too late for that," I said, putting him down. "You know where he stays?"

"If you was to go down to the end of this street and turn left, you might find a shack with a light in the window. If you took him with you, you might find he knows the place and the girl who lives there knows him."

I thanked the man for being straight with me, then picked Fletcher up and draped him over my shoulder, using his shiny black boots to bump open the door.

Outside, the air was still rank from the cattle we'd driven through the streets that morning and people were being careful of where they stepped. I found the shack and it was mean looking and poor but for the lamp in the window and the pretty red-haired girl who opened the door to my knock.

She must have recognized the soles of Fletcher's boots, for she cried out and reached for him. I shook my head at her and pushed inside, going into a room as pretty as a picture and as neat as a pin. I figured she couldn't do much about the outside of the shack, but she had made the inside real homey. I laid Fletcher on the brass bed and then stepped back to let her get at him.

"Who did this to him?" she said.

"A man named Moss."

"Daddy? You must be joking, Cowboy. My daddy never in his life hit anything he shot at." She was taking off Fletcher's boots, though why she started there I didn't know, since it was his arm needed tending. Maybe she wanted to keep him at home and figured that without boots he wouldn't take a chance at going out among the cow flops.

"Well, the wind must have been just about right," I said. "For he sure as hell shot your fancy man."

"Oh, pooh! He ain't my fancy man. Me and him's married."

I was some surprised by that. I said, "You'd best be telling your daddy then, cause he don't know it and like to killed Jack over it."

"I won't tell him nothing! I can be just as stubborn as him. Didn't Jack tell you Daddy just wants to keep me out on the prairie so I can cook for him and his crew? Didn't he tell you...?"

"Ma'am, he didn't tell me much of anything and I don't think I want to know any more." I was figuring her for empty-headed and I thought that if I let her get too much of a start on rattling her tongue she might never stop.

She went back to work on Fletcher while I held the lamp close, finally getting to his arm and cleaning and bandaging the gouge the bullet had made. "You see? Daddy did almost miss him again."

Jack came to himself and told her all that had happened and my part in it, and told her it was thanks to me he wasn't bleeding to death back in that saloon.

"You wouldn't have died from that little scrape, honey," she said kindly. "It was just the sight of blood that made you weak. Why, if you'd ever seen Daddy skin out a buffalo..."

"Ma'am!" She wasn't looking at Fletcher but I was and he looked about to pass out again.

"Oh! Goodness!" She put a damp cloth on his forehead. "Cowboy, we're grateful to you but you'd best get out of town while you still got a chance. My daddy will be looking for you and while he ain't much of a hand with a pistol, he can get you with a skinning knife quicker than you can say scat."

Well, I couldn't leave, not since Wayne had taken sides against me. Doing that would be the same as letting him call me wrong and I'd never yet let Wayne get away with doing that. I didn't tell any of this to the girl, but I did say, "He'll be coming for Jack, too, and I guess Jack ain't no hand for a fight."

"Jack? Oh, pooh! Why, Jack used to be the best gunfighter in these parts until Hickok came to marshal the town. He could shoot off Daddy's ears left-handed if he wanted to."

I was fuddled again, but not so much that I couldn't talk. "Then why the hell didn't he do it?"

"I can't shoot my own father-in-law," Fletcher said.

"He shot you!"

"That's his look-out, not mine."

"But you're the one with the hole in you."

"That's true." He looked kind of thoughtful. "He is getting better at it, so likely I'll have another one or two before he's through with me." He didn't say it at all like he was scared, just like it was something that was bound to happen.

"He won't shoot back because I won't let him," the red-haired girl said. "Besides, up to now Daddy never even came close."

Those cobwebs were filling up my head again. "Did you ever think to just tell him you're married?"

"No, and he never thought to ask us if we were. So there!" I think if her daddy had been there, she'd have stuck out her tongue at him.

Heading for the door, I said, "Well, you two do what you want to about your part of the fight. But if that ugly old man comes looking for me, I'm going to be where he can find me."

"What about your friend?" Fletcher said.

"I guess he'll find me, too."

"I'd better tag along with him, Mary." Fletcher sat up in bed. "He's bound to get himself killed. I never saw a more clumsy draw in my life."

She chewed on her lip for a minute, and then nodded. "You take your gun, Jack."

I thought that was more like it. Maybe I was heading into a fight I couldn't win alone, but now I had the second-best gunfighter in Abilene to side me. I felt pretty good about everything until Fletcher opened his mouth again.

"I don't need my gun, honey. Moss is bound to get tired of shooting at me sooner or later." He kissed the tip of her pretty nose. "Besides, it was my gunfighting and gambling made him dislike me in the first place and I've got to convince him I gave it up. If I was to shoot him, he'd know for sure I'd gone back to it."

"Don't you come home dead, then."

That was too many for me, so I got myself out of there and headed for the saloon. Fletcher followed but we didn't talk–me because my head was still spinning from the last talking we'd done, him because he was in his sock feet and was kept busy cussing the cows we'd driven through town.

I hadn't hardly had time to take a drink of my beer before Moss came into the saloon wearing a bandage across his nose. Wayne and the little ratty man flanked him, all three of them with their pistols in their hands and all three of them looking mean as hell.

There wasn't a thing I could do but push myself away from the bar and stand facing them. Then I took a couple of steps sideways to put more room between me and Fletcher. He was a gunfighter and he was siding me, but he didn't have a gun and he did have a way of drawing fire from Moss.

We all stood there for a long minute with the saloon so quiet I could hear beer dripping from the tap in the keg. I licked at my lip and wondered if everybody had mouths as dry as mine. Then it came to me that, before they cut me down, I had at least one chance to make some sense out of this whole business.

"Mary sends her love," I told Moss. "She wanted you to come to the wedding, but couldn't get word to you."

"What?" Moss reared to his full height, looking like a big red bear. He swung on Fletcher. "Is that true?"

Fletcher nodded. "We got married about a month ago."

"No, by God!" Moss roared. "She wouldn't do it unless

you put up your guns and quit gambling."

"Dammit, Moss, you been trying to shoot me off that piano stool for three weeks, now. What the hell did you think I was doing there?"

Moss' shoulders began to shake and I didn't know whether he was choking or laughing. Then he pointed to Fletcher's socks. "I thought it was some of the same bullshit you been walking in."

There was another long minute of silence while Moss worked his face through a whole range of expressions, all of them ugly, then he said, "Well, I can't be shootin' kinfolk and you can't play the piano with a busted wing, so you'd best be getting home to my little girl."

"Why don't you come with me, Moss? I know Mary would admire to see you."

Moss scratched at his head. "I reckon I could do that."

"Good," Fletcher said. "First, though, let's stay a bit and see how this plays out

I finally let out the breath I'd been holdin'. I'd gambled everything on telling Moss they were married, but damned if it hadn't worked out.

"Well, it ain't our fight no more," Moss said. "So let's get out of the line of fire. Ain't no sense makin' Mary a widow and a orphan." Over his shoulder he said, "Rat, you come with us. It ain't your fight either."

"Damn, Moss! You said I could help shoot Fletcher."

"Well? There he is, damn you. Go ahead and shoot him. But you mind that he's kin to me now and I'm a vengeful man."

"Oh, never mind."

My mouth kind of hung open while the three of them moved aside and took seats at a table. Now it was just Wayne and me out there in the middle of the floor, with all our grudges to settle and only one way to settle them. I was keeping my eye on Wayne and, to his credit, he was looking about as bothered by the whole business as I was.

Truth is, I'd started feeling bad about the whole thing. I'd known from the time I hit Moss that I was borrowing trouble for us, but I never figured we'd end up owning the whole thing. Yet I knew Wayne and I knew myself, and now I knew there was no good way for either of us to back down.

So, we stood there for what seemed a long time. Wayne had slipped his gun back into his holster, giving me the fairest chance he could, but I was thinking he was much faster than me and that my better aim wouldn't count for much if I was the first to be hit.

"Draw, dammit!" Moss bellowed.

Wayne's eyes met mine and I saw his smile as he went for his gun, his hand moving slow.

Wayne missed me, mainly because I was doubled over laughing at him. It went right over my head and I heard it thud on the floor behind me. Then I got enough control over myself that I was able to get my own gun out of my holster.

"Now, Roy Lee, don't you do it. Don't do it, now." Wayne was backing away from me with his empty hands open and up, palms out toward me and laughing fit to kill. "Now, come on, Roy Lee. You know that'll hurt."

I aimed low and he jumped, but not high enough. My pistol caught him on the right knee and he grabbed his leg and commenced to howling and hopping around on one foot and then he fell to the floor, still holding his knee. I couldn't tell whether he was laughing or crying, but he was sure cussing up a storm.

"You ever see Texas gunfighters go at it before, Jack?" Moss asked.

"A time or two, but never quite like that," Fletcher said, looking thoughtful. "Though it does seem to save on bullets."

Moss was scratching his red hair. "But how do they know who won?"

"Hell, they're Texans," Fletcher said. "It don't matter who wins just as long as they get in on the fighting."

"Well, I believe I'll shy away from Texas," Moss said. "It's too confusing."

I got my laughing all done and helped Wayne to his feet, then scooped up my gun and put it in my holster. A man brought Wayne's pistol to him, looking at the weapon and at Wayne in a funny way.

The man leaned close to me and whispered, "His gun was empty."

"So was mine," I told him. "We shot up all our bullets and clean forgot to buy more."

The man looked like he'd sudden tasted something sour. "Gunfighters," he said, walking away and shaking his head.

"That's right," Wayne called after him. "Texas gunfighters. Hellbenders."

"I been thinking about that, Wayne. I think we'd better go see Mr. Winslow in the morning and see if he needs bodyguards to help him get home with all that cattle money."

"Since when did I let you start deciding what we'll do?"

"Since right now," I told him. "Unless you want your other knee popped."

Well, we did exactly that and Mr. Winslow did let us ride home with him, but not until he'd locked our guns up in the cook wagon again. Neither one of us was put out about it, though. Whether we had guns or not didn't seem to make a lot of difference.

"I don't know what a hellbender is," Pap said.

"Neither do I. It's something Wayne made up that summer."

"Why didn't either of you ever tell that story before?" Pap said, looking from one of us to the other.

"Well..." Wayne kind of poked at the low-burning campfire.

"Never mind. I know why." Pap looked at Wayne and then at me. "It's about the kind of behavior I'd expect from a couple of dumb pups." He stood and took his blanket roll from the cook wagon. "Now we'd all best get some sleep. I hope you don't dream about pigs, Roy Lee."

"Hold on, Pap" Wayne put up a hand. "You ain't told us a secret about Velvet."

"Oh." Pap scratched his head, then fingered his grizzled jaw. "Okay, here's one. She's got a strawberry birthmark."

"That's good," Wayne said, kind of chuckling. "Where is it, Pap?"

Pap grinned. "Just above her left nipple."

"Why, that ain't so, Pap!" I blurted. "I never saw any such thing!"

Both of them whipped their heads around, staring at me with wide eyes.

I realized what I'd done and so I picked up a stick and commenced to digging in the dirt between my legs, hoping they'd just let it pass. Wayne didn't.

"Roy Lee McAllister, what in the hell is wrong with you today?"

"Nothing." I stood up and shook out my bedroll, not looking at either of them. I knew what was wrong, but there was no way of explaining it to them, even had I wanted to explain it.

Before I even met her, Velvet had got her brand on me.

The Velvet Brand

Chapter Three

Jessie and the Rangers

In spite of how I thought I was feeling about Velvet, I knew I had to go on over to the schoolhouse and say goodbye to Jessie. She'd never much liked it when I went off up the trail and liked it even less when I came back dead broke, but so far I'd been able to explain to her that my being penniless was mostly Wayne's fault.

She knew of some of the trouble Wayne had gotten me into, but she didn't know all of it for there were some things it wasn't fit to mention around a lady, and if they was to be mentioned I expect that lady would have never spoken to me again.

I left Wayne and Pap to watch Rambler building up our herd and rode slow to the one-room schoolhouse in Waco. There was many a time I'd dreamed about me and Jessie being alone in that schoolhouse, but it hadn't happened yet and I was hoping it might happen this afternoon, hoping she would be so sorry to see me go that she'd want to send me off with some proper loving to make sure I came back to her.

I guess I'm not that much different from other men. I was already determined that I was going to meet Velvet at the end of the trail and that I might be spending the rest of my life in her arms. But at the same time, I needed to know whether Jessie truly loved me and truly wanted me to come back to her. I guess I really didn't know which one of them I cared about the most, and it was bothering me more than somewhat.

Jessie and me had spoken for one another when we were twelve and would probably already have married if not for her Pa. I knew Velvet was only a dream, but I put a lot of stock in dreams and the way she had pushed Jessie out of mine was a marvel to me.

By the height of the sun, school lacked a bit of being let out for the day, so I knew I'd have to wait a bit to talk to Jessie alone. About the time I'd made up my mind to do that, I saw a man sitting on the step of the schoolhouse, his reins in his hand with a quick-looking little pony attached to them. One jaw was pooched out from the tobacco he was chewing on, and his eyes were little and mean.

"Howdy," I said, tying my own horse to a low branch of the shade tree.

"Howdy." He was wearing a star pinned on his shirt, so I knew right away he was a Texas Ranger.

"Come to arrest some school children?" I said, grinning.

His tight mouth told me he didn't take the joke. "Rangers don't arrest chirren. Not until they grow up and turn to robbery and cattle rustling and flimflammin'."

"I guess you got a kid in this school, then?"

"Now, why would I have a kid in school or anywhere else when I have to be runnin' all over the state chasin' desperados and flimflammers? Rangers don't have kids."

I could see he wasn't a friendly kind, but it wasn't in me to let it go that easy. "Generally, men with kids has got a wife to take care of the kids while the men are off chasin' desperados."

"Rangers chase desperados. Everyone else sits on their ass and waits for us to catch 'em." He shifted his chaw to the other side.

I grinned at him. "Maybe you could teach the desperados

to sit on their asses. Then you wouldn't have to ride so far to catch 'em."

"Say, you got a smart mouth, don't you?"

"It's been mentioned a time or two," I said.

"You'd best not let it get you crossways of the law." He spat a gob into the dust and watched it roll. From the way he studied it, I guessed it didn't take much to amuse him.

"Well, I didn't know funnin' a Ranger was against the law," I said, sticking out my hand. "My name's Roy Lee McAllister."

He looked up and his little eyes narrowed, but he didn't take my hand. "I've heard of you. I ain't takin' your hand, though."

"Hell, it ain't hardly dirty."

"Rangers don't make friends." He spat into the dust again. "Might have to arrest 'em and hang 'em one day. Most men that want to shake your hand turn out to be horse thieves." After he'd studied his spit, he looked up again. "You got papers on that horse?"

"I do."

"You here to court Miss Jessie?"

Well, I was some surprised by that and I figured the only way he'd know of me was what he'd heard from Jessie and the only way he'd be interested in my courting her was if he was here to do the same. So, I narrowed my eyes at him and set my mouth tight. "Matter of fact, I am."

"Won't do you no good. I'm fixin' to marry her my own self." He spat again but this time he didn't take much interest in it. "Reckon I could fight you for her, if it'd make you feel better."

Now, he looked like if he stood up he'd be about my height but he was wiry where I was mostly muscles. He'd likely be quicker than me, but when I hit him, he'd stay hit. Of course, when it came to gouging and biting and such, size and quick don't make much difference. All in all, I figured it would be a welcome change from fighting Wayne.

"Now, just how would I feel better?" I leaned down and put my face close to his, but kind of to the side so I wasn't in his line of spit. "Whippin' your ass or laughin' myself to death at you thinkin' you can whip mine?"

"Rangers don't lose fights." He shifted his cud again, so I took a step sideways to give him room to spit.

"You'll have to make some changes in your rule book after we tangle," I said.

He stood up and stepped backward so that he stood on the step, making him a head taller than me, and hitched up his gun belt. "You want fists, knives, or guns?" he said.

I saw the door behind him move so I quick put up my hands. Jessie stood in the door with her mouth open, but the Ranger still hadn't noticed for he was trying to figure what I was doing.

She was sure pretty standing there, even though she looked surprised. Her shiny brown hair was done up in a bun, the way she'd been doing it since she'd started teaching school, but I could remember how it looked when she'd let it hang loose and how the sun put some red in it every summer. She wore a checkered dress with a wide skirt and a high neck, and there was a lot of buttons up the front. Many times, I'd thought about how it would be to undo those buttons and take the pins out of her hair.

"I don't know what the problem is, Mr. Ranger, but I can't take a hand against the law."

He shook his head hard. "What the hell are you talking about?"

"What are you talking about, Lawrence? What's Roy Lee done?" She had him by the elbow, making him half turn toward her, and it was the same way I'd seen her do with the pupils in her school.

"Well...nothin', yet. But he..." I think he swallowed when he should have spit for he got a sick look on his face.

"No, and he wouldn't do anything, either. I know Roy Lee and I know he respects the law."

"He don't neither!" the Ranger said. "Why he just..."

"You might have mistook me for someone else, Lawrence," I said.

"My friends call me Larry! I don't like Lawrence!"

"I thought you told me Rangers didn't have friends."

"You see, Miss Jessie? There he goes again with that sassy mouth!"

Jessie looked from him to me and back again and I thought I saw the corner of her mouth twitch. "Why, I didn't hear any sass in his tone. It was just a statement."

"Well...He knows how to sass without bein' sassy."

Now Jessie did smile, but she patted his arm while she was doing it and I didn't much like that. "Lawrence, sometimes you should listen to what you're saying."

I just kind of shrugged.

"Now, you two get off the porch so I can let these children go home," Jessie said.

While the children were leaving, most of them taking good looks at us while the others busied themselves with hair-pulling and such, the Ranger tied his horse to the hitching rail, then snooped around my horse, looking close at the brand and fingering my saddle and saddlebags. "Reckon you got a bill of sale for this nag?"

"I already told you I do. There's a bill of sale in that

saddlebag you're itching to get into, Lawrence. Go ahead and look, I don't mind." There wasn't else in it but a few biscuits I'd saved from breakfast, so I didn't care.

He opened the saddlebag and stuck his hand down in it, then pulled it out and snickered. "Looks like you been stealin' biscuits."

Jessie was coming toward us, so I raised my hands again. "Yes, sir, you've caught me. I waylaid an old woman in El Paso just this morning and took all her biscuits from her at gunpoint."

"Lawrence! What are you accusing him of now? How ridiculous are you going to be?"

"It ain't me bein'...It's him and his smart...You couldn't get from El Paso to here...And he keeps putting his hands up...Oh, I don't know!" Then he came over and leaned in at me, sticking his finger in my face and waggling it. "One riot, one Ranger. Remember that!"

"Okay." I grinned at him. "One riot, one...What was the rest of it?"

"Ranger, Goddammit!"

"Lawrence!"

"I'm sorry about the cuss word, Miss Jessie." He put on a real good hangdog look. "But he provoked me."

"I think each of you is provoking the other and I think the best thing to do is to separate you."

"I'm all for that," the Ranger said. He made a smug smile that caused his cheek to pooch out even further.

Me, I just grinned and shrugged. "Can I put my hands down now?"

"Dammit! I never told you to put 'em up!"

"No profanity, Lawrence." I hoped she'd crack him with a ruler, the way my teacher used to do to me.

"Rangers can't lose their temper," I said.

He grabbed off his hat and kind of wadded it up in his hands, his eyes somewhat rolling about. "Miss Jessie..."

"Yes, Lawrence. Let's you and I go inside and talk." She took his arm and they started inside, but then she turned and smiled at me. "And then I'll talk to you, Roy Lee."

"Oh, don't you do it, Miss Jessie. He's confusin'."

"I know how to handle him, Lawrence," she said, just before the door closed.

I'd guess they were inside that little white schoolhouse for about a quarter of an hour. I went over to the pump and wet my head, trying to slick down my wild hair so I'd look nice for Jessie, but before I got my hat on again I could feel my hair springing back to where it had been before.

I felt a bit forlorn, thinking of all the years me and Wayne and Jessie had learned our lessons in this same schoolhouse, thinking of all the times the teacher had caned me for writing notes to Jessie on my slate and then holding it up for her to read.

When the door opened again, Jessie came out first, followed by the Ranger. He still had his hat in his hands and seemed bent on crushing it into a wad, but he had a kind of smirky look on his face.

"Guess I showed you, Roy Lee," he said.

"Now, Lawrence, you promised you wouldn't start anything."

Me, I just put my head down and toed at the ground. If he'd showed me anything at all, it was that Jessie would accept a marriage proposal even from a stupid man. Figuring that didn't make me feel any better, though. I could be forlorn about Jessie hitching up with such a man and I was just as forlorn over my own loss.

Even so, I put out my hand to him, forgetting that Rangers don't shake hands. He just looked at my hand, shifted his wad, and spat in the dust.

"You should be more polite, Lawrence. Roy Lee offered you his hand."

The Ranger grinned real big, showing yellow teeth. "His hand ain't the one I want."

Jessie and me both looked at him and I saw her mouth had dropped open a little. So before she could say anything, I said, "Maybe, but I've got something you do want."

"I doubt that, Cowboy."

I shrugged. "Well, you can step over here with me or you can wonder about it for the rest of your life."

"Now, Roy Lee, you be nice."

The Ranger's curiosity got the better of him and he followed me over to the tree where my horse was hitched, out of earshot of Jessie. I opened my saddlebag and pretended to be rummaging around in it.

"You ain't going to show me nothin' out of there. I done seen it all." He snickered again. "'Less you're fixin' to hit me with one of them stolen biscuits."

"I ain't fixing to hit you at all," I said. "But if you plan to keep on being a Ranger, I think you need some remindin' about your Ranger oath."

"Of course I'll keep on bein' a Ranger. Why would I quit?"

"You might have to quit if you marry."

"Now, just what do you think you know about that?"

"Just what you told me, Lawrence." I made myself look sad and shook my head slow. "Now, if a Ranger can't have friends, how's he going to have a wife? Can you have a wife and not be friendly to her?"

"That's a different kind of friend!"

"Well, still...Who's going to be her friend when you're riding all over the state chasing desperados and flimflammers?"

"Now, you don't say that about..."

"I've known Jessie for years and I know she's a good woman. But who's to say some flimflammer won't come along and dazzle her away from you while you're off chasing another flimflammer?"

"By God, I believe you're a flimflammer!"

"Nah. I'm just a biscuit thief tryin' to remind you of your duty."

"I don't need you to..."

"I think you do, Lawrence. Why, you're the one told me Rangers don't get married. Are you gonna go back on your oath?"

He looked puzzled. "I don't think that's in the oath."

"I'm pretty sure it is. You told it to me. What happens when Jessie wants a baby? Are you just going to keep the parts of the oath that suit you?"

"Rangers don't do that! With Rangers it's whole hog or nothin'!"

"Now, see? That's my point." I put my arm around his shoulders and his head was bent like he was studying hard at something. "Why, if you just kept the parts of the oath that suited you, you'd be no better than a flimflammer yourself."

"Rangers ain't flimflammers." He didn't sound as certain as he had before.

"Of course not. No one said you were. And you don't want to become one by marrying a high-steppin' girl like Jessie and having to worry about her taking up with other flimflammers every minute of every day."

He smiled at me with his yellow teeth. "Jessie's a high

stepper?"

"Not that kind, or I'd have known by now."

"Say..."

"I mean I'd have heard talk, Lawrence. No, Jessie's a high stepper because she's educated. Now I reckon, given time, she could teach you to read and write and maybe even do sums."

He was nodding his head like it was an enjoyable prospect.

"But by the time she learned you all that, you'd both be too old to enjoy your conversations anyway."

"I am a bit slow."

"Of course you are, but it ain't no sin. Hell, you didn't have time for book learning and such. You had to be practicing how to draw your gun and how to shoot straight. You had to learn about desperados and flimflammers and such."

"That's true." He was still nodding his head.

"Sure it is. How else could you have become the Ranger you are? Why, if you hadn't studied all that–or if all your learnin' came from books–you might not be able to handle a riot when one came along."

He grinned at me again and nudged me in the ribs. "You did remember that, didn't you?"

"The way you taught it, Lawrence, I'll probably never forget it."

"I was in a riot once." He sounded glum and thoughtful, almost like he was talking to himself.

"Were you, now? How'd that turn out?" I was moving so that my back was toward where Jessie waited on the schoolhouse steps and the Ranger had to turn to face me.

"Well...not too good that time. They took my gun away and beat me up. But I learned some lessons for next time."

"I'll just bet you did. Did you practice more on the fast

draw?"

"Sure did."

"Show me, Larry."

"Aww...Now...I don't want to draw down on you, Roy Lee."   He leaned closer to me.   "Not many understands Rangerin' like you do."

"Well, I didn't mean for you to shoot me. I just wanted to see that fast draw."

He whipped his pistol out and gave it a fancy spin that surprised me and that spin gave me time to throw up my hands and back off a step.

"Lawrence!" Jessie yelled. "What are you doing?"

The Ranger looked at the gun in his hand like he was surprised to find it there. "Why, Miss Jessie, I was just..."

"I saw what you did!" She came flying off the steps and jerked him around to face her. "How can you arrest Roy Lee when he hasn't done anything?"

I kept my hands up and backed off another step.

"Aww...I ain't gonna arrest him, I guess." He looked a mite confused. "Was I arresting you for something, Roy Lee?"

I put my hands down.

"No. You was just tellin' me about how proud you are to be a Ranger, and how nothing is gonna keep you from bein' a good Ranger, loyal to your oath."

"That's right." He holstered his gun and hitched up his gun belt. After a minute of studying the ground he said, "Why did I draw my gun, then?"

"You wanted to check the loads. Rangers have to be prepared."

"Oh. Right." He squared up his hat on his head. "Miss Jessie, I'm afraid our wedding is off."

Though she was beside me, I saw Jessie's mouth drop

open.

"I know it pains you, ma'am. It pains me, too. But I can't be a proper Ranger when I got to be worryin' about you traipsin' around the state with every high-stepping flimflammer that comes along. Why, if I was to marry you I might have to hang you someday."

"Might have to hang your own chirren, too," I said.

"What?"

"Well, if she was traipsin' around like you accused her of doin', them boys of yours would probably grow up to be horse thieves."

"Right." He jerked a nod at me. "Without no momma, they'd do that."

"Well...Lawrence...Uh, if you think that's best..."

"I'm sorry, ma'am, but I do think so." He tipped his hat at her. "Now you'll excuse me."

The Ranger went to where his horse was tied, and mounted. Then he remembered the reins was still tied to the hitching rail, so he dismounted and untied them and mounted again. He rode over to where we were standing and pointed his finger at me. "One riot, one Ranger," he said, then rode away.

"I won't forget," I called after him.

Jessie moved until she was standing in front of me, her hands on her hips. "Roy Lee, what in the world was that all about?"

"Oh, we was just talkin' about Rangerin' stuff."

"What was he saying about marriage?"

"Did he ask you to marry him?"

"Hmmm...no. I mean, I don't think so." She folded her arms and tapped her lips with one finger. "Once or twice I felt he had something on his mind other than what he was talking about, but...Well, he seemed a little confused about everything."

"What did he want to talk about?"

Jessie cocked her head to one side and smiled. "Now, that may just be none of your business, Roy Lee. Are you jealous?"

"I might be."

She threw her arms around me and kissed me, then put her head on my shoulder. "Oh, I love you, Roy Lee."

Looking back, I know I should have felt guilty as sin for what I had been thinking and dreaming about Velvet, but I didn't. Fact is, Velvet wasn't on my mind at all right then. It felt so good to be holding Jessie again after such a long time, that there wasn't room in my head for anything but thoughts of her.

She kept her head against my shoulder and now her hand moved around to play with the ends of my neckerchief while I kept my arms about her. "I might as well tell you anyway," she said. "He stuttered and stumbled a lot, but I think he wanted to escort me to the barn dance over at the Treble place next week."

"Did you tell him you'd go?"

"Of course not! Why, I only met him for the first time yesterday!"

I wondered if she could feel the grin that spread across my face.

"I thanked him kindly and told him I couldn't possibly go to a dance with a man I didn't know, even if he was a Texas Ranger. He sure sets a lot of store by that badge."

"He does that," I said.

Jessie giggled. "You know, I think one of the reasons he stuttered so much was because he couldn't find a place to spit!"

She stepped away from me then and turned and put her head down, but kind of looking at me from the corner of her eye. "When he mentioned the dance, I started hoping you were here to ask me to go with you."

Now, I like barn dances. I know I ain't as graceful as some, but it is fun to fling myself out and I always have a good time. Some of the best times were had when Wayne and me got into a fuss about something or other and one of us would end up with a swollen ear or a black eye.

"No," I said slowly. "Not unless you tell me your Pa's in Laredo or Ohio."

"You know he isn't, Roy Lee," she whispered. Then she looked out toward the road that ran by the schoolhouse. "He'll be coming for me in the wagon, soon."

"Well, then..."

"Oh, I know you can't take me, Roy Lee. I just wish Pa liked you the way I do. I just wish he could see what I see when I look at you."

I was pretty sure I knew what he saw when he looked at me, for he'd told me often. To him I was nothing more than a shiftless cowboy, forever getting into fights, forever frittering away my money on gambling and liquor, forever going off up the trail for months at a time. I didn't much like her Pa, but I couldn't fault him for being right.

"Jessie, you got to prepare him."

She faced me with her eyes wide. "Prepare him for what?"

"We're takin' a herd up the trail, probably just a day or two from now."

"Oh. You'll be gone all summer, then." She seemed sad about it.

"I expect so. But this time it's our herd, Jessie. Mine and Wayne's. We ain't workin' for wages this time."

"But you'll be broke when you come home. You always

are."

"Not this time, Jessie. And if the cattle bring a good price...You just tell your Pa to expect me to come home and buy some land."

She threw her arms around me again. "Oh, Roy Lee..."

"Roy Lee, you take your hands off my girl!"

We both turned to look. I don't know why we hadn't heard her Pa come up in the buggy and I don't know what he'd heard. But I knew I couldn't fight him, for Jessie's sake, so I stepped back away from her.

Jessie had her head down. I knew she was cowed by him, her whole family was, but there wasn't ought I could do about it except try to hold on to my temper. "Roy Lee was just telling about how he might buy a ranch, Pa," Jessie mumbled.

Her Pa was a big man with a black beard and he carried the buggy whip with him when he got off the wagon and stepped over to me. "Well," he said. "Tell me. I like a good joke."

"I see you ain't laughing," I said.

"No, I ain't. But I'll tell you this, Roy Lee McAllister. The day you buy a ranch is the day I'll eat supper with the hogs."

It was in my mind to tell him to start working up an appetite, but because of Jessie I held my tongue.

"Nothin' to say, huh? I thought as much!"

"No." My own voice was low. "Nothing to say, Mr. Meacham." I went over to my horse and mounted him.

"Say! Did either of you kids see a Texas Ranger pass this way?"

Before I could answer, Jessie said, "I saw him. What about him, Pa?"

"Oh, nothin', I guess." He took her over and helped her

into the wagon. "I just thought it peculiar and I felt sorry for him the way he was walkin' his horse slow and mutterin' to himself. Said he'd lost his wife and kids all on the same day. Cholera, I expect, though I hadn't heard about any in these parts."

Jessie was hiding a smile behind her hand and I tipped her a wink Pa Meacham didn't see. "And yet he was out doing his duty," I said. "My, my."

"Yes, he was." Pa Meacham sounded testy. "You could learn a lot from that poor Ranger, Roy Lee."

"Reckon you're right," I said.

Riding away, I doubted that Ranger was any more confused than me. On the one hand was Jessie, warm and willing and soft in my arms but with a daddy who'd as soon shoot me as take me for a son-in-law. On the other hand was Velvet, no more than a dream for the end of the trail, but so far my dreams were better than what was real.

Chapter Four

On the Trail

Three days later, we got the herd lined out and started up the trail to Dodge City. It was a well-worn trail, for cattle had been going to Kansas for several years now and the only time any thinking was required would be when the trail forked. The cattle trade had started in Abilene, but as the railroad moved west and south, the cattle buyers moved with it, mostly because the trail was shorter. So, at different times the trail had ended in Abilene, Ellsworth, Newton, and Wichita.

As the cattle buyers moved, the saloons, gamblers, and fancy women moved with them and so did the law. Each town became rowdy and wide-open in its turn and then kind of curled up and took a nap when the cattle trade moved on.

We moved on up the trail, but there wasn't any rowdiness among us. To keep from answering questions about my moping and dreaming, I'd took to doing most of my talking with Harvey. He was as simple as folks said he was, and a conversation with him was likely to be long and pointless, but right then I needed simple a lot more than I needed complicated.

Wayne and Pap was still fretting at one another over the horses Pap had brought for the remuda. The day after Pap had joined us in camp, Wayne looked over the horses and then came back to the morning campfire. He didn't say anything, just hunkered down and looked thoughtful for a minute. When he realized he was hunkered on his spurs he kind of shifted around and didn't look so thoughtful anymore.

"Well?" Pap said. "Are you goin' to give us the benefit of your years of experience with horseflesh?"

I hadn't yet looked at the horses, so I was as interested in Wayne's opinion as Pap was. But Wayne seemed determined to take his time and play it out, sitting there and poking a stick in the fire while side meat sizzled in the frying pan.

Pap looked at me and I could see the devilment in his eyes. "I guess when you don't know what you've been lookin' at, a judgment takes a whole lot more considerin'."

Times past, I'd have had some snappy remark ready so I could join Pap in deviling Wayne, but the last few nights had been hard ones and I wasn't feeling up to it. So I just said, "I reckon."

Both of them looked at me like they was somewhat disappointed, but I didn't know what else to say. To keep from meeting their eyes, I busied myself by sticking a fork in the side meat and turning it over.

"How much did you say you promised to pay for them horses, Pap?" Wayne said.

"Well, I didn't say, but it was thirty dollars apiece."

"Same price for the blind one?"

"Dammit, Wayne, that horse ain't blind," Pap said. Then some of the heat went out of his words. "I believe he might be nearsighted, though."

"Might be nearsighted." Wayne's words were flat, more like an echo than a question or a statement.

"I believe he might be, yes. I said so, didn't I?"

"Then it might be we could stop in Fort Worth and get him fitted for some spectacles."

Pap opened his mouth three times before any words came

out. "I ain't talkin' to you about that horse any more. You ride him and see if I ain't right."

"No, I don't believe I want to be ridin' over a cut bank or steppin' into gopher holes because the horse can't see," Wayne said.

"Don't nobody ride him on point, then," I said.

They both looked at me and I guess they were some surprised for it was the first time all morning that I'd spoke up about anything. "Ride him on drag," I said. "Even if he's nearsighted, he can surely see a herd of cattle in front of him."

"Now, that's so," Pap said, nodding hard. "Roy Lee is right."

"And what if he's blind?"

"Then whoever's the nighthawk can ride him. Dark won't make no difference to a blind horse."

Wayne looked at me for a spell, and then realized I was funning rather than being serious and his mouth went into a slow grin. "Welcome back, Roy Lee."

I gave his grin back to him while Pap got up muttering about dumb pups and went to saddle a horse. The nearsighted horse didn't look bad. He had a deep chest and legs that looked to be strong, but he kept moving his head from side to side in a way I'd never seen. Maybe he was wary that someone was going to saddle and ride him without first telling him about it.

As I saddled a different horse, I thought about what Wayne had said. I didn't really feel like I was back. I'd dreamed about Velvet again and it troubled me, though I don't know why. It was pretty much the same dream as the first time, except that I woke up sooner, before any of my clothes got shucked off, but it lasted long enough for me to know that Pap had been right about that strawberry birthmark.

Now we were out on the trail with that old bull Rambler

doing most of the work for us, and I found myself thinking that I was a full day away from Jessie and tomorrow I'd be two days away from her and that kind of troubled me, too. With Wayne and Pap still testy to one another about the nearsighted horse, I started talking to Harvey Nodder.

I'd been riding drag, but Rambler was watching the herd more careful than I was. He'd stay up on point most of the time, but then he'd come back to the rear of the herd and if there were any stragglers he'd chouse them up, bellering at them and sometimes threatening them with that long horn. Then he'd take another look around and go back to the point, checking the other flank of the herd as he went.

So I pulled away from riding drag, knowing Rambler would handle it for a while, and went over to the left side of the herd where Harvey was driving the cook wagon. He kept it far away from the herd, trying to stay out of the dust cloud they stirred up, but from the taste of the food he wasn't always successful.

When I rode up alongside the wagon, he looked at me and grinned and nodded. "Good day, Roy Lee."

"Good day to you too, Harvey."

He kind of frowned. "No. I think I meant this was a good day, Roy Lee."

"Oh. All right, then."

"Are you sayin' it's not a good day?" He looked up at the blue sky with the fleecy white clouds. "I don't see any rain clouds or tornadoes, Roy Lee."

"By God, you're right, Harvey. I don't see any tornadoes either."

"Good. It's a good day then, Roy Lee."

Harvey Nodder looked to be about forty years old, with pale blonde hair and dark brown eyes. No one around Waco knew much about him. There were a lot of vacant houses and shacks left behind by people who had gone busted and moved on, and one day it was found that Harvey was living in one of them and working a garden out behind the place. Nobody much cared about that because most folks can't live in but one house at a time anyway and those who were still living around Waco were pretty much settled in and just waiting to go bust so they could move on.

Some of the women made courtesy calls when they found out Harvey was living on the old Rickert farm, and it was them that came back to their families and the church meetings and said they guessed he was simple and that was too bad because he was kind of an attractive man.

I don't recall anyone ever saying why they thought he was simple, but you didn't have to talk to him for very long before you started thinking they must be right. The way he said your name almost every time he spoke to you made you think it was his way of keeping track of who he was talking with.

"You ever have much woman trouble, Harvey?"

"All the time, Roy Lee."

I hadn't expected to get an answer like that. As far as anyone around Waco knew, Harvey lived alone and had never been seen in company with a woman. Since most gossip is done by women, I guess they held that any man that wasn't trying to get to any of them must be simple.

He'd show up at a sociable or a barn dance with some dish he'd cooked up and then he'd just sit off by himself and watch the others enjoy it. People were polite and they did say Howdy and Thank You to him, but I don't know of anyone ever said they spent the evening talking to him. When the sociable was over, he'd take his empty pot and go on back to the old Rickert place.

He was a good cook, and truth to tell there was only that one time I knew of when he'd forgot to skin something before he cooked it. There was talk about last year's Easter Sunrise meeting, though. When the folks were finished praying the sun up, they sat down to platters full of breakfast trout that Harvey had cooked up but forgot to gut. Me and Wayne was on the trail with a herd at the time, so I couldn't say about the truth of that talk.

I'd opened the subject of women with him because I was looking to talk about my own troubles with someone. I knew if I tried to talk to Wayne or Pap, they'd end up offering an opinion or a judgment and I didn't want any of that. That left only Rambler and Harvey to talk to, but now Harvey had made me curious.

"What kind of trouble you been having?" I asked.

"They're always wantin' to know things about me, Roy Lee. They want to know why I ain't married and whether I ever been married and am I ever gonna get married and do I have a sweetheart somewhere and do I have any children and do I have any folks hereabouts and what do I think of the weather and am I gonna come to the barn dance and will they see me in church next Sunday."

"Do tell," I said.

"And then they want to know about my cookin', Roy Lee, but I won't tell them about that. They want to know how I learned to cook and when I learned to cook and where I learned to cook and did my Mama teach me and is my Mama living and was my Pa a farmer and do I have any brothers or sisters and what kind of spices and flavorin's do I use and how long do I cook things and why do I cook things the way I do and why don't I pay more attention to skinning things before I cook them."

"Well..."

"I don't like it when they complain about my cookin', Roy Lee. If they don't like it they don't have to eat it and if they do like it they don't have to eat so much of it that others don't get any 'cause I always try to cook enough for everybody but then somebody will bring some cousins or other kinfolk to the meeting and then there isn't enough to go around and that vexes me, Roy Lee, because I'm always tryin' to do my best for people and then they act like it just ain't good enough for them, like the time that fat old Mrs. Washburn came to me at a barn dance, laughin' and gigglin' and saying my apple turnovers was delicious but I should have made more of them, and her sayin' that after me spending the better part of two days and three nights trying to bake enough for everybody, Roy Lee, and then for her to come up to me and say that and I was so vexed about it that I was gonna set fire to her house but they went busted and moved away before I got around to it."

"Women are a caution," I said, putting spurs to my horse to chase after a stray and wishing I'd talked my troubles over with Rambler.

***

At supper that night, while I was sopping up the last of my gravy with a biscuit, Harvey came over and took my tin plate and poured more coffee in my cup. "You rode away before I finished talking, Roy Lee."

"Oh. Well, we'll get back to it on a day I ain't so busy."

"Don't forget, Roy Lee. I might get vexed if you forget." He went away and I heard the sounds of him washing pots and pie plates.

"What's he talking about?" Pap said.

"I'm helping him out with some woman troubles."

"Old Harvey?" Wayne said, laughing.

I quick shushed him.

In almost a whisper, Wayne said, "I guess still waters do run deep."

Simple waters, too, I was thinking. I shook out my blanket roll and laid down with my head on my saddle and my hat over my eyes.

"Just don't complain about his cookin'," I said. I wasn't real serious, I was just setting Wayne up. "No matter what it is, just eat it and keep quiet about it."

"Now, why would I do that?"

I grinned, knowing it was the last thing I was going to say that night and knowing Wayne would probably lay awake for a long time puzzling about it.

"If he gets vexed, he might set fire to the herd."

***

All the days of the cattle drive were easy, but most of my nights were still hard.

Wayne finally rode the nearsighted horse and said it was only half blind, so him and Pap weren't arguing about it anymore.

After a few days, when I thought I could stand it, I had another talk with Harvey and I stayed with him until he run down. It didn't take too long, for I'd remarked on how favorable the weather was. Once Harvey had run through tornadoes and hurricanes and rainstorms and prairie fires and fog and lightning and thunder and flash floods and blizzards and blue northers, he was pretty well played out and told me I'd better go away and quit bothering him so he could fix some supper.

I didn't need to be told twice. I spurred away from the cook wagon before he could get vexed and set fire to me.

The dreams about Velvet were still happening most every

night. By the time we'd been on the trail for almost a month, there were probably only a dozen nights when I'd been too tired to dream anything at all.

I found myself wishing I was back in Waco so I could talk to Granny Davis about the dreams.

Granny Davis claimed to be a hundred years old and since she had no kinfolk to dispute her claim, most of us believed her. She was an old darky woman, shrunk down to where she was only four feet tall, but still spry enough that she raised her own garden truck and traded vegetables and fruits for pigs and cows that she butchered herself. She said she'd never been a slave, that she'd been born up around Boston and had made it a point to never go south until after the war was over. Maybe it was because she'd never been a slave and was well spoken that most folks around Waco treated her just like they treated one another. She could talk on just about any subject and had a wealth of stories to tell, but her specialty was telling the meaning of dreams.

One time at a barnraising on a hot August day, before me and Wayne got to be cowboys, I got tuckered and had to sit for a while. Granny brought me a dipper of cool water and asked about my health and the next thing I knew I was telling her about a dream I'd had about Jessie. By that time, Jessie's Pa had threatened to shoot me if I ever came around his place again, so I was staying away, but I was still dreaming.

Jessie was at the barnraising, of course, but I hadn't been able to do more than sneak glances at her all day. When I did that, I generally found her Ma giving me a hard look or her Pa hefting his hammer like he was thinking of a new way to use it.

"Jessie Meacham? The schoolteacher?" Granny said when I was done. "I didn't know you two was that close, Roy Lee."

"Well...maybe you're confused, Granny. We ain't as close

as we were in that dream."

"Oh, I know that. Now you be still and I'll tell you about your dream."

We were sitting on a bench that ran in a circle around the trunk of a big live oak tree. The shade was cool and a little breeze had come up and I was feeling some better after the drink of water. I still didn't know what had made me tell Granny about the dream, except for maybe knowing she was an expert on such, and now I was kind of embarrassed about the whole thing even though I'd been careful to not tell her all the details.

"Maybe we'd best just forget it, Granny," I said. "I didn't mean to..."

"No, now you got to know about it because you said you've had the same dream before. That's what we call a repeating dream and that means it's true. If it hasn't happened yet, it will happen and you got to be ready for it when it does."

Well, that gave me some hope because what happened in the dream was surely some of what I wanted to happen between me and Jessie, but I didn't need to be made ready for it because I had been ready for a long time.

"Now, you said the dream starts out in the schoolhouse and you're sitting at a desk and Jessie is up front writing on the big slate board with chalk. That all has to do with learning and that means you need to learn something you don't already know. What is it you don't know, Roy Lee?"

"I don't know what I don't know," I said. I thought the dream had started in the schoolhouse because Jessie was the schoolteacher, but I knew enough to admit Granny probably understood a lot more about it than I did.

"Don't be cagey in your answers, Roy Lee. I can't abide somebody looking for truth who can't speak the truth."

"Yes, ma'am."

"Now, you said you fit into that desk just like you was the right size for it. That means you were dreaming you were a little boy again. My oldest boy, Justin, used to always dream he was little and that he was still nursing on my teat, and he was having that dream up till the time he died. He was thirty-nine years old when he died of the mumps and it was hard on him the way those things are always hard on a man, but I had the comfort of knowing he still thought of himself as my little boy, sucking on my old teat..."

"Uh...Granny, maybe we'd best save this for another time..."

She laughed and slapped my knee. "Why, Roy Lee, you're blushing! Now you know I got teats—or at least did have—and you know mothers suckle their young. It's a natural thing, just as natural as what's going to happen between you and Jessie."

"Well...Can we get to that part, then?"

"Directly. We will directly. Now, you said it was a hot day and there weren't any other children in the schoolhouse, there was just you and Jessie. That means you're wanting to be alone with her so you can learn something. We still don't know what it is you want to learn, because you won't tell me what you don't know and that means you're ashamed about what you want to know. But since you put Jessie in the role of a schoolteacher, we can be pretty sure that it's her you want to teach you something. And you said the door was closed and locked and that might be more of wanting to be alone and have some privacy while she teaches you. Or it might be that you think something else is locked up where you can't get to it. Which is it, Roy Lee?"

"Lord, I don't know!"

"Never mind. I'm about to tell you. Now, you said Jessie

was fanning herself with a palm fan and walking back and forth and studying you, and directly she undid the top button of her dress and you could see a bead of sweat run down between her bosoms. You must have been looking awfully close to see that and the reason you saw that is because sweat is a symbol. It usually means water or a river or something like that, so you've got to think about how moisture of some kind might play a part. You said she was breathing kind of heavy and you didn't think it was all from the heat and when you looked down you saw you was naked, with your little thing standing up."

"Granny, all I said is that I thought I was naked!" And it was at that point, when I realized I was naked, that I had woke up from the dream.

"Well, if you was naked and there was a woman in heat in the room with you and the door was locked so nobody else could come in and catch you, it's a cinch your little thing would be standing up, ain't that so? I got to fill in the details you left out, Roy Lee, because everything in a dream is important. Now, the fact that your thing was standing up means you were paying attention, because it was standing to attention, just like a little soldier. You see the connection, don't you? And that all means you've been paying a lot of attention to Jessie, thinking about her a lot, and your thoughts haven't always been pure."

I put my elbows on my knees and put my head in my hands. "I reckon."

"Now, you said she came over to where you sat at your desk but she didn't seem to notice you were naked. That's because you were the only one who knew you were naked and that's just some more of those impure thoughts you're always having about her. The reason you were the only one who noticed you were naked was because you were ashamed of it and ashamed of the way your thing was standing up and pointing at Jessie.

"You said she leaned over your desk to help you with your lesson, but instead of looking at your slate you looked down her dress that she'd opened and you saw the ripe swelling of her bosoms and the darker shadow between them and..."

"Dammit, Granny! I mean...Beg your pardon, Granny, but all I said was that she had opened her dress a button or two."

"Well, if she undid those three or four buttons then you could see down her dress and you could see how her bosoms swelled and how they kind of heaved with her heavy breathing and how there was moisture where her sweat had run down between them. And there's that moisture again. You seem to think about sweat an awful lot, Roy Lee. I used to have those thoughts a lot myself when I was young and married to my first husband. We'd be doing it and I'd be sweating and yawping and he'd be sweating and saying 'Yeah, yeah, yeah' and then I'd throw my legs up around his waist and..."

"Granny!"

"Huh? Oh, yeah. Well, then you just stuck your hand right into her dress and grabbed onto one of her bosoms. That's that teat thing again, Roy Lee. You got what we call a fixed idea about that, I'd say, and that's why it's coming out in your dreams. Dreams are always full of symbols and bosoms are symbols, though I'd be willing to bet Jessie's symbols aren't as big and as ripe as you dreamed they were. They never are.

"Oh, don't tell me you didn't say anything about grabbing her, Roy Lee. You didn't have to say anything. I know you did it, because any healthy man in your place would have done it. Jessie's an attractive woman, even if she did lose that tooth when she was young. I'm surprised there aren't a lot more young bucks around here dreaming about her, though maybe they just haven't come to me yet. And it don't do any good for you to sit on this bench with your head in your hands moaning like that. What's been done has been done and moaning won't change a bit of it. Or maybe the moaning is a sign you're wishing right now that you could do it again."

"I just wish I was somewheres else."

"Yes, and I'll just bet you do. You're wishing you was back there in that hot old schoolhouse with the door locking the two of you away from the world and your hand down her dress and feeling her rosy nipple getting hard between your fingers and you kissing her and trying to stick your tongue in her mouth like you did before and feeling her hand stealing slowly down over your chest and belly until she's gripping your hard little thing."

"Well..." I had to admit there was something to what she said about my wishing, even though my dream hadn't gone nearly that far.

"And you're thinking about how you got right up out of that desk and you picked her up and laid her down on that dusty old schoolhouse floor and you're remembering how the dust motes rose up and sparkled in the sunlight streaming in the windows. You're remembering how you raised up her dress and how she tried to protect herself, but didn't try very hard, and you brushed her hands away and tore down her pantaloons and then you stuck that hard little thing in her secret place and she moaned with the pain and the sweetness of it all.

"And I'll bet you're remembering how she laid still for a while and then matched her movements to yours, meeting your thrusts with thrusts of her own, and just how she locked her legs around you so the heels of her high button shoes were in your ass and how she grabbed her ankles and pulled on them to get you in deeper and how sweat was running off her face and that big vein in her neck was pulsing in time with your rhythm and how your sweat was dripping down on her and how she was licking it off her lips and smiling at you so soft and gentle and then all of a sudden saying 'Oh, hurry, Roy Lee, hurry!' and how you stepped up the pace until both of you were yawping and yelping and thrashing around on that hard old floor until the waves of ecstasy rolled over you and then you fell over and lay on your sides, looking deep into one another's eyes and exchanging slow soft kisses and watching the dust motes make a golden sparkle in the air."

"Damn!" It was all new to me but it was surely wondrous the way she told it.

From the other side of the oak tree I heard Jessie's voice as plain as day. "Oh, my!"

"What's it all mean, Granny?"

She stood up and she was so short her dark eyes were about level with mine. "It means you're an unmitigated son-of-a-bitch, taking advantage of that poor young woman." Then she slapped me across the mouth, hiked her skirt, and went to where the other womenfolk were gathered.

From the other side of the tree, I heard a young boy say, "Somebody help me over here. Miss Jessie's fainted from the heat."

Thinking about it now, I decided that maybe Granny wasn't the one I needed to talk to, even though it was true what people said. She did have a way with dreams.

***

I was thankful there wouldn't be any dreams for me this night, for they tended to wear me out so that I felt like I hadn't rested at all. I was also worried that I might speak out in my dreams, like I had on that first night, that I might say something that would tell Wayne or Pap who I was dreaming about. If it happened, I didn't know whether I could handle all the deviling

I would have to take.

On this night, I had the nighthawk duty. Because our crew was small, we split it in two. I would take the first half while Wayne slept, and then he would take over so that I could sleep the rest of the night. Because of being in the saddle most of the day and then riding nighthawk for half the night, I was usually too tired to dream and those were the only nights I felt like I got any rest at all.

I was of the opinion that we didn't need a nighthawk at all. Those cattle were so old that by the time we stopped for the day they was more tired than we were. And we had Rambler to help us out. He did a pretty good job of watching out for the herd at night. Even though he must have been as old as the other cattle, he didn't act like it and I'd never seen him slow down or shirk. With the rounds he made during the day, he was working harder than any of us. If we'd been able to train him to wake one of us when he started getting sleepy, we might have got by with only one man doing nighthawk duties.

The campfire was burning low. Wayne and Pap had already spread their bedrolls and were about to settle down for the night. I was drinking my last cup of coffee before going out to start my slow rides around the herd, and Harvey was getting the biscuit dough ready for the morning. I always felt good about eating a mess of Harvey's biscuits. They rested nice and heavy in my stomach and there was nothing he put into them that needed skinning.

"Reckon we'll strike the Red River tomorrow, Roy Lee?" Wayne asked.

"Tomorrow or the next day, I'd say."

"Remember the first time we done it? How the older hands talked about it for days ahead of time, lettin' us know how fearsome it could be? And then when we did get to it, it was as gentle as a lady."

"I remember," I said. "But I wouldn't want to cross the Red or any other river if it was in flood."

"That's so. What do you think, Pap?"

Pap was getting situated, squirming around to make a hole for his hip to lay in. "Up until now, I've done all my river crossings in boats and ferries. But I am anxious to see that Red River, no matter how I have to cross it."

"Well, you'll be a sure-enough cowboy by the time we finish this drive," Wayne said. "Ain't that so, Roy Lee?"

I gave Wayne a big wink. "Not until we've shaved him."

"Now, what's that?" Pap sat up in his blankets, looking hard at first one of us and then the other. "No one's putting a razor to my throat except me."

"It's got to be done, Pap," Wayne said. "Tell him, Roy Lee."

Wayne was throwing it back to me because he didn't have the least idea what I was talking about, but I could tell he'd follow any lead I gave him.

"It's about crossing the Red, Pap," I said. "Everyone goin' up the trail for the first time has to get his head shaved after crossin' the Red."

"Be damned if anyone is shaving my head." His look had got suspicious. "How come I never heard you boys mention this after your first drive?"

"Just embarrassed, I reckon," Wayne said. "You might recollect we never took our hats off for a long time after we got back home."

"I don't remember any such thing."

"Well, they shaved mine to look like there was a cross on top and for Wayne they left just a little topknot."

Pap's eyes got narrow and then he kind of smiled. "Well,

if you boys went through it, I guess I can get through it, too. What kind of shavin' did you have in mind for me?"

"Why, I hadn't thought about it a lot, Pap. I figured you'd kick and fuss so that we'd just either make you completely bald or maybe patchy." Wayne looked at me. "You got an idea, Roy Lee?"

"Oh, sure. I figured to shave him bare as a baby's backside on top but leave it mostly alone on the sides. Make him look like he's about ninety years old so the whores won't be botherin' him."

"Maybe we can get that scruffy beard off him while we're at it," Wayne said.

"I see," Pap said. "Well, I said I'd go along with it and I will, though it's not to my liking." He settled down in his blankets, then raised up again, grinning at Wayne. "By the way, what kind of design do you dumb pups have figured out for Harvey?"

"It's time for me to go do the nighthawkin'," I said. "You tell him about that, Wayne."

As I was riding out of the circle of light, I heard Wayne saying, "Well, it's just a custom. That don't mean we have to do it, though."

"So I can be a real cowboy without getting' anything shaved?" I could hear the chuckle in Pap's voice.

"You're a cowboy, Pap. Now get some sleep."

I rode around the herd for half the night, and though they didn't need it, I sang soft and low to the cattle. When I judged the stars had moved far enough, I went back to the camp to wake up Wayne and let him take his turn.

There was still a bit of light coming from the campfire and I could see Wayne was sleeping sound. Just as I was about to wake him up, I heard him mumble something, though it was too low for me to make out. I decided to try something I'd seen done on one of our other drives when one of the cowboys started talking to old Larry Fish, who was known for talking in his sleep. Old Larry had answered him back plain as day and we all had a good time funning him about it the next morning.

So I leaned kind of close to Wayne and spoke low so that I wouldn't wake Pap. "Talk to me, Wayne."

He kind of smacked his lips and turned toward me.

"Talk to me, Wayne. Tell me what you're dreamin' about."

"Aww, Velvet, honey, you know what I'm always dreamin' about."

I stood up and kicked at his feet. "Time to get up, Wayne. You got some nighthawkin' to do."

"Well, damn, Roy Lee. Don't be so testy about it." He sat up and put on his hat and then his boots, looking at me all the time.

Me, I just went to my bedroll and snuggled in. I didn't want to dream about Velvet again that night, but I damned sure didn't want Wayne to be having my dreams for me.

The Velvet Brand

Chapter Five

The Runaway

We struck the Red River two days later, toward the middle of the afternoon, and it was an easy crossing in spite of Wayne trying to argue it to death.

We were a little bit ahead of the herd, still following a well-marked trail, and when we saw the line of trees stretching across the horizon we knew we'd come upon a river of some kind. It was about midday then and the cattle were moving slow behind us, so I turned and let out a whoop for Pap to hear and then Wayne and me rode ahead. We went slow at first, giving Pap a chance to catch up, then the three of us set spurs to our horses and went hell-for-leather toward the river.

The crossing was well marked. Someone who'd gone up the trail before us had cut long stakes and driven them into the riverbed, and I figured that as long as we kept the herd between the stakes we wouldn't lose any of them to quicksand or drop-offs.

"It don't look like the Red River to me," Wayne said.

"That might be because this ain't where we crossed it before. The last times we went on a drive we were on the Chisholm Trail."

"Well, what trail is this?" Pap said.

"I don't know that it's got a name," I said. "But it's more to the west of the Chisholm Trail because Dodge City is closer this way."

We were all still sitting our horses, leaning on the saddle horns and studying the flow of the river. It was a strong flow, but I could see the high-water marks on the bank across from us and the level of the river was well below that. As long as we crossed today, we wouldn't have to worry about the river being in flood.

"It still don't look like the Red," Wayne said.

"It don't look red to me at all," Pap said.

"I hope you're not fixin' to tell us you expected the water to be red."

Pap gave me a hard look. "All my life I been hearin' songs and stories about the Red River Valley," he said. "And yes, by God, I did expect the water to be red. If this is the Red River, I'm some disappointed in it."

"Well, I've never seen any red water and I don't believe there is any."

Wayne surprised me by agreeing with me. "That's right, Roy Lee. Hell, I'm older than you and I've never seen any either."

"You ain't but six months older, Wayne," Pap said, still testy. "So that didn't give you a hell of a lot more time for lookin', now did it?"

"I was keepin' my eyes peeled that first six months." Wayne's shoulders were shaking, but he managed to keep a straight face.

"I sure don't think much of a trail drive that can't show me a red river when I need to see one," Pap said.

"Well, I'm sorry as can be about that, Pap," I said. "You'd best go back and get the cook wagon brought up. We'll cross the wagon first so Harvey can have supper waitin' when we get the herd across."

"What are you boys gonna be doin'?"

"We're going to ride this crossing, find out how deep it is and whether any quicksand has grown up in it since they set them stakes."

"All right, then. You boys find any red water, you set it aside so I can see it when I come back with the wagon."

Wayne and me looked at one another and busted out laughing, then spurred our horses down the bank and into the river.

The crossing was firm all the way across and from one set of stakes to the other, so I guessed not many herds had crossed it yet this season. That was another piece of good luck, for if we were one of the first herds to arrive in Dodge, we might get a higher price per head. As old as most of our cattle were, we needed every advantage we could find.

Thinking about the age of the cattle with the Velvet brand reminded me that I wanted to ask Pap when Velvet had left Waco and why she had left. There hadn't been anything in my dreams to answer those questions, even when I tried to do what Granny Davis had taught me about filling in the missing parts.

In fact, there were too many missing parts in those dreams, parts that would have placed me where I really wanted to be which was in Velvet's bed and locked in her arms. Seems like something always woke me up just before I got there. It was troubling me, but the whole idea of having such dreams about a woman I'd never met was just as worrisome.

"Want to have some fun with Pap?" Wayne said.

"I thought we just did."

"Let's not join up with him till he gets closer with the wagon."

Looking back toward the herd, I could see that the wagon was only about eighty rods away and I wondered why Wayne needed it to be much closer. But I played his game and waited, and when Pap came riding out ahead of the wagon Wayne yelled at him to stay put.

"I got somethin' to show you, Pap!" he yelled.

Then he went back into the river, took off his hat and scooped it full of water, and started for the herd. "Come on," he told me.

We rode up to Pap, Wayne carrying that hat full of water and trying not to slosh it out.

"Pap, it don't look red in the river cause there's so much of it," Wayne said. "But you get a hatful or a bottle full off by itself and it's red sure enough."

Pap came closer, leaned from his saddle and peered into Wayne's hat. "Looks black to me."

"That's 'cause my hat's black. You got to look really close." Wayne was starting to snicker and I knew he was going to give the whole thing away, even though I was only guessing at what he had in mind.

Wayne didn't see it happening, but I did. Pap splayed one hand out big and got it under Wayne's hand but not touching him. Then he did what Wayne was fixing to do to him. He made as if to look closer into the hat, then whipped that water right up into Wayne's face.

"That tears it!" Wayne flung his hat at the ground and took off after Pap toward the river.

Pap was going at a fair clip, spurring his horse and looking back over his shoulder at Wayne, and laughing fit to kill. If he'd remembered he was riding the nearsighted horse, he might have paid more attention to where he was going. That horse ran right into a cottonwood tree, Pap went off of him ass over teakettle, and by the time I caught up with them him and Wayne were standing over the horse and arguing about its condition.

"I say he's dead," Wayne said.

"He ain't dead," Pap said. "He just knocked hisself out when he was tryin' to kill me."

The horse was lying on his side and I thought I could see a knot between his eyes.

"I never heard of an unconscious horse before," Wayne said, doubtful.

"Well, you have now." He threw his hat to Wayne. "Go scoop up some more of that red water and throw it in his face."

Wayne did as he was told, and after he threw the water in the horse's face that horse kind of whuffled and got to his feet, shaking his head. He kind of looked at Wayne and Pap and then looked toward where I still sat my horse, but I doubt he recognized any of us since he never had before.

"I'll put him back in the remuda for a day to two," Pap said, putting his wet hat on his head. "Likely he's gonna have a headache for a while."

The wagon was up with us by now so me and Wayne hitched our lariats to the left side of it, him in front and me in back, stayin' on the upstream side of it and ready to haul back on our lines if the current hitting it broadside tried to sweep it away.

We made the crossing without any problems and Wayne and me took a breather while we watched Harvey getting situated beneath a cottonwood tree, and then we rode back across the river to start crossing the herd.

Pap took the lead, staying on the downstream side of the herd but close to the far bank. Wayne took up the same position on the near bank, the Texas side of the river, while me and Rambler drove the herd across. When the last of the herd was in the water, Wayne joined me and we choused them up the far bank and into territory called the Indian Nations.

It was early evening by the time we got the herd bedded down, the sky going purple off to the west and a cooling breeze coming up that felt it might be strong enough to keep the mosquitoes off of us for a change. All in all, it was looking to be a good day ending until I looked at our campfire and saw three people standing where there should have been only two.

"You reckon that's trouble?" I asked Wayne, pointing.

He studied for a minute and then said, "No. If it was trouble, Pap would have managed to get off a shot."

"I guess that's true," I said, not thinking that there are some kinds of trouble you can't shoot at.

The third person at the wagons was a girl of about my own age, which was twenty-two at the time. She was wearing a shapeless dress that had been made out of flour sacks before it got covered with mud and she was barefoot, with mud splashed up on her legs to where the dress ended just above her knees. Her hair was probably light brown, though there seemed to be a lot of mud there, too, and it was tangled until a bird wouldn't have nested in it for fear of getting dizzy and falling out. Her face was smeared with mud too, but even so, I could tell she was pretty.

"Where'd you find her, Pap?" Wayne asked.

"She was just here, jawin' with Harvey, when I came up out of the river."

"You know anything about her?" I said.

The girl looked kind of meek, standing with her hands behind her back and her head hanging down. One foot seemed to be trying to scrape mud off of the other, but she had a long way to go before she was clean.

"I don't know a damned thing except that it's all peculiar," Pap said. "She was talking to Harvey and I came up to 'em and grinned real big and said 'Howdy' and the next thing I know she was down at the riverbank flingin' mud on herself."

"I know about her," Harvey said, stepping forward.

"Well, Harvey, maybe it'd be a good thing if you told us what you know so we'll know what to do about her," I said.

"Don't send me back!" the girl cried. "I won't go back!"

"Honey," Pap said kindly, "we're not going to send you nowhere you're afraid to go." He reached out like he was going to pat her on the shoulder.

Real quick, the girl squatted down, that short dress hiking itself up on some fine looking legs, and commenced to throw dirt on herself.

"By God, I've heard of that," Wayne said. "That's an Indian thing she's doing. You remember when Ranse Tucker told us about that, Roy Lee?"

"I do." I looked at Pap. "She's afraid of you, Pap. She's dirtyin' herself up so you won't be taken with her and tryin' to get to her."

"You mean she's tryin' to make herself look ugly?"

"That's the way of it," Wayne said. He climbed off his horse and undid the cinch strap, stealing a look at the girl now and then, and I did the same.

Pap laughed. "Well, it ain't workin', boys. First off, she ain't no Indian. And underneath all that dirt she's still just as pretty as..."

The girl started throwing dirt on herself again.

"Maybe you'd best not talk to her or get too close to her, Pap," Wayne said.

I went over to Pap and put my arm around his shoulder and my lips close to his ear so the girl couldn't hear. "Ranse told us that sometimes Indian woman will pack sand right up inside themselves so they can't be taken."

Pap backed off several steps, looking like he was either

scared or amazed. Wayne threw his saddle down under the tree and then went to the girl. On his way, he thumbed back his hat so a lock of that dark curly hair was showing, a thing he always did when he was trying to make up to the ladies.

Wayne walked right up to that girl and took her by the hand and she came to her feet just as pretty and as graceful as you please, looking right into Wayne's blue eyes all the way up. Then she gave Wayne a little smile and started trying to dust herself off. I wondered what she would have done had it been me instead of Wayne.

Wayne tipped me a wink and grinned real big at Pap. Pap opened his mouth three times, but no words ever did come out so he just sat down and folded his arms across his chest and sat there looking mad.

While all this was going on, Harvey had been shifting from one foot to the other and I knew he was just busting to tell us what he knew about the girl. "Go on and tell us, Harvey," I said.

"Wait a minute," Wayne said. He still had the girl by the hand and now he looked right into her eyes again. "While Harvey's tellin' us what he knows, little lady, would you like to take some soap and go down to the river and clean up?"

She nodded, kind of shy, and then gave him that smile again.

"Now, what if she escapes, Wayne?" Pap said.

"Escapes from who? She ain't no prisoner, Pap."

Without being told to do it, Harvey moved as quick as I'd ever seen him move and got a bar of fresh soap out of the cook wagon. He tipped his hat when he handed it to the girl and if her smile hadn't been covered in dirt, I bet it would have been real pretty.

Wayne finally let go of her hand and she started for the

river. We all watched her go until she turned aside and got some brush and bushes between us, and the way me and Wayne both shook our heads I know we was both thinking the same thing–that underneath that flour sack was a fine looking woman. It was just too bad that she'd got so scared of men that she had to throw dirt all over herself.

"All right, Harvey," Wayne said. He went over to Harvey's dishpan and washed the mud off his hand. "Now you can tell it."

"Well, Wayne, she's running away from some buffalo hunters that took her from her home over by Ogallala one night when she was out walkin' and lookin' at the moon like she sometimes took a notion to do, only Ogallala ain't really a town, it's just a trading post and a couple of shacks 'cause that's all Indian Territory, you know.

"Anyway, they may not have been buffalo hunters, Wayne, they may be Comancheros or they may be Comancheros that hunt buffalo when there ain't nothing else to do, she wasn't sure about that. She wasn't real sure about living in Ogallala, either, come to think of it, cause she also said she was from Fort Smith over in Arkansas, but I know where Fort Smith is from here and that's a long way east for Comancheros or buffalo hunters to be going, unless they had to go way out of their usual stomping grounds in order to find a girl as pretty as that out looking at the moon, and I mean she is pretty, you can see that under the mud, so I guess they probably took her from Ogallala after all.

"But she don't think they were purposely looking for a girl, Wayne, 'cause when they found her and picked her up and threw her over a spare horse they happened to have with them, tied hand and foot and with a rag in her mouth so she couldn't cry out, she thinks it was just a whim they had and not something they'd been planning to do until they seen her out walkin' alone in the moonlight and the whim come over them real powerful.

"The next thing she knew, Wayne, was that they was crossing a river and then ridin' hell-for-leather across the plains with her layin' face-down across that saddle and being jounced ever which way and her belly was sore for days afterwards, even though at daylight when they could see no one was after them they let her sit up on the horse and tied her feet together under the horse's belly so she couldn't jump off and go run and hide in the brush where they might never find her and she'd starve to death and her kin would never know what had become of her, they'd probably think she had run off with that whiskey trader that had been in town a few days before she was kidnapped and they'd think awful bad of her if they thought she'd done that."

"Damn, Harvey!" Wayne was scratching his head. "Are you going to finish the story some time this week?"

About the time Wayne said that, I was beginning to wonder if Granny Davis had ever taught Harvey how to fill in missing parts.

"Don't vex me, Wayne, 'cause there's a lot more to tell. The buffalo hunters or Comancheros or whatever they might be rode for several days across the Territory and they're camped somewhere west of here in a ratty old camp that smells of buffalo hides and some of them had at her when they got her into camp and that's when she heard from some little feller among them about how Indian women throw dirt on themselves but it didn't do a lot of good when she tried it because some more of them had at her a few days later and she just figured that buffalo hunters and Comancheros or whatever they are just don't care what their women look like, but that

little feller who'd told her about what Indian woman do didn't
have at her when his turn came even though the others was
devilin' him to take his turn but he said he was feeling poorly
and would get to her later so that night she climbed into his
bedroll with him and lay in his arms nice and sweet and
sneaked his skinning knife out of its holster and held it to his
throat while they walked real soft to where the horses were
hitched and she made him saddle his own horse for her, though
how she kept the knife to his throat while he did that is
something I can't figure out unless it was that he felt sorry for
her and was glad to help her escape, and anyway she got on
that horse and rode away from the camp but it wasn't until the
sun came up the next morning that she could figure which way
was east and so she started east and then she found the river to
follow and here she is and that's all there is to it and I know it
ain't much of a story, Wayne, and I'm sorry about that but it's
all I was able to get out of her before your Pap came up and
started scaring her into throwing mud on herself."

"By God, I never did!" Pap said. "All I did was grin and
say 'Howdy.'"

"Well, there's something about you that scares her, Pap,"
Wayne said, touchy-like. "Maybe you remind her of one of
those buffalo hunters or Comancheros or whatever they call
themselves. Maybe if you'd shave now and then you wouldn't
look so much like a damn buffalo your own self."

"Now, by God, that tears it, Wayne!" Pap got to his feet
and balled his fists and I swear there was the same fire in his
eyes that Wayne always had when he was coming at me. I'd
never seen Pap that mad before, though he'd come close to it
that time Wayne painted all the chickens blue, but I'd been
around Wayne long enough to know that there ain't anything
like a pretty woman to bring out feelings most men don't even

know they have.

Before Pap could take even one step toward Wayne, he froze, except for his mouth dropping open. We all turned, expecting to see that Indians had snuck up on us, but it was something more dangerous than that.

That girl came walking up from the riverbank just as naked as the day she was born. Her dress was wet and was draped over her arm and kind of held in front of her, but not held so that it hid anything of the nicest looking bosoms I'd ever seen. Her legs were as shapely as her bosoms, though in a different way, of course, and the swelling line of her hips was like something out of one of my dreams about Velvet.

"Well?" she said. "I don't know why the hell y'all are looking so surprised. I had to wash my damned dress, didn't I?"

"Oh. Oh, sure," I said. "That dress was dirty."

"Well, the son-of-a-bitch is clean now. I soaped it good and pounded hell out of it on some rocks." She giggled then. "Probably like to wore holes in it. Would you like to see if it's clean enough to suit you?" She held the dress out to me and the last mystery of her was uncovered.

"No. No, that's all right. I can see from here that it's whean as a clistle."

She giggled again. "I'll just bet you're Roy Lee. Harvey told me you were the shitkicking kind."

I just nodded and tried to quit toeing at the ground. I didn't know how Harvey had had a chance to tell her anything.

She turned to Wayne. "So that would make you to be Wayne."

Harvey had gone to the cook wagon and now he came back with a blanket for her to wrap herself in.

"Why, thank you, Harvey. I was gettin' a mite chill in this

ol' night air."

I was scratching my head, wondering what had happened to the scared little girl she'd been before she cleaned herself up.

"Harvey," Pap called. "When you get done hanging her dress on that bush, heat me some water. I believe I'd like to shave tonight."

While Pap shaved and cussed about water that was half mud and not even of a color a man could get interested in, me and Wayne and the girl made ourselves comfortable around the campfire. I was kind of glad I sat across from her because that blanket kept slipping every now and then, and while she fixed it back in place she'd usually give me a wink or a smile.

She said her name was Maggie and that she had been taken from Ogallala and how old Harvey got all mixed up about Fort Smith was something she just couldn't understand.

"Now, tell us about these buffalo hunters or Comancheros or whatever they were, Maggie. How many of them are there?"

She kind of chewed on her lower lip for a moment. "More than ten, Wayne."

"How many more?" I asked.

"Now, I just don't rightly know. You see, I can only count up to ten and I did that, but then here was some left over."

"Why didn't you start over and count up to ten again?"

She made her eyes wide. "Why, what on earth difference would that have made, Roy Lee? There would have still been ten of them with some left over."

I thought on that until it felt like my head was kind of spinning. I opened my mouth twice to tell her how it was done, and in the end I decided she was right.

"Do you think they know about us?" Wayne asked. "Do you think there's any chance they'll try to hit our herd?"

"Now, I don't rightly know about that, either." She chewed on a thumbnail and her blanket started to slip, moving far enough this time that a pretty nipple peeked out. She tucked it up around her bosoms again. "Do y'all have any buffalo in your herd?"

"Not the last time we looked. But if they're Comancheros, they may not care all that much whether we got buffalo or not."

"Don't you have any clearer idea of what they might be, Maggie?" I asked. "Did you see any buffalo hides anywhere around the camp?"

"Well, the camp smelled of dead things." She looked thoughtful. "So did the men, for that matter." Then she kind of giggled. "I know they had at least one damned old buffalo robe, though, cause that's where they laid me down when they had at me."

"That's a real sorry thing," I said.

She took it wrong. "Well, I am sorry about it, too, Roy Lee, but at the time I didn't know I was supposed to be scoutin' their camp for you." She was kind of flared up, her eyes narrowed, and her tone sharp. "And I think you'll appreciate that it's damned hard to learn much about a camp when you're flat on your back buck naked with your goddamn legs up in the air."

The coffee I'd been about to swallow choked me and I went to coughing and spitting.

Maggie was grinning at me and then she turned her grin on Wayne. "He is kind of a shy shitkicker, isn't he?"

"Yes, he is," Wayne said, grinning right back at her. "Never much been that way myself."

"Well, I think it's kind of cute."

Wayne was quick. "I have been that way a time or two, though."

She reached up to the bush where her flour sack dress was spread out and felt of it. "Well, it's mostly dry. I suppose I'd better get dressed."

She stood up and let the blanket fall, stretching and yawning, then she turned her back to us and pulled that dress on over her head. I don't know why she bothered to turn away but it was comforting to know that her backside looked as good as her front. Then she laid down with her head on her saddle and the blanket pulled up to her chin and went right to sleep.

"What do you think, Roy Lee?"

"I don't know just what to think. This is all one too many for me."

Wayne nodded. "We'd best get Pap in on this. It's gonna take some talking about."

"If y'all are going to talk about me, would y'all mind going over by the cook wagon so I can get some sleep? I've had kind of a hard day." All the time she was talking, she kept her head on the saddle and her eyes closed, looking calm and peaceful.

Wayne and me looked at one another, surprised that she'd fooled us into thinking she was asleep, and then I got my wits about me again. "Well, she has had a hard day, what with putting on mud and washing it off and one thing and another."

"I expect that's so," Wayne said. "Though that whole thing is puzzling, too."

"Just in case you boys are wondering, or might be thinking about getting at me in the night, I didn't put no mud up inside me."

"I don't think we was wonderin' about that, Maggie," Wayne said.

"I ain't really scared of your Pap, either."

"Well, maybe I'll tell him that and ease him some," I said.

"All right. Good night."

Being quiet about it, though she probably wasn't asleep, me and Wayne got up from the fire and went over to the cook wagon where Pap had finally finished shaving the brush off his face and Harvey was asleep under the wagon.

"Now, what's this?" Pap said. "I was just fixin' to come over and see if that little girl was still scared of me."

"I'm not so sure she ever was scared of you, Pap. I think there's a lot of lies mixed in with the story she's tellin' and I think it's time we hashed it out and see what we know for sure."

Pap nodded, fingering his jaw like he was sorry he'd bothered to shave. "I been thinkin' on some of it. First off, there haven't been any Comancheros around for years, not since the Rangers killed off most of the Comanches."

"Now, that's good, Pap. That's just the kind of things we got to turn over and look at real good." He looked at me and grinned. "What about you, Roy Lee? You formed an opinion about anything besides the way she looks naked?"

I could have took offense at that but I didn't. I just gave his grin back to him because I knew he'd been studying her form as hard as I was. "Matter of fact, I do, Wayne. I noticed that she's well-spoken when she's not cussin', which would mean she's been educated. But she says she can't count and if that's true, that means not much of an education. So maybe she was just raised around people who were educated and spoke well. Whether she can count or not, she must come from a good family."

"Another thing," Wayne said. "She acted at first like she was scared to death of us, then all of a sudden she changed her mind and got real friendly. I can't figure that one."

Me and Pap nodded.

The night was full dark now and a bright half-moon was

in the sky. I looked back to where Maggie was sleeping on the far side of the dying fire, but what I saw in my mind was a young girl in a short flour sack dress, walking out at night to look at the moon.

"I ain't got to hear her say much," Pap said. "But what I did hear sounded more like Georgia or Alabama than it did like Arkansas or Texas."

"All right," Wayne said. "So we can figure that much. Now, I wouldn't believe anything about the buffalo hunters except for her knowing that Indian thing about throwing dirt on herself."

I agreed with that but only part way. She could have heard them stories elsewhere, same as me and Wayne had, though usually you wouldn't think of a young girl being around people who told such stories. It seemed like the more we worried at it, the more puzzling it got.

"Why wouldn't you believe that?" Pap said.

"For one thing, that's a fine-looking horse and saddle rig she's ridin', better than I'd expect you could steal from a hide hunter. You'd best tell him the rest, Roy Lee."

"Damn, Wayne, why me?"

He kind of hung his head and mumbled, "Because Pap don't like me talkin' to him about things like that."

"You damned pups! What kind of things?"

I kind of put my head down and mumbled it. "Pap, she was telling us about how they laid her on a buffalo robe and a bunch of them had at her and it was like she hadn't minded it much." When I realized I was toeing at the ground again, I made myself stop.

"Buffalo robe, huh?" He was feeling of his bare jaw again. "Maybe I oughta think about gettin' one of them for myself."

"Pap!"

"Oh. Uh...Well, boys, you're the ones heard her tell about that. Do you think she's simple?"

"I guess either she's simple or she was enjoyin' it all," I said, looking to Wayne. His face was kind of pinched up, like he didn't want it to be true either way, but he was nodding some agreement with me.

"Well, enjoyin' it is out for sure," Pap said. "So she must be simple."

"How do you figure that, Pap?" Wayne said.

"Now, dammit, Wayne! You're old enough to know women don't enjoy doin' it. Not unless they're whores and then they only enjoy it because of the money involved."

"Or the pigs," I grinned.

"Right! Or the pigs..." Pap stopped and gave me a look like he was speculating. "About them pigs, Roy Lee..."

"If the women I was with didn't enjoy it," I said quick, "then they sure put on a fine show."

"That was likely in a whorehouse," Pap said. "Puttin' on such fine shows is what they do." He shot a glance at Wayne. "Anyway, that's what I hear from other fellers."

"Well, now, Pap, me and Rose..."

"And where did you find Rose?"

"Uh...in a whorehouse, I guess." Now Wayne was toeing at the dirt and I was glad Maggie wasn't awake to see him do it. She already seemed a bit taken with him and I didn't think it was a good idea for him to get ahead of me. "But all she did there was to sling hash and dust the furniture, Pap."

There was my chance to tell him he was wrong, but I couldn't see my way clear to making a fool of him in front of Pap. Besides, it had been a long, confusing day and I was too tired to enjoy a fight the way it ought to be enjoyed. When I'm fighting Wayne, I like to go at it whole hog, with nothing else on my mind.

"Now, even if that's true, Wayne," I said, "she could have done some talkin' with the whores and learned some of the things they do."

Wayne gave me a black look. "Sometimes, you talk like you know Rose, or know more about her than you're sayin'."

"All I know is what you've told me," I lied.

"Don't matter," Pap said. "Both of you just proved my point. The only women who enjoy doin' it are whores and they're just play-actin' so's they can get your money."

"Are you sayin' that Maggie's a whore?" Wayne asked. He looked like he'd just been hurt.

"I ain't sayin' anything, yet," Pap said. He looked at me. "Has she asked anybody for money or pigs?"

"Now, what the hell do pigs have to do with all this?"

Pap gave him a dark look. "Ask Roy Lee sometime."

"Anyway," I said, changing the subject. "We got to figure what we're going to do about her and we got to think about whether them men she was with might try to take our herd."

"How many men were there?" Pap asked. "Did she say?"

"More than ten."

"Well? How many more?"

"I'd just as soon not start on that," I said. "Last time I tried to figure it I got a headache."

"What do you think, Pap?" Wayne said. "Let her trail along with us or send her on her way?"

Pap rubbed his jaw some more. "We're goin' north and she says she was goin' east. Might be she'll want to keep on goin' east. But if she wants to trail with us, I'd say let her. She's one more hand if they do hit our herd and she's got a fine Sharp's rifle on that saddle of hers."

"But can she shoot it?" I said. "And which side would she be on if they did attack us?"

"That's a chance we have to take," Pap said.

"Now, I don't see it that way," Wayne said. "Why do we have to take any chances at all on her?"

Pap grinned and fingered his smooth jaw. "Because there's a chance she may not be simple."

Chapter Six

Maggie

The way I was seeing it, nothing was simple. Only a few weeks ago, I'd spent most of my time with Jessie on my mind and then Velvet had come to replace her in my thoughts. When I crawled into my bedroll after the talk with Wayne and Pap, I was doing a lot of thinking about Maggie and of how she'd looked when she came walking naked back from the river. And then I thought some more about how she'd looked with the campfire light and the night shadows playing on her and that blanket slipping off her shoulder ever now and then.

Maggie was a fine-looking woman who didn't pretend to be ashamed or embarrassed about any of her qualities and didn't seem to mind men taking stock of those qualities. More to the point, Jessie was back in Waco and Velvet might or might not be in Dodge City, but Maggie was right here in our cow camp and the night was warm and full of stars and had the good smell of prairie grass. It was troubling.

Wayne had the first turn at nighthawk, and we thought it was especially important tonight. I believe we all had the thought that Maggie could be an advance scout for rustlers, someone to get into our camp and find out how strong we were and how likely we were to fight for the herd. If that was the case, our small numbers should have caused her to just stand up and yell, "Come on in!" to whoever might be lurking in the dark, but she hadn't done that yet.

When I shook out my bedroll and laid down, Maggie was still asleep on the other side of the fire. Pap took a spot near me after Wayne pointed out that he didn't need to be near enough to Maggie to get her spooked again. Pap grumbled about it a bit, but then his grumbles turned into snores, Wayne moved off to do his rides around the herd, and I was left alone to think about Maggie.

It was in my mind that any of us could have her for a kind word or a trinket, and maybe for less than that. But no matter how fine she looked without her clothes on, I decided I wasn't even going to try.

Now, that wasn't an easy conclusion to come to and I only got there after turning a lot of things over in my mind. On the one hand, there was the notion that me and Wayne would end up fighting over her. And then add in Pap and the way Harvey was taken with her and it could turn into a four-way fight.

After that, I had to think about my being true to Jessie and Velvet. Even though it was a cinch that I was never going to amount to enough of anything to impress Jessie's Pa, I still had strong feelings toward her. The memories of her that last day in the schoolyard, when she'd thrown her arms around me and said she loved me, were just as fresh as the day they'd happened. As for Velvet, there was still in my mind that vision of her that Pap had given me and I had my hopes that she would live up to that vision and would favor me for bringing her cattle up the trail.

The last thing I thought of was that Maggie might really be simple and that if she were simple it would be a mighty low thing to take advantage of her. In the end, I decided the best thing I could do was to stay true to Jessie and Velvet and to protect Maggie from Wayne and Pap, if need be.

We were in the one-room schoolhouse, the door locked

and dust motes dancing golden in the shafts of sunlight that streamed in through the closed windows. Jessie was at the front of the schoolroom with her back to me, writing on the big slate board. She was naked, her wet dress hung over one arm and her dark brown hair hanging damp on her creamy shoulders.

I couldn't make out what she was writing, but then she turned to face me and said, "The lesson for today is about love."

"Yes, ma'am."

"Do you know anything about love, Roy Lee?"

"I get uncertain of it from time to time."

"Did you do your homework about being faithful, Roy Lee?"

"Uh...Well...No, ma'am, I guess I didn't."

"Oh, that's naughty, Roy Lee. You can't ever learn about love if you don't know how to be faithful." She wore a big smile, showing where that tooth was missing from near the front of her mouth. "I like it when you're naughty, but you'll still have to be punished." She put the dress on her desk and picked up a yardstick, then came back to where I sat at the desk and took me by the hand. "Come into the parlor and take your punishment, Roy Lee."

It all made sense to me then, so I got up and followed her through a doorway that hadn't been there before. As we entered a parlor that was lit by a dozen or more lamps, I could see that her hair wasn't reddish at all but was more of a light brown color. And what she held in her hand wasn't a yardstick. It was a Sharps rifle.

"Sit over there, Roy Lee." She motioned with the rifle toward one of the overstuffed chairs and I did as I was told.

"Take off your boots, Roy Lee. Oh, hell, just take off

everything."

Again, I did what she told me to do, and pretty soon I was sitting in the chair naked, looking at a naked Maggie who was pointing a gun at me.

"Now, you can have me, Roy Lee, but first you've got to tell me how big your herd is and what it's worth. My partners need to know if it's worth their trouble to take it away from y'all." She sat down in an easy chair across from me, letting the barrel of the rifle point at the floor while she put one leg over the arm of the chair. "You do want me, don't you?"

"Yes, ma'am. A thousand head and they should be worth fifty dollars apiece in Dodge," I said.

"That's good, Roy Lee. That's very good." She grinned at me and then beckoned me to her. "I guess y'all have earned the right to have at me."

I went to her and she stood and we put our arms around one another and kissed and I felt her tongue go way back in my mouth and decided I liked that French way of kissing after all. She pulled away after a minute, both of us breathing heavy, and said, "Not here. In my bedroom."

She took my hand and led me through another doorway I'd not seen before. There was a big four-poster bed with a white canopy on it in case of a hailstorm. Velvet led me to the bed and lay down on it, her golden hair spread across the pillow and her green eyes watching me as I climbed in beside her.

She pulled me to her and we kissed some more. Her hands were roaming over me so I thought it was safe to let my hands roam over her and every now and then, depending on where I touched her, she would let out a little gasp or a moan. Finally, I knew I was as ready as I was ever going to get so I rolled her over onto her back and moved over her.

"Not yet, Roy Lee. Please."

"I hope you're not fixin' to ask me about pigs," I said.

"Of course not, Roy Lee," she giggled. "But a woman has to prepare herself, you know."

"Oh." I didn't know for sure, but I was willing to take her word for it. "Sure, I know."

"Good." She moved her legs apart and bent her knees so that her feet were flat on the bed. "Now, you can't watch me do this, Roy Lee."

"I'll close my eyes."

"That's fine," Velvet said. "But before you close them, reach over to the nightstand and hand me that box of dirt."

"Dammit! I'm sick of hearin' about dirt!"

"Maybe you shouldn't sleep in it, then."

I got my eyes open and saw Maggie walking back from the direction of the herd. When she got closer to the dying fire she said, "You've done rolled off your bedroll and got face-down in the dirt." She giggled. "Kind of looked like you was humping it, Roy Lee."

"I never did."

"Well, anyway..." She laid down on her own bedroll and covered herself with the blanket. "Good night."

I suppose I was still coming awake, for all of a sudden I realized where she'd been coming from and a rage started building in me. A check of the stars told me it was a good hour before Wayne was due to wake me up, but I thought it best that I go find him and see whether we still had a herd to guard.

I rode out easy so as not to wake Pap or Maggie, and when I got out to where the herd was bedded down I dismounted and waited in a grove of cottonwoods. Wayne would be coming by on his rounds soon and I wanted to be set for him.

When I heard the sound of his horse walking easy, I stepped out into the moonlight and called his name soft.

"That you, Roy Lee?"

"It ain't Maggie."

"Too bad about that, I reckon," he laughed. "What's doin', Roy Lee? You got another hour before it's your turn at nighthawk."

"I got something on my mind. Dismount and come on over here."

Wayne got off his horse and came over to where I stood. When I judged the distance about right, I swung an uppercut that staggered him back a few paces. "That one was for Maggie," I said.

Wayne was fingering his jaw and shaking his head, but he was coming back at me. I swung a roundhouse right that knocked him to the ground. "That one was for me."

He was sitting on the ground, knees drawn up, his forearms resting on his knees and his hands dangling while he kept shaking his head.

"You gonna just sit there?" I said. I still needed to wallop him for stealing my dreams about Velvet.

"Until I find out if you got any more damned mail to deliver, I believe I'll do just that."

"Not good enough." By God, if he wouldn't stand and fight I'd just kick the hell out of him. I swung my boot, but Wayne was quick. He grabbed my foot, raised his arm above his head, and I went down in the dirt flat on my back with the wind and the rage knocked out of me. When I sat up, he still had my boot in his hand and was looking at it kind of queer.

"Would you like to tell me what this is all about? Or are you waitin' for me to get up and whale the tar out of you?"

"That was a low thing you did, Wayne. I never would have thought it of you." I got my foot back from him and sat Indian fashion in the dirt.

He kind of hung his head. "Well, it was stupid, maybe even ornery, but I don't see how you figure it was low-down."

"You don't see how I figure?" I took off my hat and threw it in the dirt. "Wayne, for all we know that girl is simple and it ain't right to take advantage of simple people."

"What the hell are you talking about?"

"The same low-down dirty deed you're talking about, I reckon."

Wayne laughed and that surprised me. "No, I don't think so. The ornery thing I'm talkin' about is getting Harvey to ride nighthawk so I could catch a few extra winks."

I gave him a narrow look. "If that's so, when did you spell Harvey?"

"Oh, within the last half hour. I just got to make one round of the herd before you came out here and ambushed me."

"Damn."

"Now, what made you to think I was out here dallyin' with Maggie?"

I told him about how I'd woke up and seen Maggie walking back from the direction of the herd and how she'd seemed kind of bright and bouncy.

"Well, if anybody made her feel bright and bouncy it wasn't me," Wayne said. "It would have to have been..."

"Harvey?" I said.

"Nah, not Harvey." Wayne laughed again. "I don't think she's that simple."

I laughed with him. "You're right. Old Harvey would still be trying to talk her out of that dress."

"Come to that, I don't know that I agree. She seems to like sheddin' that dress."

"Well, I kind of like it when she does it, too. But then I got to thinkin' about how she was probably simple and that the best thing I can do is to keep you and Pap from tryin' to get to her."

Wayne cocked his head at me. "And you figured the best way to do that was to leave her alone with Pap?"

"Damn!" I got to my feet and dusted myself off.

"Don't be in such a hurry," Wayne said. "Hell, Pap's too old for that, no matter what he might think."

"I hope I never get that old." I picked up my hat and put it on. "Well, I guess nothin' happened. Might be she was just payin' a call on nature. I guess we got to expect things to be different now that we've got a woman on the drive."

Wayne nodded agreement. "You know, Roy Lee, I'd been thinkin' along the same lines as you. Only I was figurin' it would be you I'd have to keep away from her."

"Well, I'm glad to hear that, Wayne. As long as you feel that way, I don't have anyone to worry about and you don't, neither." I went to get my horse and led him back into the clearing. "You might as well go get some sleep, Wayne. I'll take over from here."

"Say, before you go, I'd like another look at them boots you're wearin'."

"Some other time." I quick mounted my horse and kicked him into the shadows.

We trailed on for several more days with me, Wayne, and Pap keeping a sharp eye out for rustlers. Maggie sometimes rode on the cook wagon with Harvey, her fine horse trailing behind, and I often wondered what they found to talk about. Other times she would ride the horse, her short dress hiked up to allow her to ride straddle, and times like those I liked to ride drag on the herd.

Drag was the worst place to be because of the dust and the smell of all the cow flops and the flies that couldn't find a good cow to bite on, but it wasn't nearly as discomforting as seeing Maggie half naked.

***

We were getting close to the Kansas border, where roamed the gangs that would stop a herd and levy a head tax on it, and we were all worried about that. Since we didn't have much cash money, it looked like it would be bad for us if we was stopped. We weren't enough to make a fight against a bunch of any size, and the best we could hope for was that they would cut the herd rather than try to take the whole thing. As bad as that would be to our chances of making money on the drive, I was already figuring that if they took any of the Velvet brand, I'd make up for them out of my share of the other mavericks.

The moon was full again and we were right close to the Kansas border when Maggie came to me in the night.

There had been times during the past week when I'd woke up and seen that she wasn't in her bedroll, but I didn't think much of it. For a woman, she did drink a sight of coffee and I figured that kept her going to the bushes in the middle of the night. Now, of course, we were getting into that prairie country where there were hardly any bushes, not to mention a serious lack of trees, but once you got off the cattle trail the high prairie grass offered some privacy.

Pap had started taking turns at being the nighthawk, complaining that his arthritis wouldn't let him sleep much anyway. Wayne and me was some surprised at that and when we talked it over we were both sure we'd never heard him mention that ailment before. Of course, he was a prideful man and he did have enough years on him that the ailments of old age were most likely starting to bother him, so we guessed he hadn't mentioned it until it became so bad he couldn't ignore it any more. However it may have been, we were both glad for the extra sleep it gave us.

He woke me up at midnight, telling me it was my watch. I untangled myself from my blanket while he threw another couple of buffalo chips on the dying fire. There wasn't enough wood in this prairie country to build even a hitching rail and we had had to lean on Harvey and Maggie to start picking up any buffalo chips or cow chips they saw, otherwise we'd have had no fire at all.

While Pap was getting into his bedroll, grumbling that there never was any leftover vittles anymore, I was getting out of mine, taking the saddle I'd used for a pillow and slinging it on the horse I'd kept tethered close to the fire. I looked back at the three of them and thought I saw firelight reflected from Maggie's eyes and guessed either Pap or me had made enough noise to wake her up.

The night was warm with a soft breeze blowing and on the air was the smell of long grass and prairie flowers. On a pretty night like this, it was easy to know why so many settlers were making their homes on the Kansas prairie, even though most of those homes had to be built of sod or dug into the side of one of the low hills. The full moon showed me the sleeping herd almost as bright as day and I could see the long grass waving in the breeze. I said howdy to Rambler when I came upon him and then he trotted off to find himself a likely spot for a nap.

I'd only made one round of the herd when Maggie came walking out of the tall grass and then climbed up and perched herself on a big boulder.

"You lose your way, Maggie?" I said, pointing. "The camp's over that way. You can just see the fire from here."

"I didn't lose my way, Roy Lee. I'm right where I want to be..." She was sitting atop that boulder with her knees drawn up and her arms resting on them and that short dress wasn't covering much at all, so I was kind of thankful for the shadows.

"You'd rather be out here settin' on a rock than to be sleepin'?"

"I'd rather be out here talking to you." She put her chin on her knees. "I'm feelin' kind of forlorn, Roy Lee. Do you ever feel forlorn?"

"I guess there's been times," I said carefully. Truth was, there had been plenty of times and most of them just lately, when I thought about how far away Jessie was and how we might never find Velvet. "What are you forlorn about, Maggie?"

"About us. About you and me."

Now something happened to me when she said that, something that went clear through my body. The nearest I'd ever come to that feeling before was when lightning struck a tree near me and my hair stood on end. I figured right then that Maggie was about as dangerous to my peace of mind as the lightning, so I wasn't going to ask any more about her feelings.

I got down off my horse and hunkered down near the rock so that she and I were looking off in the same direction. If she needed to talk, then I was going to have to answer and I figured to keep the distractions to a minimum. "What did you need to talk about?"

"About us."

"I didn't know there was anything about us to talk about." I had the reins in my hand and I found out I was tying knots and then untying them.

"Have you ever been with a woman, Roy Lee?"

"Well...I don't think that's something we should be talkin' about."

"Oh, hell! Don't be treating me like I'm some kind

of...breakable virgin. I hate it when men do that. I'm a woman, Roy Lee, can't you see that?"

"I noticed."

"Then quit knottin' them reins and look at me now and then!"

I turned my head and craned my neck, but what I saw were her bare feet and legs just over my shoulder. Right then I knew I didn't want to see more so I quick turned back and looked out into the dark prairie.

"I have a woman's needs, just the same as you have a man's needs. That's what I meant about us, Roy Lee, about us needing one another."

I kind of gulped. I'd never thought about women having needs and I was sure she was lying about that. If Pap was right and women didn't like doing it, then what difference did it make if they thought they had needs?

"As for being some silly damned virgin, I haven't been a virgin since I was twelve years old and my second cousin caught me up in the hayloft."

"Well...Uh...I'm sorry about that..."

Maggie laughed. "Hell, I'm not sorry. As far as I'm concerned, it could have happened sooner. It made those first twelve years just a damned waste of time."

"Then...I guess those buffalo hunters havin' at you wasn't as bad as what we all thought it was."

The way it was, with her up on that rock she was higher than me. Now she took my hat off and started playing her fingers in my hair, giving me chills that ran all the way down to my boot heels.

"There weren't any buffalo hunters, Roy Lee, and there weren't any Comancheros. I just made them stories up to kind of protect myself, maybe get y'all to feel sorry enough to take me with you." She slid down off the rock and knelt in front of me, taking my face in her hands and looking right into my eyes. When she spoke again, her voice was husky. "I just needed some time to get to know y'all a bit better."

"Well..."

"I ran away from home, Roy Lee, and I needed to know you weren't the kind of people who would drag me back."

"Why run away, Maggie? The way you talk, we figured you must come from a good home." It was kind of hard to talk because her fingers were touching my lips.

"Oh, yes." She sounded bitter. "A fine old southern family that got torn up by the war and wanted me to marry a man I didn't even like. All their talk about what fine stock he came from and what good bloodlines we'd pass on to our children...I felt like I was a horse about to be bred."

"I guess I can understand that, but..."

"Don't say anything, Roy Lee. I'll show you how people who need one another really get to know one another." She leaned toward me and kissed me full on the lips.

Well, I'd been sitting on my heels and the surprise of that kiss made me lose my balance. I kind of toppled over and the next thing I knew I was lying on my back and Maggie was stretched out on top of me. She kind of giggled and then kissed me again, her hair falling forward and shutting out even the moonlight, so that it was like we were all alone in some private place and when I felt her tongue touch my lips I opened my mouth and tasted the sweetness of her.

She giggled. "Aren't you supposed to be on top?"

When she spoke, I came to myself and got my hands on her shoulders to twist her off of me, but the way it ended up after her squirming around was that now she was on her back and I was over her, pinning her down.

"Mmmm...That's more like it. I'm going to like you, Roy Lee."

"Now it ain't what it looks like, Maggie." I sat up, but I was still straddling her.

"I care more about what it feels like," she whispered. She ran her hand over the front of my jeans. "And so far it feels very good."

I raised up, getting to my knees but still holding her by the shoulders. That short dress had worked itself all the way up to where it was around her waist and I admit it held my attention for a minute.

"You like what you see, don't you?"

"It don't make no nevermind whether I like it or not," I said, mournfully. "We ain't going to do it."

"Well, Goddamn, Roy Lee! You get me all worked up with your sweet talk and your pawing at me and then tell me we're not going to do it?"

"Dammit, I never sweet talked you!"

"The hell you didn't! And pawin' at me and raisin' my dress! Let me up!"

I let go of her and she sat up, her legs straight out in front of her and her pulling that dress down to cover as much as it would. "You damned cowboys are all alike. Lots of sweet talk but too damned bashful to back it up. Shitkickers!"

"Listen, Maggie." My voice sounded strangled and I wondered if the sudden tightness of my jeans had anything to do with it. There were a whole lot of feelings churning around inside me and I knew some of them were what old Granny Davis had called impure thoughts, but I knew I had to stand fast and try to do what was right–or at least not do what I knew to be wrong. "You're a pretty woman, but I just can't do it to you."

"Awww..." She put her hand on my leg and was slowly moving it up my thigh. "If you've got a problem, maybe I can..." She giggled. "No, you sure as hell don't have a problem."

Moving her hand off me, I said, "It ain't my problem. It's yours. You're simple, Maggie."

Her eyes flashed fire. "Now, that's the second time this week I've been called simple and told to go away. I can tell you I'm getting damned tired of it." She grabbed my shirtfront. "Why does everyone think I'm simple?"

I pried her fingers loose. "Well...the way you paraded naked in front of all of us. The way you didn't seem to mind what you said those buffalo hunters did to you..."

"I told you there weren't any buffalo hunters! How can you hold that against me?"

"Well...But..."

"Oh, Goddamn!"

She put her hands to her face and began to cry. I had no doubt it was genuine, for her shoulders was shaking and she was sobbing and when I put my hand on her shoulder she moved her hands and looked at me and I could see her tears glistening in the moonlight.

"All...all I wanted to do...was to learn to be easy...not...not simple!" She leaned toward me and the next thing I knew was that I had my arms around her, her head was against my chest, and I was patting her on the shoulder, trying to comfort her.

As kindly as I could, I said, "Now why would a fine girl like you want to be thought easy, Maggie?"

"You...you won't laugh if I tell you?" She kind of sniffled, the way a person does when they're trying to stop crying.

"I wouldn't laugh at you, Maggie," I said, my voice soft.

"Well...before I met up with you all...I was on my way to

Wichita...to be a whore."

Well, I had to laugh. We'd all made up our minds not to bother her and here she wanted to be bothered, maybe so she could get the experience she needed for her new job. It put a new light on my thoughts about Jessie and Velvet and I decided that maybe I didn't have to worry about them. The way I was figuring it, I could still be loyal to them and yet give a runaway girl some practice at getting ready for a new job.

"Damn you! You said you wouldn't laugh!" She pushed herself out of my arms and started to her feet.

"Now wait a minute." I pulled her back down and held her with my hands on her shoulders. "I wasn't laughing at you."

"Yes, you were!" She pushed my hands away and got to her feet, looking down at me. "I guess you think it's funny, me wanting to be a whore so I can make some good money, and I can't even get a couple of randy cowboys to dally with me!"

"Wait, Maggie. Now that I know you're not simple, I'd be proud to dally with you."

She started off through the tall grass. "That's the same thing that damned Wayne said!"

"Wayne?"

She turned and put her hands on her hips. "And I'll tell you the same thing I told him. Too damned late, Cowboy." She brushed away more angry tears. "To hell with it! I'll find some other line of work. This is too humiliatin'!"

She stomped off through the long grass, not even looking up at the moon.

I didn't see much of Maggie the next day, for she rode on the cook wagon with Harvey. When I did chance to ride close to them, it seemed they had their heads together and I still wondered how she could talk to Harvey and ever get a word in edgewise.

At about noon, we came to a fork in the cattle trail. From what I'd been told, the right fork was the old trail to Ellsworth and the left fork was the newer one that would take us to Wichita or to Dodge City. I was riding point, so when I saw where we were I called a halt and rode back to talk to Wayne and Pap.

"We're in Kansas, now," I told them. "If there's any border gangs out, they'll be posted somewhere along the trail, so we've got to look sharp and not miss any signs."

"Well, you're the one ridin' point, so it's likely you'll see sign before we do," Wayne said.

"Why don't we hold the herd here for a while?" Pap said. "It's about time for a noon stop anyway, so after you boys eat you might want to scout ahead a bit and see if you see anything."

Twisting in my saddle, I looked around. It was good grass and the cattle could do with a little rest. When I looked at Wayne, he nodded and I said, "We'll do it that way, then. Soon as we've had something to eat."

"I sure hope Harvey cooks up more than he's been doin'," Pap said, fingers drumming on his stomach. "Seems like he don't know there's five of us to cook for now."

"That Maggie does have a healthy appetite," Wayne said, grinning at me. "But I think you got a tapeworm, Pap."

"I ain't got no damned tapeworm, Wayne! I just ain't gettin' enough to eat."

I wanted to get Wayne to a place where Pap couldn't overhear so we could compare notes about Maggie trying to lay with us, and I was anxious to start the scout.

The noon meal was a bit light, except for the biscuits. Since I trusted Harvey's biscuits more than any of his other cooking, I filched a few extras when no one was looking and put them in my saddlebag. They were handy when I was out nighthawking and got hungry.

"You're sure the three of you can hold the herd?" Wayne asked Pap while we were saddling our horses.

"Now, just look at the damned herd, Wayne. Do they look like they're goin' anywhere?"

Wayne grinned at him. "They do look a sight calmer than you do."

Pap started to throw a biscuit at him, then thought better of it and took an angry bite out of it.

"We'll likely be back before dark," I said.

Wayne and me were about two miles from camp before I thought to open the subject of Maggie, but before I could say anything Wayne opened the ball.

"You done any more talkin' to Maggie, or any more thinkin' about her?"

Taken by surprise, I kind of shied an answer at him. "Some."

"Talkin' or thinkin'?"

"Both."

"Dammit, Roy Lee, I know when you're being cagey, but this is something we got to talk about. Did you lay with her?"

"Hell, no! Don't you remember we said we wouldn't do that because she's simple?"

Wayne chewed on a thumbnail and looked sideways at me. Then he kind of sighed. "I might as well tell you, Roy Lee. She ain't simple."

Still fighting shy of telling him what I knew–or thought I knew–I decided to see how much I could drag out of Wayne.

"Now, how come you to know that about her? Did you lay with her your own self?"

"No." He worried at his thumbnail some more. "But she wanted me to do it, Roy Lee."

"Why didn't you?"

"God dammit! By the time I figured out that she wasn't simple, it was too late! She lost interest in me."

"That's the same thing that happened to me!"

Now it was Wayne's turn to look surprised. First surprised and then crafty, with his eyes narrowed. "Let me guess about this. Did she come to you when you was on nighthawk?"

I nodded.

"And she told you all that stuff about the buffalo hunters was just a lie she made up?"

I nodded again, feeling somehow mournful about lost opportunities. I know I should have been examining rocks and gullies and such for signs of the border gangs, but instead I was thinking of how Maggie had looked in the moonlight and of how soft and firm she had felt when she was laying on top of me.

"And did she tell you she wanted to do it with you 'cause she'd fallen in love with you?"

"Whoa, now! She never said nothin' like that to me!" I found I was some jealous about it.

"Me neither." Now Wayne looked mournful. "That was a lie I just made up."

"Dammit, Wayne!" Looking at him, I couldn't stay mad for long. It was clear to me that he was mourning a lost opportunity, too. "Did she tell you about bein' on her way to Wichita? And what she was goin' to do there?"

"Yep." He nodded. "Said she wanted to be a whore."

"You hear that, Sim?" a voice said from behind some rocks. "They got a herd of whores."

"That ain't what was said, Tiny."

At the first voice, Wayne and I had both drawn our guns and turned toward the sound, but still hadn't seen anything.

"Come on out with your hands up," Wayne said.

"Boy, we got you and your friend covered with rifles from a can't-miss range." The voice was the one called Sim.

"Come out where we can see you, then."

Tiny laughed. "Not likely!"

"You got a whore with your herd?" Sim said.

"We did have," I said. I was still peering at the pile of boulders, hoping to see a hat or rifle barrel or something that would tell me where I could shoot. "But she left yesterday."

"Damn! You Texas boys sure know how to travel. How come I didn't see her when I was lookin' over your herd?"

"She was probably out in the grass with one or the other of us," I said. "How come you to be lookin' over our herd?"

"We're fixin' to tax you on it," Sim said.

Tiny giggled. "All nice and legal, too, ain't it, Sim?"

"Shut up, Tiny."

"How many of you are there?" Wayne said. He was turning his horse this way and that, almost like a dance, trying to see where the road agents were hidden.

"There's about thirty of us," Sim said.

"That's a damned small patch of rocks to be hidin' thirty men and horses," I said.

"Now, see there?" Tiny said. "I told you..."

"Fifteen, then, and you're still outnumbered. Don't go countin' yourself into an early grave, Cowboy."

Wayne looked at me. "I don't believe there's more than the two of them."

"Yes, there is!" Sim said.

"Well, we ain't got no cash money, so you're goin' to have to make a fight of it," I said, winking at Wayne.

"Dammit, Sim! I told you they was a hardscrabble outfit. No hands to speak of and cows I wouldn't drive into a river except I wanted to see 'em drown!"

"Shut up, Tiny! You're gonna give the whole thing away!"

"If you boys are hungry, we could probably spare you a cow," Wayne said.

"We done seen them cows! There ain't a meal in ten of 'em!"

"What do you reckon that smoke is, Sim?"

Wayne and me both turned our horses and saw a column of smoke rising from where we'd left the herd. "Indians!" I said.

"Obliged to you boys," Wayne said. "If we get back this way, we'll drop off a cow for you."

"Drop us off one of them whores, too," Tiny said.

If there was more talk, we didn't hear it. Wayne and me had spurred our horses hard and were racing back to the campsite. When we got closer we could hear gunfire, enough of it that I figured Pap and Harvey must be making a pretty good stand.

We drew rein on a rise in order to look the situation over. There were no Indians that we could see, but the cook wagon was burning and the sound of gunfire was still heavy.

"We'd best split up and go in from opposite sides," I told Wayne. "The Indians must be on the far side of the fire."

He nodded, we drew our pistols and rode hell-for-leather down that slope, first away from one another and then, as we got near the wagon, riding back in toward one another.

"God dammit! Get down!" Pap yelled. "There's bullets flyin' ever whichaway!"

One zinged close by my ear and I didn't need to be told twice. Pap was on the other side of the cook wagon from me, half hidden behind a tree, and it seemed to me the firing was coming from the wagon. I hit the ground and saw Wayne doing the same over on his side.

"Where are they, Pap?" Wayne called.

"They rode off, God damn 'em!"

"Then who's shootin' at us?"

"It's the cook wagon, you dumb pup! All our bullets is burning up."

There wasn't anything to do then but to wait it out behind something that would stop a bullet. I scooted backward until I found a rock to hide behind and since there was nothing I could do, I put my hat over my eyes and took a nap.

When all the sounds of shooting stopped, I woke up and came out from behind my rock. Wayne and Pap had did the same and the three of us stood looking at the pile of smoldering ashes that had been the cook wagon. I looked around, expecting to see Maggie and Harvey coming out of their hiding places and the first thing I noticed was that Maggie's horse was gone and so was the one Harvey had had hitched to his wagon.

"I guess you're going to tell us what the hell happened," Wayne said.

"Well..." Pap kind of toed at the ground. "I think I may have vexed Harvey."

He looked up, first at Wayne and then at me, but neither of us had anything to say.

"Now, all I did was to tell him again that he should be fixin' a little more grub for our meals." Pap looked at us again. "That's all I said to him and he got all vexed and set fire to the cook wagon. Then him and Maggie rode off together. And when the bullets in the wagon started shooting off, I couldn't get close enough to put the fire out." He folded his arms across his chest and looked like he was expecting someone to dispute him. "And that's the by God truth of it."

Wayne pushed his hat forward and scratched at the back of his head. "Why would he set fire to his own wagon?"

"He took the position that he'd just cook all the food at once and we could help ourselves when we got hungry."

"And Maggie went off with him?"

"Oh, yeah. I been suspectin' about them two, and the way they was laughin' when they rode off I guess my suspicions was right."

"I'll be damned! Wayne, that was Harvey she was with the night I walloped you!"

Pap looked from one of us to the other. "You boys fought over that little girl?"

"More like a discussion," I said. "We talked about whether she was simple."

"I can tell you she wasn't simple," Pap said.

Wayne grinned real big. "Well, Pap, now that Maggie's run off with Harvey, I guess you got all clean-shaved for nothin'."

Pap rubbed his jaw and grinned right back at him. "Nothin'? Why, you dumb pup, why do you think I took up nighthawkin'?" He looked toward the north, toward where the herd was headed, and his eyes were kind of dreamy. "Wonder if she'll be in Dodge City when we get there?"

The Velvet Brand

Chapter Seven

The Hanging

Except for the half dozen biscuits in my saddlebag and some jerky that Wayne had in his, we had no food and weren't likely to get to Dodge City or anyplace else until we got some. Now, we had plenty of beef, but Pap maintained that he doubted he could survive long without some coffee and beans to go with it.

"So what I figure," he said the next morning early, "is this. You boys ride ahead and find a town where you can trade for some food, and me and Rambler will just keep the herd here on this good grass."

"Just what do you figure we got to trade?" Wayne said.

"Trade a horse. There's always somebody wantin' a horse." He dug a hand into the pocket of his jeans. "Here's a ten dollar piece. Last one I got, so try tradin' before you spend the money."

Wayne and me set out, going north on the trail the way we had the day before. Wayne was riding the nearsighted horse, figuring that if we got any chance at all to trade her it would be good riddance. I was leading a scrawny cow on a tether and when we got to that acre of rock we'd seen the day before, we stopped.

"Sim! Tiny! You still there?"

"No, we ain't!"

"Shut up, Tiny! They probably got a posse with 'em!"

Sim said. "Listen, boys, we don't want no trouble. We was just funnin' you the other day."

"No offence taken," Wayne said. "We brought you that cow we mentioned. I'll just tie her to a bush here."

"Obliged," Sim said. "You boys are bein' real Christian."

"Did you bring us one of them whores?" Tiny called.

"Dammit, Tiny!"

"Well...they said they had a whole herd of 'em. I figured they could spare us one."

"Sorry," I said. "The last one we had ran off with the cook yesterday."

"I guess it don't matter then," Tiny said, kind of mournful. "Any whore that would take up with a damned cook must be simple anyway."

We rode on for a few more miles and then Wayne concluded to let his horse step into a prairie dog hole.

He couldn't have picked a more empty place to do it. There was nothing at all on that prairie except grass and a little smudge of smoke way off on the horizon—not a house or tree or even a fencepost as far as I could see. I made it out to be just about two shades more empty than the Staked Plains and when Wayne told me he guessed the horse would have to be shot I gave up my good nature and cussed Wayne for being a blind fool.

"Now, dammit, Roy Lee," he said. "I did too see that hole."

"Then why in hell didn't you tell your horse about it?" Then, so I wouldn't have to do what I knew needed doing, I turned away and got busy wrestling the saddle and tack off the downed horse. "Go ahead and shoot her, Wayne. You got it to do."

"Well...Sure hate to have to do it. Maybe if I..."

There was a flash of brightest light and an ungodly roar and the hair at the side of my head felt like it was crackling. I jumped up, grabbed the pistol from Wayne's hand, and flung it on the ground.

"Dammit! Don't never lay a gun barrel alongside my head when you're shooting at something!" I was yelling at the top of my lungs, but my ears were ringing so I could scarcely hear myself.

"Aww...The barrel must have wavered some when I closed my eyes."

Feeling the side of my head, I found the hair all singed. It's always been a wild head of hair, but I'd been proud of it up until now. "Oughta make you walk to the next town," I said.

But I took pity on him and we shared off, one man riding and carrying Wayne's saddle while the other one walked. Both of us were tired and sore by the time we passed the outlying farms and came into this town called Lesterville, but that didn't make us feel half as bad as knowing that we had only ten dollars and no horse to trade.

"Well, we're damned near stranded, Wayne," I said. "We won't buy much food with the money we got, 'less we can sell that saddle of yours."

"Nope. We're not sellin' my saddle."

"You ain't got anything to put it on since you took to stepping horses into prairie dog holes." I knew we were in this fix together, but I wouldn't miss a chance to devil Wayne, just like he wouldn't miss a chance to devil me.

He just grinned that big grin of his. "Somethin' will turn up. It always does."

"And just what do we do while we're waitin' for that? Why, there ain't even a tree for us to sleep under. I doubt there's a tree in the whole damned state." I was stretching it some, doing my best to make Wayne feel bad, but it didn't seem to be working. "Well, let's go see if we can find a day job to do."

We walked around town some, a chore that only took half an hour, and talked to some of the people here. Mostly they all wanted us to take an interest in a big white frame house where some judge lived, and I didn't know whether they were most proud of the house or the judge. They said the lumber for the house had been freighted in from Missouri and the judge would likely be the next state senator after he tried a horse thief named Tom Two Squaws. Those that did talk to us about jobs didn't talk our language. Even though we'd both been raised to it, I was a bit proud about not doing any more farm work and Wayne said he'd burn in hell before he ever loaded any more grain sacks.

"You remember how bad you itch once that grain dust gets down the back of your shirt?"

So, we were sitting on a bench in front of a tent saloon, considering our possibilities and considering whether we even had any possibilities, when the sheriff came up to us and looked us over real slow.

"You boys are new in town," he said. "Where you from?"

"Yessir." My old Ma had always told me to respect authority and sometimes I remembered to do it. "We're from Texas."

He gave us that long, slow look again and I did the same to him. He was a big man, well over six feet tall, and I guessed the gut on him would cause him to weigh in at just under three hundred pounds. His heavy mustache was as black as his eyes and his mean look told me that, when the fur flew, Wayne was going to get whupped good and proper. Me, I'd be on my way out of town.

"Texas hardcases, huh?"

"Regular hellbenders," Wayne said grinning.

"Don't you go getting us in no trouble, Wayne." I thought the sheriff looked a mite serious for funning.

"Well, I don't know what a hellbender is, but I guess you'll do." The sheriff pushed back the tail of his black frock coat, showing a pistol that looked to be two sizes bigger than mine, and I figured he was going to take to shooting us right where we were. But his hand moved past the gun and went to his hip pocket and when I saw it again it held two brass stars. "Stand up and get yourselves sworn in. I'm deputizin' both of you."

We stood up, me dumbfounded, and the sheriff gave us each a badge to pin on. I pricked my thumb getting it on and that gave me cause to wonder if the sheriff ever forgot hisself and sat down on a hip pocket full of the blasted things.

"Raise your right hands," the sheriff said.

"Not until we know what we're bein' deputized for."

"What difference does it make?" Wayne said. "It's a better job than totin' grain sacks."

"Ummm. Guess you got a right," the sheriff said. "We got a trial starting this morning, a horse thief trial. Wouldn't be anything to it, maybe, except that the accused is a full-blooded Cheyenne. Might be some of his red brothers don't want him tried in a white man's court. Might be a whole herd of them will ride in here and try to set him free." His black mustache was twitching and I'd have thought he was smiling if the matter hadn't been so solemn. "Might be I'll need the help of a couple of Texas hardcases to make sure the law gets carried out." His face darkened suddenly. "For it's a cinch that damned judge won't pay attention to the law."

"Sheriff," I said, "the fact is, we ain't exactly what you'd call hard..."

"We ain't exactly what you'd call hard up for cash," Wayne said. "But we'd like to know if you mean to pay us."

The black mustache twitched again. "You get fifteen dollars each, just for a day's work."

Well, that was more money and faster than I'd ever expected to earn any. It looked like taking on the job was the only way we was ever going to get out of our bind and, to tell the truth, it felt smart to be a deputy sheriff. But I still had my doubts, even though me and Wayne raised our hands and took the oath.

When the sheriff had gone on after giving us our instructions, Wayne grinned at me and said, "I told you something would turn up."

"Yeah, it did. But I got a feeling you just stepped us into another prairie dog hole."

"Now, Roy Lee, you're not going to back out on enough money to buy grub for the rest of the drive, are you? Besides, you took an oath and I never heard of any McAllister going back on an oath."

"That's true," I said, knowing he was ragging me and thinking of a few more good oaths I could have sworn at him. "But usually we poke around the edges a bit more before we get ourselves into one."

"What's wrong with this one? All we got to do is sit up on top of the hotel and watch out for Cheyennes."

"That's just it, Wayne. There ain't been no Cheyennes in these parts for years. I'm surprised they found one to steal their horses for them."

"Then there ain't a thing to worry about, is there?"

I'd heard him say that before, usually just before we found ourselves knee deep in a place where we didn't want to be.

I mulled it around some–wondering if the sheriff had been

grinning beneath that mustache, wondering why anyone would want to start an Indian scare in a town full of farmers, wondering why he needed hardcase deputies, wondering what a hellbender was—but I got no closer to the heart of it. "I'll find something to worry about," I said.

The hotel was the highest building in town, being two stories tall and with a false-fronted third story, and because the country was so flat and empty, we could see for a good many miles in every direction. There were sixteen buildings in the town, if you could call them all buildings. The hotel and the judge's big white house and the jail were the only wooden structures in town; the rest being soddies and dugouts, and the saloon was one big tent. I counted the buildings about fifteen times before I got bored with it. There weren't any people to watch, for they were all below us in the hotel lobby holding the trial.

"Tom Two Squaws," Wayne said thoughtfully. He was sitting with his rifle across his knees, leaning back in the hot shade of the false third story, his hat tilted back to show that lock of curly black hair. "Must be some kind of he-bull Indian to get hisself a name like that." He took off his neckerchief and started to polish his badge.

"Listen, Wayne, you'd better give up thinkin' about him and start thinkin' about the fix we're in. That sheriff's got something on his mind and I bet it ain't Cheyennes."

"What would it be, then?"

"That's what I don't know," I said. "And you'd better give up on that badge, too. The brass plate's coming off." I was getting disgusted with the whole setup and the only thing that kept me in it was the oath I'd taken and the need for quick money so I could get on up the trail and find Velvet. I didn't figure the oath counted for a lot, since I'd taken it before thinking it through about the Cheyennes, but the need to see that Velvet woman was still powerful. "I'm going to go down there and sit in on that trial," I said. "There's something going on here and I need to know what it is."

"No." Wayne stood up and put his rifle aside, taking a hitch at his gun belt. "You got better eyes than me so you'd best stay here and keep watch while I go down here."

"But there's nothing to watch for!"

"Just the same." He swung hisself over the edge of the building and I heard his boots hit the landing of the outside stairway. In a few minutes, I saw the top of his hat below me before he passed under the awning and into the hotel.

Well, I stood up there on the roof and waited, watching that flat and forsaken land, wondering why the sheriff had put us up here out of the way. I knew he was going to use us for something, but I couldn't figure out what it was.

Once, a long way off, I thought I saw a cloud of dust and was ready to give the alarm but then I looked a while longer and made it out to be a line of scrawny trees bordering a creek or a river. Why these people hadn't put their town closer to the water was something to work my mind on for a few minutes, but I never did figure it out.

Pretty soon, there was a loud sound of voices and some cheering. Looking straight down, I saw a bunch of men and women coming from beneath the awning. The men were talking and nodding and clapping one another on the back as they headed for the tent saloon. The women were mostly buzzing, like women do, and they stuck together like a pack of hens. I couldn't see their faces, but I'd have bet they looked righteous. Then I saw the top of Wayne's hat again and I waited for him to climb back on the roof and tell me the outcome of the trial.

Well, he soon climbed over the edge, but he wasn't near as excited as the townsfolk I'd seen. His face was kind of blotchy and his mouth was set in that dead straight line it always gets just before he sets in to whip me about something or other.

But it had been me setting up there in the hot sun while he was enjoying the trial and I wasn't of a mood to take any of his sass. I balled up my fists and waited for him to come at me.

But Wayne just gave me a passing glance and kept his mouth set tight. He went over to the false front and spat over the side, so hard and disgusted-looking I was sure he'd cleared the awning and hit the dusty street. Yet I could tell that, whatever bad thing he'd tasted, he hadn't got rid of it yet. So for a while he just stood there and cussed, not at me but at things in general, and I knew him well enough that the only thing to do was to give him room and time to get it all out of his system.

"Roy Lee," he said at last. "I never saw the beat of it. They found that old man guilty of horse stealing." He spat over the side again.

Down below, someone yelled, "Hey!"

Wayne looked over the wall, his face dark and mean. "Keep moving, sodbuster!"

"Don't start anything," a woman's voice said. "It's them Texas hardcases."

"Hellbenders," Wayne yelled.

I'd had enough of it and my curiosity was killing me. "Wayne, are you gonna tell me what the hell happened or are you just gonna stand there and spit on everybody?"

He swung around and his fists were balled up at his sides. "Don't you start in on me, Roy Lee. I'm mad enough to whip the devil and I'd just as soon take you on for starters. You got us into his."

"Me?" I squared off at him. "Now, you listen, Wayne. I didn't get us into anything. It was you stepped your horse into that prairie dog hole. It was you told me to shut up and get sworn in. I didn't do anything."

"That's just it! Didn't I sit up here in the hot sun for hours, waitin' for you to go back on your oath and you wouldn't do it? Damn right you didn't do anything!"

"Now, that tears it, Wayne." I started for him, my fists up and ready. "You tell me what happened or I'll whip you for fair."

"I done told you. They found him guilty." At that, he commenced to looking sickly and set his mouth in that tight line again.

I eased back. "Tom Two Squaws? The Indian stud? Well, of course they found him guilty, Wayne. He's an Indian."

"He ain't no stud no more, Roy Lee," Wayne said sadly, shaking his head. "I make him out to be about sixty or maybe seventy years old and I ain't even sure he's in his right mind." He took off his hat and threw it down, but it was more forlorn than furious. "Listen, what came about is that the old man just likes to ride horses, see? Only he's just some poor-devil Indian and don't have a horse of his own. But that oily damned judge has got a set of matched bays and this old Two Squaws stole one and took it for a ride the other night. I could tell the sheriff didn't like to do it, but he had to swear he saw Two Squaws bringin' it back to the judge's barn when he was through with his ridin'."

"That don't sound like much to me," I said. "If he just used the horse some and then brought it back, that ain't horse stealin'."

"No, it ain't! But the judge don't like Indians and he gave

the jury a long speech about making Kansas safe for women and children. Told them that if he was state senator he'd see to it that all the Indians would be swept out of the state and then he told them he was directing them to bring in a guilty verdict. About that time I asked the sheriff what Tom could get out of it and he just looked mean and said, 'Thirty days, or else by God I'll show them a thing or two.' But, dammit, Roy Lee, that judge sentenced old Two Squaws to hang!"

I started to accuse Wayne of making it all up, but if he had he'd have grinned by now. So I sat down and thought about it for a minute, getting chilled clear through when I thought of how close we were to all of this, and then I said, "We'd better find that sheriff and resign."

"No, what we'd better do is get on your horse and get out of here and just mail him his damned badges. That sheriff is more upset than any man I ever saw, and I'd just as soon we stayed out of his way."

I mulled it over for a bit. "Guess there's nothin' we can do for the Indian, is there?"

"Not without breakin' the law."

"Then we can't do it." Yet, I still didn't feel right about it.

"But, hell, Roy Lee! We are the law!"

"That's why we can't break it." I was pacing the roof, knowing things weren't right, smelling something out of place. "But we'll go see the sheriff and resign the right way." Then it hit me what was wrong. "Do you smell smoke?"

Wayne jumped up and looked over the false front. "There's a fire all right. Wonder if Harvey and Maggie are here?"

"Cheyennes, by God!" I reached for my rifle, but then I thought of how the citizens of Lesterville had acted happy and pleased when the trial was over and I let it lay. Let the

Cheyennes take Two Squaws, I thought. Let them burn the whole damned town, starting with that judge's big white house.

"It ain't Cheyennes or Harvey," Wayne said. "Way it looks to me is that the sheriff has set fire to the jail."

I jumped up to see, and sure enough there was the sheriff standing in the middle of the street with his prisoner and waving a shotgun at the bucket brigade, keeping them at bay.

We beat it on down there, figuring we was still deputies and it was our place to side the sheriff, at least as long as it took for us to resign. Fact is, though, we both felt right smart to be standing up for anything that town was against, even if it was only a fire, and our badges gave us a right to be there. Besides, it looked like that big sheriff might have his hands full trying to guard Tom Two Squaws and protect his fire at the same time.

"Indian set fire to the jail!" someone yelled.

"Oughter hang him for it," someone else answered.

"Damn you idiots!" the sheriff bellered. "That's just what this is all about." He tilted his scattergun up just a bit, cocked both hammers, and yelled, "Now hide out, damn you all!" With that, he let go a blast from one barrel, the shot just barely over the heads of the crowd.

They broke and scattered in every direction, dropping buckets as they ran. For a minute, the town seemed empty except for us four, and then I saw the townsfolk peering at us from windows and doors and from behind watering troughs.

I did some peering myself, taking my first good look at the prisoner. Tom Two Squaws was just about the poorest excuse for an Indian I ever did see. He was naked except for a breechclout and a necklace made out of what appeared to be old raccoon tails. Lanky, thin gray hair hung to his shoulders and his ribs stuck out like a bunch of crooked railroad ties. But he was a happy Indian, nodding and grinning all the while, with not a single tooth showing in his head. I thought it was a sorry day that such an old man had to be hung for riding a horse and an even sorrier day when a whole town of farmers seemed to want it that way.

The sheriff had a long coil of rope over his shoulder and it was giving him fits as he tried to reload the scattergun. The old Indian reached up, took the rope and hung it over his own shoulder. He was so short the coils reached his knees and he nodded and grinned and commenced to busy himself playing with one end of the rope.

About that time the walls of the burning jail fell in, showering us with sparks, and we all moved further out into the dusty street. Now the big sheriff was grinning beneath his black mustache and I was glad to see he was feeling better about things.

"There she goes," he said. "These hypocrites don't deserve the good law I tried to give 'em nor the jail I built for 'em. To hell with them all. Guard the prisoner, boys."

He handed Wayne the loaded scattergun and walked across the street to the livery stable. We could see him talking to a man and pointing to a horse, then money changed hands and it wasn't hard to figure what he was doing. He was going to string that old Indian up and then whip the horse out from under him, the way Pap had told us some of the big ranchers did in the early days.

It gave me a kind of sick feeling to know what was going to happen and how it was going to happen, and I looked at Wayne. He nodded slowly, letting me know he didn't feel any better about it than I did. "A sure-enough scaffold might at least let him die with some kind of pride," he said.

"What the hell would you build one with? There ain't a

stick of wood anywhere on this damned prairie." Come to think on it, I hadn't seen any tree of a size to hang a man from, unless the sheriff intended to take Two Squaws all the way down to that creek.

"You should have seen them people at the trial," Wayne said. His jaw was tight and his eyes were squinted near shut when he turned to look at the people who were coming out from under cover. "Their eyes were lit up, let me tell you. I bet they ain't had any excitement like this for a long time." He shook his head. "Makes you wonder why farmers live like they do."

"Well, I won't have it," I said. I spat in the dust while I tried to collect some thoughts out of all the feelings that were churning around inside me. "We got the scattergun and we got the Indian and I say can't nobody hang him unless we let them. You with me in this, Wayne?"

Before Wayne could answer, the sheriff came back to where we stood in the street. He was riding the horse he had bought and there was an old warbag tied behind the saddle. Now I had an idea of what he was going to do and knew he'd had to plan it ahead of time. He sat there a minute, looking over at what was left of the jail, then unpinned his star and chucked it over into the ashes.

"I tried to give them good law," he said. "But that damned politician judge is bound to have his way."

I had it figured that the sheriff felt as bad as we did about hanging old Two Squaws, so I said, "Maybe we could just kind of drag our feet until the Cheyennes get here and take him away from us."

"There won't be any Cheyennes," the sheriff said. "I started that tale a-purpose, hopin' I could scare everybody into going easy on this old man. All it did was to get me the two of you for deputies." He nodded sharply. "Well, you're Texas hardcases. Likely you got more stomach for this business than I have."

"What's to keep us from quitting?" Wayne said.

"Nothing. You can do it just as easy as I did." The sheriff jerked his head. "That crowd of farmers down the street will likely be glad to lynch the prisoner."

I looked to where a dozen or so men were standing in front of the tent saloon, nodding and talking and nudging one another and jerking thumbs in our direction. "Reckon we'll stay," I said.

"Then you're the law in Lesterville and you got the sentence to carry out," the sheriff said. "Hang him by the neck until he's dead." He put the spurs to his horse and was soon out of sight.

"God damn it, Roy Lee!" Wayne spit in the dust and threw his hat at it, the backward way of doing it showing me just how worked up he was, then commenced to cussing while Tom Two Squaws grinned and nodded like he was enjoying the whole performance.

I admired it myself, for I'd never seen Wayne fling himself out with quite so much style, but at the same time I knew we were in bad trouble and weren't about to get out of it by cussing.

"Roy Lee, I won't have it! By God, I won't! I resign, right here and now!"

"There ain't no one left to resign to, Wayne. All you can do is quit."

"Then I quit! You just do this all by yourself, Roy Lee, if you're so damned set on it. But don't you ever come 'round me again." He turned and had stomped off about three steps before I called to him.

"Where you ridin' to, Wayne? And what are you ridin' on?"

He stopped short and spun around quick. "You think you got me, don't you? Well, you ain't, because I'm takin' your horse."

"You know what we do to horse thieves in this town?"

His eyes widened in surprise and then he grinned that cocky grin. I didn't even have to look to know his fists were balled and he was ready to come at me. "By God, you'd try it too, wouldn't you?"

I shrugged.

"Come on, Roy Lee. I know you don't want to see him lynched and that's good. That's fine. But don't you see where that puts us? I can't do it, Roy Lee. Just look at this poor old man."

I took another look and saw that Tom Two Squaws was having fun with the rope. The greater coil of it still hung on his scrawny shoulder, but he'd fashioned a slipknot and had a noose around his neck. When he caught me watching he pulled up on the rope, slipping the noose tight, crossed his eyes, stuck out his tongue, and giggled till his whole body shook.

It made me thoughtful and I said, "Wayne, I don't think he gives a damn whether he gets hung or not. And come to think of it, neither do I."

"You'd better not act like you mean that, Roy Lee."

I ignored him. "Come on, Two Squaws. Let's go find a place to hang you." He nodded and grinned and made as if to hand me the coil of rope. "No," I said. "You keep it on your neck. It'll come in handy."

He patted me on the arm, nodding and grinning some more, then pulled up on the noose, crossed his eyes, and gurgled. His long tongue hung out of that toothless old mouth, but he looked bright and happy.

We turned away but Wayne hopped in front of us, holding that scattergun up across his chest to block our way. His face was screwed up like he was ready to cry. "Look at him, Roy Lee. He does everything you tell him to do. Hell, he ain't got no more sense about this than a newborn pup. You can't do this to him."

"It ain't what I'm doing," I said. "It's what these blamed farmers started and I got a notion to let them finish it." I know my face was stony hard. I had to keep it that way to keep my own feelings from getting the best of me. But I couldn't keep it that way for long so I gave in to my feelings and grinned. "You can come with us, Wayne, or you're going to miss out on the most fun you've had in a year."

"You mean we ain't gonna hang him?"

"I mean we're still wearing badges and we're goin' to do our level best to see that the law is served and the sentence is carried out." I'll bet my old Ma would have been proud to hear me talk like that.

"You ain't makin' much sense," Wayne said.

"Well, the judge and the jury didn't make much sense either, did they?"

Wayne grinned sudden-like. "You got a plan, don't you?"

We walked down the middle of the dusty street, Wayne with the scattergun, me with my saddle gun, and old Two Squaws with a coil of rope over his shoulder and the noose around his neck. People stood aside to let us pass and we looked neither right or left, keeping our faces grim and hard and marching as though we owned the town. We'd have made a finer show of it if only old Two Squaws hadn't tightened his noose and gurgled every time we passed close to someone. We left a few fainted ladies behind us, but we kept on marching.

Our first stop was in the tent saloon. It seemed every man who wasn't out in the street was in there having a drink and talking over the excitement of the day—the trial, the loss of the jail, and the prospect of a hanging. When the three of us walked in through the flaps, all the talk stopped and about thirty pairs of eyes were watching us.

"Fine boys," someone said. "They take their duty serious."

"Texas hardcases, I heard they was," someone else said.

"When you gonna hang that critter, deputy?" someone called out.

"Pretty quick now," I said. "But first I want to meet the men who were on that jury."

There was some milling around, some elbowing and shoving, and pretty soon we had twelve men standing before us grinning and nudging one another and looking like they was right proud of the work they'd done that day. Then Wayne threw down on them with the scattergun and herded them all into one corner of the tent.

"The rest of you men hide out," I said. "We got personal business with this jury." I glanced over my shoulder. "Barkeep, you stay. Give the Indian a drink or two of something good."

"It's against the law for me to serve an Indian," he grumbled, but he was quick about setting up the drink when Wayne kind of pointed the scattergun his way. "You can bet the judge will hear about this."

"Sooner rather than later, I'd say," Wayne told him.

It was hot and smelly in the tent, what with the Kansas sun beating down and untrimmed kerosene lamps trying to make some light in the place. Sweat was rolling down my face as I turned to face the jury.

"Y'all voted to find the Indian guilty," I said. "You let that judge talk you right into it. So now you're goin' to have to take a vote to see which one of you is going to be the hangman."

There was a lot of pushing and shoving and backing away until there was a tight little knot of men backed into that corner. But, like scared men will do, they got the job done, several of them laying hands on the smallest man of the bunch and throwing him out to me. He tried to crawl back into the crowd but I grabbed his foot and hung on.

"Listen, mister," the little man begged. "I can't do this for you. I got three little ones to home and they just wouldn't understand it."

Wayne grabbed the man by the front of his coat and hauled him to his feet. "Don't you want to protect them little ones from this murderin' savage?" He shook the man so hard I'm surprised I didn't hear his teeth rattle. "Don't you?"

"But...but...He didn't murder anybody! Did he?"

"Don't make no difference." Wayne's grin was so hard and wolfish it almost scared me. "Murderers or horse thieves, they all hang the same way. By the neck."

Two Squaws yanked on the noose and gurgled.

The little man's eyes rolled back in his head and he went limp, only Wayne's grip on his coat keeping him from falling. "Passed out," Wayne said. "I expect it's from the heat."

"Then we'd best let some air in here." I waved my saddle gun at the jury. "The rest of you men lay hold of these tent poles here and tear them down. There ain't a tree in the whole state and no lumber to be found so we're going to have to use whatever wood we can find to build a scaffold. Get to it."

"By God, that's enough!" the barkeep yelled. "You pull them posts out and the whole tent comes down. I won't have it!" He came up with a short-barreled scattergun, but Wayne dropped the little man and got his own scattergun going first. He put a load of shot alongside the barkeep's head, busting a lot of bottles and letting some daylight in through the sidewall of the tent. The barkeep thought it over, dropped his gun, and legged it out of there.

The jury didn't wait any longer. They grabbed hold of the two poles and started pulling at them while me and Wayne and the hangman and Two Squaws went out into the street to wait. The tent fell, rippling as it came down; then the kerosene lamps busted and a dozen fires started right away. We waited to make sure the jury got out from under the burning canvas, then took a good look at the two poles they drug into the street.

"Flimsy," Wayne said.

"It's a start." I turned to the jury. "All right, you men. Get on over to the hotel. I want that outside staircase and the posts that hold up the front awning. Move!"

As they walked away, talking among themselves about how to get the job done, I heard one man say, "You can call it what you like, Carson, but it's the most fun I've had since the last time it rained."

"Well, I will give it that," Carson said.

Our hangman had come to himself enough that Wayne didn't have to drag him around any more, so I gave him the coil of rope to carry. "Mind you don't trip or lag behind, now. We don't want old Two Squaws to strangle to death before we have a chance to hang him."

The little man looked confused. "What difference would it make?"

"You wouldn't want to hang a man with a sore throat, would you?" Wayne said. "Besides, the law's got to be served."

"Now, that's real fine talk, Wayne," I said, tipping him a

wink.

He grinned. "I think I'm getting the hang of this deputy business."

Some of the jury had got ropes and others had gone away and come back with horses. I saw enough smiles and grins among them to make me think they had got over being afraid and was starting to enjoy the work we'd set out for them. I didn't give it more than a minute of thought for I figured a man who'd stick a plow in the ground had something wrong with his thinking anyway.

They took hitches around the stairway and around the awning supports, then whipped at the horses. The staircase and the awning came down with a crash and raised a cloud of dust. When the dust cleared, I could see that the awning was still attached, but in swinging down it had busted every window in the front of the hotel.

We were beginning to have a right smart pile of lumber in the street. Waving my rifle, I sorted the jury into two groups, telling the first group to get hammers and saws and whatever else they needed and then start in on building a gallows tree. "The rest of you come with us. We're going to get some planks for building a solid platform."

One of the men from the first group stepped forward and took off his hat. "Mr. Deputy, sir, I don't know where you expect to find any planks but if we're going to have a platform and all, maybe we oughtn't to bust up them steps. They'll come in handy for walkin' up on to the platform."

"Now, that's a good idea," Wayne said. He called to the rest of the group. "This here man is the honcho. You all build it like he says."

The man went back to the group, walking proud.

On our way to the judge's house, we stopped by the

smithy and I told the farmers to get what they could carry in the way of pry bars and such.

We were making some good headway on tearing down the big white house and Tom Two Squaws was having the time of his life, nodding and grinning and bearing a hand where he could, the little hangman almost passing out every time Tom crossed his eyes or stuck out his tongue. The jury worked fast and had ripped off half a dozen whole planks plus pieces of others before the judge came running out of the house and around to where we were working.

"What in the hell is going on here?"

He was a short man, fat and bald. I saluted him, not knowing exactly how a deputy should act before a judge but figuring I'd be as proper as I knew how to be. "Just getting boards for the scaffold, your honor," I said. I leaned close and whispered to him. "Sure wish you'd sentenced him to be shot. Do you know there ain't a tree or a lumberyard in the whole state?"

"Of course I know it! Every stick of wood in this house was freighted in from...My God! You men, there! I'll have an end to this. Where's the sheriff?"

"He burned down the jail and quit," Wayne said. "We're the law now."

"You? My God!"

"Yessir. And I was wonderin' if I could have a new badge. This one I got is tarnishing."

The fat judge turned red. It started at his stiff collar, worked its way up his cheeks, and then went right across the top of his bald head. I admired how complete it was and thought it wondrous to see a man get so wrapped up in what he was doing, and I told him so.

He narrowed his eyes and squinted at Wayne and me.

"You're those Texas hardcases."

"Hellbenders," I said.

"Um-hm, um-hm." His eyes and his smile got crafty. "Well, I think I know how to deal with you. You two come on up to my office where we can have a cigar and a drink and talk this over."

Wayne and me looked at one another and shrugged, deciding to give it a try. "You're right, Wayne," I said. "He is oily."

I took the rope from the hangman and let Two Squaws carry it, since it seemed to give him so much pleasure, and we three followed the judge into the house and up the stairs to a fancy office with a big desk and cases full of books and whatnot.

"Now listen, men. I want to be reasonable and it may just be that we can come to some kind of lucrative agreement about how the law in Lesterville is best served. But I cannot have you tearing down my house around my head." He gave us the same kind of smile I'd seen on stump speakers running for office. "It is necessary for me, in my aims to higher office, to have the respect of these people and if we let them tear down my house...Well, I'm sure you see my point."

"We don't want the whole house," I said. "Just another thirty or forty good planks, enough to build a nice, strong scaffold." I widened my eyes and tried to look innocent. "We kind of thought you'd want to give as much as you could, since it was you wanted old Two Squaws to hang."

"Yes, yes, of course." He looked kind of sickly. The red had gone out of his face and now he looked more the color of paste. "Ah...I did sentence him to hang, didn't I? But you must understand...My God! What is that heathen doing?"

Tom Two Squaws was hoisting himself with the noose,

crossing his eyes and gurgling at the judge.

"He's practicin' for the hangin'," Wayne said. "Stop it, Tom." Then Wayne came over and tried to lift a corner of the judge's desk. He stood there, fingering his chin and looking like he was thinking hard, and then he said, "I think it'll do." He nodded to himself. "By God, it will do."

"What is he talking about?" the judge asked me.

"Listen, Roy Lee, we don't need no scaffold and we don't need to bother the judge's house any more. This old desk is plenty heavy to hold the weight. We'll just tie one end of the rope to it and then chunk old Two Squaws right through that window."

"Let's do her." I took the coil of rope and made a hitch around the leg of the desk.

"You men are insane!" the judge yelled. "Take him clear out of town and hang him! That's an official order!" He was starting to get red again.

We stopped fooling with the rope and Wayne scratched his head. "I ain't so sure about that, Judge. Do we have any authority once we're out of town?"

"You have authority all the way to the river." He sounded tired and was mopping at his head with a handkerchief. Then he brightened and sat up straight. "There are trees down by the river, men. I'm sure you can find a good one."

There was a loud screeching of nails as another plank came off the house.

"Is that your official sentence now? You want him to hang from a tree?"

"What?" He seemed to be listening for the sound of more planks being ripped off his house. "Yes. Yes, it is. That's the official sentence. Just hang him from a tree. I don't care how you do it as long as he hangs." He slapped one fat hand down on the desktop. "There, that makes it official, just like with a gavel, you see?"

"What about our pay?" I said. "Likely we'll just keep on going after it's done, so maybe we ought to be paid now. The sheriff mentioned thirty dollars."

"Of course, of course." He dug out his wallet and gave each of us thirty dollars. "There. Done and done."

"What about old Two Squaws?" Wayne said.

The judge blinked hard, and then stared. "What about him?"

"Man oughtn't to die broke."

"What difference does it make?" The judge was fairly shouting now.

"Makes a difference about buryin' him," Wayne said. "I'll deputy for thirty dollars, but grave diggin' costs more."

"Oh, all right." The judge got out more money and gave it to Tom. "There, now. You use that money to pay these men for burying you."

I swear, I thought he was going to pat the Indian on the head and he might have, but old Two Squaws was grinning and nodding and trying to find a way to stuff the money in his breechclout.

"Well, gentlemen?" the judge said. "We seem to have an agreement here, so be on your way and tell those men to stop tearing down my house."

"It ain't that simple, Judge," I said. "We need a horse for Wayne and one for Two Squaws. Can't make an old man walk all the way to that river. Hell, he could die of heat stroke before we got him hung."

"I'm sorry," the judge said. "I can't give you horses. That's final."

Wayne leaned across the desk, his scattergun kind of

accidentally pointing at the judge's nose and said, "You got them two matched bays. They'll do."

"Now, wait just a minute! You can't..."

There was another loud screech as a plank came free. The judge put his face in his hands and I thought I heard him sob. "Oh, all right! Take the horses and leave me alone!"

"We'll take a bill of sale, too," I said.

Like a desperate man, the judge grabbed for paper and a pen.

We left the town in ruins behind us and maybe we'd left the judge's ambitions in ruins, too. Wayne and me felt pretty good about the whole thing. We were riding those matched bays, with Two Squaws mounted behind me, for my old horse was loaded with the supplies we'd bought before leaving town.

We came to the creek, which in my understanding was the county line, and there we stopped.

"Well?" Wayne said. "We can't take him to Dodge with us." He kind of grinned. "Even though Pap might like to have him for a pet."

"Don't I know that? Get down, Tom, and hand me your rope." I threw the coil over a likely branch and then took a hitch around the trunk and made it fast. Then I took the noose off Two Squaws' neck, untied it and let the rope hang loose. "You notice the judge forgot to say about hanging by the neck? Or about hanging till he was dead?"

"For a fact," Wayne grinned.

"Tom, you grab onto that rope and hang on for as long as you can, you hear?"

Two Squaws nodded and grinned, grabbed the rope and commenced to swing back and forth on it. We told him goodbye and rode away, figuring his arms would give out before he starved to death and figuring we'd carried out the judge's law to the letter.

Some ways down the trail I remembered we'd forgot to tell the jury to quit tearing down the judge's house, but it was too late in the day to go back.

The Velvet Brand

Chapter Eight

The Velvet Escape

Wayne and me felt mighty prosperous as we headed back to camp, reckoning Pap would be proud of us. We had the two bays we were riding and our packhorse was loaded with pots, pans, and food, more than enough to see us through to Wichita and Dodge City. The man who ran the general store in Lesterville was the same man we'd picked for a hangman and he had been so eager to see us get on with the hanging without his help that we got all we needed and still had twenty dollars cash money between us.

We were close to where the herd was being held, coming on that acre of rocks where Sim and Tiny lived. There was the glow of a fire coming from the center of the pile and I had an idea to be kindly to them, since it seemed their road agent business wasn't doing too well.

"Hey, in the rocks!" I called. "You fellers got a coffee pot?"

There was a bit of cussing and mumbling that I couldn't quite make out.

"I asked if you had a coffeepot."

"Here, take the damned thing!" In the half-light of the evening, I saw a battered pot come sailing out into the road and landing with an empty clatter.

"First time I ever been robbed of a coffee pot," Tiny said. "Damned road agents don't leave a man nothin'."

"If you'd been standin' your damned watch, they'd never have got the drop on us," Sim said.

"Now, how can I stand watch while I'm tryin' to cook that damned cow?"

Me and Wayne was both laughing and I got off my horse and picked up the coffee pot, then went to the pack horse and dug out a pound sack of Arbuckle's and stuffed it down inside the pot. "Here it comes back," I yelled, heaving the pot at the glow of their fire. "There's coffee inside the pot."

"Dammit!" I guessed Sim was cussing at the shower of sparks I saw fly up in the air. It looked like I'd landed the pot right in their campfire. "Now they're tryin' to burn us out!"

"There's something in the pot," Tiny said. "But if it's coffee it won't pour."

"You boys cooked that cow yet?" Wayne called.

"Are you the fellers that gave us that cow?" Sim answered back.

I told him we were.

"Well, it's a damned poor cow! Wouldn't stand still for being cooked, so now we got to go out in the dark and try to find it."

I was trying to mount my horse, but then I got to laughing so hard I couldn't do it. I didn't know what they'd done, but there was a picture in my mind of the two of them trying to build a fire under the cow. I reckoned Harvey could have done it, but I wasn't sure about these two.

"Was I you," Wayne said, "I believe I'd kill it and butcher it before I tried to cook it."

"Oh."

"Obliged," Tiny called. "This is damned thick coffee, Sim. If it ever does pour, likely we'll have to chew it to get it down."

"Don't show your ignorance," Sim said. "That'd be New Orleans coffee."

Wayne and me rode on. We could see Pap's fire from a long way off so we kind of hurried up the horses in order to get there before full dark. I'd left the rest of my biscuits with him that morning, but I figured that unless he'd set fire to a cow he was probably getting pretty hungry.

"About damned time you got back," Pap said when we came into the circle of firelight. "Now, I sent you out this mornin' with two horses and you come back with three. What kind of tradin' is that?"

Wayne got mad, but not so mad that his hat hit the ground. "If you'd take a closer look, Pap, you'd see that one horse is loaded with beans and coffee and stuff to cook it all in."

Before we had left that morning, we'd sifted through the ashes of the wagon and took stock of the cookware. Except for one big old skillet, everything else had at least one hole in it from where the ammunition in the wagon had burned off.

"I'll be damned," Pap said, inspecting the packhorse. "You boys remind me of me when it comes to making a good trade. Ah...is anyone likely to be after you about them two bay horses?"

"We got a legal bill of sale for 'em, Pap, signed by a judge."

"Well, I hope so. I reckon you know what they do to horse thieves around these parts."

Wayne and me looked at one another and I was doing pretty good at holding it all in until he tipped me a wink. When it started, I got around to the off side of my horse, putting it between me and Pap.

"What's wrong with Roy Lee?"

"Whoopin' fit, I reckon. He's had an interesting day."

Finally I got myself under control and took the saddle off my horse, carrying it to a spot near the campfire. When I laid out my bedroll, it came to me that I was kind of going to miss having Maggie to watch out for. On the good side of it, I thought that, with Maggie gone, maybe my dreams about Velvet would be less confusing.

"You boys ever goin' to say how you made such a fine trade?" Pap asked. Supper had been eaten and now we were just drinking coffee and smoking cigarillos to keep the mosquitoes away.

"It wasn't so much tradin', Pap," I said. I looked at Wayne and caught his nod. We'd tell Pap about it someday, but not now. "We managed to get ourselves a day job."

Pap looked at the truck we'd taken off the packhorse, then from one of us to the other. "I don't know of any day job that pays that good."

"You're forgettin' there was two of us workin', Pap."

"Well..." He didn't say any more but he still looked doubtful.

"Listen, Pap," I said, "You never did tell us why Velvet quit Texas or why she left her cattle behind."

"No, and I don't believe I will since I know you're funnin' me about them day jobs." He crossed his arms over his chest and set his mouth tight the way he always did when a matter was concluded.

"I'll trade with you, Pap," Wayne said. "You tell us about Velvet and I'll tell you what kind of day job we had."

"You first." By the light in his eyes, I knew Pap's curiosity was burning hot.

Wayne crossed his arms over his chest. "Nope." He set his mouth tight.

"If you two are gonna see who can be stubborn the

longest," I said, "then I'm goin' to turn in."

"Oh, hell," Pap said. "I guess I'll tell it. But you mind, Wayne, I never had anything to do with Velvet till after your Ma died."

Wayne nodded. "I don't doubt you on that, Pap."

***

Velvet and her man came to Waco just before the war (Pap said). Yeah, she had a man but I don't know if they were married and I never asked her about it. Mayhap I didn't want to know.

Anyway, he built her that fine house you know about on the south of town and it wasn't no ranch or farm, just a house set off a ways from the town. The ranchin' part didn't come until later and it was kind of accidental, like I told you before. That's why all her cattle and livestock were allowed to roam free, because they didn't have a whole lot of acreage, just a town lot or two. But in time, some fellers that had more land than livestock gave her more acres and it become a fine ranch.

When the war came, the man went away. I didn't know him myself except to nod to when I passed him in town, but people who lived there said that on the day he left he was wearin' a fine gray officer's uniform with gold braid for a hatband. As far as I know, he was never seen back in Waco after that time.

Well, there was a lot of men went off to war and never came back and you never asked their kin about it unless you was willing to hear a tale of sorrow and loss, so when I did come to know Velvet I didn't ask about him. The war was still goin' when she left Waco, so I never knew if he came back or not. If he did, I guess it was to wherever she was then.

The way it came about that I knew her was that I started hearin' stories about the gatherings in her parlor on Saturday nights and sometimes of a Friday, too. It was Tim, the blacksmith, told me about it first, I reckon, but after that I brought the subject up with some of the other men I knew and by their smiles and winks I knew something was going on.

Now, just like you two pups did, I figured her for a whore. Any woman that entertained menfolk in her home without their women bein' present just had to be that kind, or so I thought. Waco was a good-sized town, even in them days, and it did have a whorehouse. I'd been there once, but found it to be a mean place. There was a feller sat by the door with a Navy Colt in his lap and there were two sisters, Velma and Vashti, to take care of the business. And business is all it was. Pay your cash money, climb into a crib with whichever one wasn't busy or sick, and get it over with quick.

After your Ma had died, I let Tim talk me into going to Velvet's house one night and I found out I was wrong about her bein' a whore.

A darky maid let us in, a big old woman that had to go through doors mostly sideways. She asked for our hats and I wouldn't give mine up until Tim laughed and told me it was all right, that I'd get it back when I left. See, in those days I didn't know about fine things or about the way fine folks lived and did things. I guess everything I know now is what I learned from Velvet.

After she had put our hats on a rack that already held about six other hats, that maid led us into a big parlor. I think there must have been about a dozen kerosene lamps burning, plus some candles, and I just wasn't used to that kind of light after dark. You know, at home, we never had more than two lamps burning and if you left the room, you took one with you to light your way into the next room. But Velvet's house had lights going in every room whether there was anybody in the room or not. It was strange to me and kind of uncomfortable, too, to think of all that oil being burned for nothing, but it sure was better than the half-dark house I lived in.

It was a clean house, too. There were stuffed chairs and things I learned were called settees and davenports and there wasn't a pair of overalls hangin' on any of them. There was no dirt on the floor and nothin' piled in the corners and no truck in the way that you had to walk around or step over to get where you wanted to go and no rafters to hang things from.

Thinkin' about it then, I could almost believe the other fellers there felt the same as I did. Her bright-lit house was so different from what we knew that we were drawn to it like moths to a flame, but that was just the first thing I thought. A few minutes later, I learned different.

Me and Tim sat down on one of those davenport things and I nodded howdy to a few of the fellers I knew by sight. Then I waited for something to happen, and by God, it did.

Velvet walked into the room.

Before that night, I'd never seen her. I didn't get into Waco often and when I did, I was at the general store buyin' truck we needed and then right back home. So even though I knew about her from what Tim and others had told me, when she walked into that room it was like the wick in every lamp had been turned up.

She was wearing a green silk gown that matched the green of her eyes. Her hair was gold and wasn't pinned up or in a bun the way most women did, but was let loose to fall down to her shoulders in soft waves. Her skin was fair and it was plain she hadn't spent any time out in the sun or the wind. And she had a smile for every man in the room. Seeing Velvet, I knew what had drawn us in and would keep drawing us back.

She went around the room sayin' hello to every man there

and callin' him by his first name, touchin' some of them on the shoulder, some of them on the cheek. When she got to me, I stood up and tried to swallow while Tim told her my name. I put out my hand and she took it in hers with a touch as light as a cloud and said, "Welcome, Gerald, to our little gathering. I hope you'll become a regular visitor."

"I brung you a pig," I said. Tim had told me about the custom of the house and I had a pig to spare so I had brought it along. But I was so tongue-tied in telling her that I could barely get it out and I felt stupid and clumsy after I did.

"Why, how nice of you to think of my needs," she said, smiling at me. "It's so hard for a woman alone, especially with this terrible war going on. Have you heard the latest news from Richmond?"

Now, you see? That's the way Velvet was. She knew I felt stupid and awkward so she took the attention right away from me and let me feel at ease. That's the way she always was in them days, and I hope the years haven't changed her.

***

"Damn, Pap," Wayne said. "I thought you started in to tell us why she left Waco."

"Let him go on, Wayne. This is a good story, the way he tells it." In my own mind, I was looking forward to having the same experience Pap had had when he first met her and I was thinking about how my first meeting with Velvet might be only a week away.

"You'll never understand how terrible it was she left if you don't know how good it was she was there in the first place," Pap said.

***

Well (Pap went on) I did become a regular at her place. And when I wasn't tending my crops, I'd be out in the brush poppin' out mavericks to take to her. I figured it was the least I could do to help a woman alone and I even had Tim, the blacksmith, make me up a branding iron with the letter V, so that when I took them cows over to her all I had to do was to turn 'em loose and give her the tally.

Now I didn't know all the customs of Velvet's place, not at first, so I didn't know she had her own set of tally books and that she kept a book on every man who visited her. I should have known, I guess, for sometimes when she was making the rounds of the parlor she might say something like, "That was a poor hog you brought last week, Fred. I'm afraid you'll have to bring me another one," or "Tom, you've got credit for a bull whenever you want to cash in."

So it was one day durin' the middle of the week, with no entertainin' goin' on, that I drove about five more mavericks over to her place and gave 'em to the care of the old Mexican who worked for her. He was a sharp old man and he always earmarked ever cow I brung over. Since I was doin' my own brandin', he needed to make sure I wasn't bringin' the same cows twice.

Velvet came out on the back porch and seen me talkin' to the Mexican and she said, "Gerald, you'd better come in here for a minute." It was the first time I'd ever seen her by daylight and she was just as pretty as she was in the lamplight.

I followed her into the house and into the parlor, but since I was in my workin' clothes I wouldn't sit on the furniture, figuring it was too fine for my dirt. She was wearing a red gown with a white shift under it, her hair fallin' loose the way she liked, and she put her hands on her hips, cocked her head and grinned, and said, "Gerald, just what am I going to do about you?"

"I don't believe I understand," I said. "I didn't know I'd

done anything wrong."

"You've been bringing over all those cattle and you haven't yet allowed me to repay you."

"Well..." I found myself kind of toeing at her fine carpet. "Miss Velvet..."

"You don't have to call me 'miss.' Velvet will do just fine."

"Well, I've been drinkin' your whiskey and eatin' sandwiches and fried chicken, and..."

"Gerald, that's what the boys pay for when they bring a pig or a brace of chickens, like most of them do. But you've started a fine cattle ranch for me and you're entitled to much more."

***

Wayne laughed. "Pap, I never took you for no shitkicker."

Pap kind of shook himself out of his memories and bridled at that. "Well, I wasn't! I was just play-actin' until I seen where she was going with her talk."

"The way you tell it, you was doing a damned good job."

"Do you want me to tell it, or don't you?"

"Go on, Pap." I was a bit sick and a mite jealous at what I felt was coming, but I had to hear it all.

"Well," Pap said, "I knew what she was getting at and so I didn't waste no more time. I just scooped her up into my arms and carried her out of that parlor and into a bedroom where there was a bed with a big canopy on it. I never did figure that canopy out unless it was to keep the rain off when the roof leaked, but I didn't really care.

"I put her down on the bed real gentle-like and hiked up that shift she was wearing so I could see the promised land clear and then I undid my belt and dropped my pants and climbed right into that bed with her."

I thought the wind in his talk had shifted quite a bit, but I didn't say anything. If there was any truth there, it might come out later. What I knew was that most of us don't remember things the way they were, we remember things the way we wish they had been, and if we tell about them, we do it to put ourselves in the best light.

"And that was it?" Wayne said.

"Well, not quite. She stopped me. Said I couldn't be coming to her bed with my boots on and while I was at it I'd best take off my work clothes, too." Pap grinned real big. "But before she said that, she'd got a look at me and I can tell you she was some surprised."

Wayne tipped me a wink and said, "She wasn't used to tiny men?"

"God damn you, Wayne! I oughtn't to even tell you any more!"

"Just funnin' you, Pap."

"Huh!" Pap shot him a sideways glance. "Anyway, I did what she asked, even though I felt funny about doing it. I'd never been stark naked with a woman before. When I did turn and get back in the bed, damned if Velvet wasn't stark naked, too. First time I'd ever seen that in a woman, I mean without one stitch of clothing on that pretty body."

Now I was real jealous of that, for I'd been with a few women myself by that time, in sporting houses that we found at the end of the trail, but them women never took the time to get full undressed and I'd always felt somewhat cheated by that.

Pap's eyes were soft with remembering and he was fingering that scar over his eye.

"I guess now you're going to give us the details of every time you laid with her," Wayne said, laughing. "Just tell us about that first one and forget the other one."

Pap didn't rise to the bait the way I thought he would. His eyes stayed soft and when he spoke again his voice was soft. "I was with her for seven months, Wayne. Right up until the time she left Waco. I guess I'd have gone with her, but...Never mind."

"Are you gonna tell us you was in love with her?" Wayne said.

Pap just looked at him and nodded kind of slow. "I don't know that it was love, but I do know I was mighty taken with her."

"If that don't beat all! To fall in love with a..."

"Don't you say it, Wayne!" Pap said. "Don't you call her a whore! And you might want to think about where you found this Rose you're always moonin' about!"

"Don't you go callin' Rose a whore!"

Seeing the fire in Wayne's eyes, I knew for sure it wasn't going to be me calling Rose any names.

"Why'd she leave, Pap?" I said. "That's what you started in to tell us."

"Pap, was she takin' other men to her bed?"

Yes (Pap said), she was takin' other men to her bed. I knew of it and was some jealous, but she explained to me it was the only way she had of thankin' 'em for the livestock and such that they'd brung her. I knew the truth of that and so I made myself to look the other way when I was there for an entertainment and she would lead one of the other fellers off into that bedroom with the fancy bed.

Tim, the blacksmith, was one she took by the hand several times that I saw, and that dimwit Donnie Spoon that had an ugly wife and more cattle than he knew what to do with, and I guess there was a few others that I did my best to ignore.

Some nights there wasn't any of those trips to the bedroom

goin' on and Velvet would just play the piano and sing sad songs while we sipped at our whiskey and played checkers and such. No one ever got loud or rowdy, for if he had the rest of us would have shown him to the door real quick. And there was never any gamblin' at cards, cause that can lead to fights and arguments.

Generally, on nights like that, I'd lag behind until all the others had left and then Velvet and me would climb into that fancy bed and have at it until we were too tired for any more and then I'd tell her goodnight and make my way across the dark fields back to my own house. But it was nights like that, too, that her and I would talk and she'd tell me about how I never again had to bring her a cow or a pig if I didn't feel like it, for she wanted me bad every night and I was the one man in the crowd of regulars that she most wanted to be with no matter what.

So, naturally, I popped the brush harder than ever to get more cattle to bring her.

***

"Pap," Wayne said. "Maybe you should've gone off with her. Hell, if she cared for you that much..."

"There was a lot of things against it," Pap said. "There was that feller that had brought her to Waco and then gone off to the war. I had you to raise and...Oh, hell!"

"What?"

"About a year after she'd gone, I got to tellin' Tim about how I felt about Velvet and how she felt about me. He said she'd told him the same damned things she'd told me. Now, I knew Tim could stretch the truth when it suited him, but I didn't have no heart to call him on it. And I never talked about it with any of the other fellers because I didn't want to know. But after he told me that, I gave up all thought of ever seein' her again 'cause I didn't want to find out she'd been lyin' to me. There wasn't a hell of a lot of things to believe in after the war so I guess I just held on to what little I had."

***

Anyway (Pap said), some mean talk started going around Waco about the kind of entertainments Velvet was putting on. Pigs and horses were mentioned and there was even talk of her layin' with two or three fellers at a time. I think the tales was started by Velma and Vashti, them two sister whores I told you about, and there wasn't a man who knew Velvet that put any stock in them.

But the women...Hell, a woman will believe anything bad that she hears about anybody. That's why they're such damned gossips, 'cause they'll believe anything they're told and can't wait to pass it on to someone just as gullible.

When the rumors started, Velvet started packing and she even shipped some things to Missouri. I remember how dark it was in her place after she'd shipped out a bunch of the lamps and other breakables, along with trunks full of clothes.

I guess it's a good thing she didn't wait until the last minute, because that came sooner than I would have thought. One night a whole posse of women showed up, carrying torches and a rope. Old Granny Davis was the one leadin' 'em and keepin' 'em stirred up. She claimed she'd had a dream and that the dream meant they were to take Velvet out and hang her because Velvet was the devil come to earth and once they hung her the South would be purged of the sin of slavery and the war would end and all the boys would come home safe and sound.

I don't know how many of the women believed that nonsense and how many just wanted to keep their men home at nights. And I guess there was some that was just tired of lookin' for a chicken to cook or a pig to butcher and not finding any where they thought they'd be.

Tim was the biggest of us, being a blacksmith with big arms and wide shoulders, so we sent him out on the front porch to talk to the women. Granny Davis yelled that he was Satan's helper and them women like to scratched and kicked him to death while the rest of us was out back loadin' a wagon with what Velvet had already had packed. We got her and that darky maid out of the house into the wagon and whipped the horses to give them a good start, then went around to see what we could do for Tim.

He was taking a beating all right and there were many men there who could have drug their own wives out of the fray, but then they'd have to admit they were there. After that dimwit Donnie Spoon pulled away his own wife and got beat about the head with an axe handle she happened to have, no one else was willing to do more than slink back into the shadows.

Some of them women tried to set fire to the house, but me and some of the single men that wasn't afraid to show themselves got it put out pretty quick.

When I figured Velvet had a good head start, I yelled, "They're getting away! Look down the street!" and them dumb women took off running after that wagon, but never did catch it. They all felt some good about it, though, and next time I went to church they was still talkin' about how they'd run Velvet out of town. I didn't care how they saw it and Tim was thankful he'd only got one ear half chewed off.

Me, I went on back to my old farm and started tryin' to forget about her, except when some traveler happened by and brought me some word she wanted me to have. I always made it a point to ask if they'd brought any word for Tim, but none of them ever admitted to it if they did, so I guess he was lyin' about the whole thing. Carpetbaggers shot him in '66, so I couldn't go whale the tar out of him when I found out.

***

"And that's all there is to it," Pap said. "Until you boys come around mentioning the Velvet brand, I hadn't thought about her in a year, since I had word last season that she was plannin' on moving to Dodge City." He fingered that scar over his eye and grinned. "We did have us some times."

"That sure was a story, Pap," Wayne said. "Go on now, Roy Lee. I promised Pap you'd tell him about the day job we took on."

"Dammit, Wayne, you promised you'd tell him." I laid back on my saddle and slid my hat over my eyes. "I'm going to get some sleep."

What I heard of the story Wayne told was mostly wrong, but I didn't care. Pretty soon his voice was just like a soft buzz that was putting me to sleep.

Velvet and me were back in her parlor with all the lamps lit, standing in the center of the room like we had before. She was wearing that same white gown that looked like it had been made out of clouds, her hair falling soft and golden around her shoulders, her green eyes bright with promise. She touched her lips with her tongue and then took a step closer to me, kind of leaning her head back and closing her eyes.

I took her in my arms and kissed her, my tongue slipping between her lips, and I felt her kind of nibble on the tip of it for a minute before she opened all the way and her tongue touched mine, making crazy circles that caused a shiver to run through me.

"Oh, Roy Lee..." she said, leaning her head against my chest.

I started to kiss the top of her head, but before I could do it a big man who looked strong enough to be a blacksmith pulled her away from me. "My turn, Velvet," he told her.

She smiled at him. "Why, so it is, Tim. Roy Lee, I'll be right back."

They went off, holding hands, through that door that I knew led to her bedroom. I heard something like the shuffle of feet and I looked around. There were four other men in the room with me, though I hadn't noticed them before, and they were kind of grinning and nodding and them that were sitting close enough were nudging one another with their elbows.

"Got to take turnabout, Cowboy," one of them said.

"Not me," I said. "I'm special to Velvet."

He nudged the man sitting next to him and grinned, but there wasn't any time for me to teach him his manners because Velvet had come back into the room and was coming back into my arms. I noticed her lip rouge was kind of smudged, but I didn't say anything.

There was no sign of Tim so I reckoned he'd gone out the back door I hadn't known about until now.

"Now, where were we?" she said almost in a whisper.

"I was teachin' you how to kiss." Our lips touched again and then she moved her head just a bit so that she had my lower lip between her teeth and was nibbling on it kind of soft and then she sucked my lip between hers and moved her head back so that she was pulling on it for a minute before she let go of it and giggled real soft.

"Is that what you were teaching me?" she asked.

She was pulled out of my arms again and a tall, lanky fellow led her off toward the bedroom. She looked over her shoulder and said, "You wait right there, Roy Lee."

I did wait, and in a few minutes she was back. Her hair was kind of mussed and the gown had slipped so that one white shoulder was bare and the color she used around her eyes was kind of smudged. I noticed one of her earbobs was gone, but I reckoned she'd find it in her bed. She came back into my arms and laid her head against my chest, breathing heavy, and she made a little gasp when I slid my hand inside that gown and took hold of her breast.

"Oh, God, Roy Lee! The things you make me feel..."

I had her nipple between my thumb and finger, kind of rolling it around and listening to her moan way back in her throat. Her head was thrown back, her lips parted, and I kissed her soft white neck. I guess it was good that I didn't have a tight grip on her nipple because she was pulled away again, this time by a grizzled old man who looked a lot like Pap.

"I'll be back, Roy Lee." She almost lost her footing as she stumbled after him, and did lose one slipper.

They closed the bedroom door behind them, but I could still hear a lot of whooping and hollering.

When she did come back, her gown was open all the way down the front, her hair was wild, and she had misplaced one of those long dark eyelashes. She was limping from the loss of that slipper and she kind of staggered back into my arms and shook her head like she was trying to clear it or trying to remember something.

"Oh," she said. "Of course." Then she slid her hand down the front of my jeans and commenced to open the buttons. I thought it was real talented of her to be able to do that with one hand, but she got it done and I could feel her fingers touching me soft. "Ummm, Roy Lee, you are just so..."

She was pulled away again, and this time it was best that she hadn't had a tight grip on me or I'd have gone with her. She kind of staggered after the portly man that had her by the hand, not saying anything but just waggling her fingers at me to let me know she'd be back

I looked around and the room was empty except for me and I knew my special time with Velvet was next on the list. I went ahead and shucked out of my boots and clothes, making a neat pile of everything on the floor.

The bedroom door opened and Velvet started through it, then stopped. The white gown was completely gone, her golden hair was almost covering her face, and she was as naked as I was. She started toward me again but got only one halting step before she had to stop and lean her back against the doorjamb.

"Velvet, honey?"

"Oh, shit!"

She slid right down to the floor, her back against the doorjamb and her pretty legs splayed out in front of her, and sat there with her head down, shaking it from side to side. "No more," she said almost mumbling like her lips were thick. "Can't take any more. Wore me out."

Then she looked up and brushed the hair back from her eyes and saw me standing there with my male pride. It was like she was noticing me for the first time. "Oh, one more." She made like she was going to stand up, but then plopped back down and giggled. "Never mind." She patted the carpet. "We'll do it right here on the floor."

"Velvet, I don't think..."

She reached up and grabbed me by the only handle I had and was pulling me to her while I was trying to back away, not wanting to see her or even know about her in that bedraggled state, not wanting to go where so many men had gone before.

"Come on, Roy Lee, it's your turn."

"Dammit! I don't want a turn now!"

"Get up and take your turn anyway," Wayne said, kicking my foot. "It's your go on nighthawk."

I got up, whuffling and snorting like a horse on a frosty morning, the cobwebs of the dream still sticking in my mind while I saddled and bridled a horse.

While I was making my slow rides around the herd, I had time for a lot of thinking. I could figure that my dream had been all mixed up with what Pap had told us about Velvet, but it was discomforting all the same.

I was sure in my mind that I still wanted to find Velvet, that I still wanted to hold her and love her the way I had when the dreams first started, but at the same time I had to wonder what old Granny Davis would make of that last part, when I had been trying to escape from her.

Somehow, my thoughts and longings about Velvet were all of a mix with my longings for Jessie and it came to me that I was going to have to do some serious thinking about taking Velvet back to Texas with me. I worried about it all the next day while we were making our way up to Abilene, but I never did feel like I got any closer to the center of it.

It was only after a long argument between Wayne and Pap that we had turned the herd for Abilene. Being this close, Wayne didn't want to wait another minute to see Rose and make sure she was still true to him. Pap's position was that we could sell the herd in Dodge like we'd planned, then Wayne could go to Abilene or to hell, but in the end Wayne proved to be the more stubborn of the two.

I sided with Wayne, but only because I needed more time to think about Velvet.

"Well, I'll do her," Pap finally said. "But I don't know how in hell you expect me to keep holdin' this herd by myself. I been mighty lucky, so far."

"Hell, Pap, you're the one sent us off yesterday."

"Yesterday was an emergency. Rose ain't no emergency."

"Never mind," Wayne said. "I think I know where we can get help." He winked at me. "Want to ride along, Roy Lee?"

Sometimes it was easy to know just what Wayne had on his mind and this was one of those times. Fact is, I'd had the same idea yesterday, but at that time I didn't figure we was quite desperate enough.

"I'll go," I said. "Those boys tickle me."

We left Pap looking somewhat puzzled and somewhat riled and rode back out to that acre of rocks again.

"Sim! Tiny!" Wayne called. "Come on out."

"We ain't here," Tiny said.

"Dammit, Tiny! You know that didn't work yesterday," Sim said. "We might as well go on out with our hands up. Likely they got the drop on us again."

"Let's go out shootin'" Tiny said.

"No need for that," I called. "We came to offer you a job of work."

The two of them talked among themselves for a minute or two, but I couldn't make out what they were saying until Tiny raised his voice. "I'd rather go out shootin' than to take a job."

"What kind of job is it?" Sim called.

"You'd be helpin' my Pap with the herd while me and Roy Lee ride ahead to look for my girl."

"Little girl, I guess?" Tiny said. "We ain't seen no little girls pass by."

"A woman," Wayne answered.

"Seems like a full-grown woman would be easier to keep track of. How'd you come to lose her?"

There was movement in the rocks now and it looked like they'd made up their minds to come out. After a minute they appeared, scrabbling over the last of the boulders. The one I took to be Tiny was a little feller and he had the open sack of Arbuckle's in his hand and kept dipping into it with the other, while his mouth worked at chewing up the coffee beans. The other was about a head shorter than me with a black beard and lanky black hair and I didn't think Pap would have any trouble whupping either of them if it came to that.

"I didn't lose her," Wayne said. "I just have to go look for her."

"Well, that sounds contrary," Sim said. "Does this job pay anything?"

"We'll give you enough for a stake," Wayne said. "Ten dollars to see the herd toward Dodge and stay with it until we get back."

"That's enough for a whore and bottle," Sim said. "I'm in."

"Not so fast," Tiny said. "You got real coffee that don't come in beans?"

I told him we did.

"Get your horses and guns and go on back down the trail," Wayne said, pointing. "There'll be a man with the herd and that's Pap."

Both men commenced to look kind of sheepish.

"No guns or horses?" I said.

"Nary one."

"Pap's got horses you can ride, but you'll have to do it bareback," I said, jerking my thumb over my shoulder. "Might as well start out walkin'."

They started off down the trail, Tiny still eating coffee beans and Sim saying, "Maybe this Pap will be reasonable and not make us take off our shirts to ride his blamed horses."

"Pap's gonna like them two," Wayne said. "They'll make

him feel right smart."

We kicked up those bay ponies, figuring a good hard ride would put us in Abilene by nightfall. Wayne was in high spirits at the prospect of getting to see Rose so soon and some of his mood must have rubbed off on me, though not because I was in any hurry to find Rose. The fact was, I was trying to think up some lies in case she let Wayne know she recognized me. But it did feel good to be out in the open country, able to see for miles when we topped a rise, riding under a blue sky with fleecy clouds and not thinking about anything except the feel of the horse under me.

I knew I should be doing that thinking about Velvet that I had to do, and I wanted to do some thinking about Jessie. In spite of the fact that her old pa had made us part, Jessie had never taken up with another feller. The few times we talked she told me she still had hopes that I'd amount to something and I guess she was prepared to wait until I did, especially since I'd told her that this time I'd be coming back with a hatful of money. But if I came back to Waco with Velvet on my arm, she was going to be more than a little put out, I reckoned.

Then again, there was the last dream I'd had, when I'd been tryin' to pull away from Velvet, and I knew I had to do some thinking about that and about what it all might mean.

But I put it all out of my mind, enjoying the ride, and it was a good thing I did for it was the last good day Wayne and me would have for a while.

The Velvet Brand

Chapter Nine

The Cheyenne Kid

When Wayne found out Rose wasn't waiting for him in Abilene, he got so mad he flung his saddle at his horse and missed. I'd seen him mad before, for he's got a temper as short as his trigger finger, but I never thought I'd see him get mad enough to want to shoot it out with the Cheyenne Kid, especially since the Kid was only ten years old at the time. But Wayne does have a wide jealous streak and the Kid would have fought a sack full of wildcats to get what he wanted.

"She was supposed to wait for me, Roy Lee," Wayne kept saying while he stomped around the stable where we'd left our horses when we got to Abilene. We'd gone over to where Rose had last been working and it was there Wayne had got his bad news. "Dammit, we made promises."

"Well..." I scratched at my head to make it appear I was thinking. Fact is, I was glad Rose was gone and hoped that wherever she was it was far away, maybe Ohio or Iowa or some place like that, for if we found her it was likely she'd remember me as a customer. "Maybe she just forgot. Let's get drunk and tree the town and tomorrow we'll go back to the herd."

"No. The man in that house where she worked said she'd gone to Newton to open a hash house, so that's where we've got to go."

"I don't recollect him sayin' anything about a hash house."

"He said she'd bought a business there and that's what she does."   He was looking at me like he expected me to dispute him, but I almost held my tongue.

Instead of holding back, I tried to sneak up on the subject edgewise.   "Suppose she went off up there with another man?" I said.

That was when Wayne threw his saddle and missed the horse.

Newton was another thirty miles or so up the trail from Abilene and I didn't feel like making another long ride that day, but I could see Wayne was determined.   I gave in and helped him saddle up proper, knowing we would go.   It had been a long and thirsty day and now that we were in a town, I was itching to have a spree.   But Wayne ain't no fun when he's mad, unless I'm the one that makes him mad, and I could figure he was going to be this way until we found Rose.   So, I decided to save my spree for Newton.

We were almost there when Wayne adopted the Cheyenne Kid.

Rather than ride all night, we'd made camp short of Newton for our money was too thin to be wasted on hotels and such.   Wayne was edgy and I was leaving him alone, listening to the night sounds in the brush and trying to figure one that didn't quite fit when he said, "Dammit!   A man ought to feel good about marryin'.   How come I just feel mad?"

Now, that was the first time Wayne had ever mentioned marriage and I guessed I was finally being told what kind of promises they'd made last summer.   But I knew I couldn't say anything directly against Rose unless I was willing to get shot, so I said, "Maybe it's because we won't be partners no more." There was a lot of hope in my tone, but I couldn't go back and say it any different.

"Aw, you always got a place with us, Roy Lee. I got it figured that with Rose to cook for us we can buy the old Potter place and make a good ranch out of it."

It didn't take more than a minute for me to think about that arrangement and decide I didn't want any part of it.

"No," I said. "You can marry Rose or you can trail along with me, but you can't do both. Hell, you don't want me living with you two." Besides, I'd already ate some of Rose's cooking and figured she'd be more of a success as a whore.

Ducking his head and looking kind of sheepish, Wayne said, "I kind of hoped you'd see it that way." Then he looked up and stuck his chin out at me. "But you've got to understand that I made promises to Rose and I can't go back on them."

"You're the one that's upset about them, not me."

He picked up the frying pan full of beans and shoved it into the fire, moving his mouth like he was holding back a lot of words.

Me, I sat there feeling lonesome for all the good times we'd had and wouldn't ever have again once Wayne was married. It wasn't all his fault, of course, because the same split would happen when I took up with Velvet or Jessie.

Not knowing which of the two women I wanted to be with made me wish I'd stayed behind in Abilene and had my spree. And it was while I was thinking this that I heard that noise in the brush again. "Someone's out there," I said. "You'd best go see about it, Wayne."

He kept a hard grip on the frying pan. "You go see."

"No, you're a faster draw than me."

"That won't make much difference if he's already got the drop on us." He gave me a hard look. "Besides, you could unshuck your gun right now."

"You're right about him probably havin' us covered." I

shrugged and laid back, knowing I could get Wayne into trouble faster than he could do it himself. "I guess we'd best just surrender."

"By God, I won't surrender till I know who it is!"

"Then go see, Wayne," I told him, waving toward the brush. "Go see."

He stood up and hitched up his gun belt, fixing his hat so that a lock of his curly hair showed in front and making me wonder if he'd got confused and thought it was a lady out there. He gave me a black look and started for the brush. "Who's out there?"

"Hey, Cowboy sumbeech, you got food?"

Wayne froze, his eyes getting big and his face turning red with rage. "By God, that tears it!" he said, and went for his gun.

He got it out right fast, the way he always does. Then he commenced fanning the hammer. You can't hit a damned thing shooting that way, but I never could get that idea into Wayne's head. Fact is, he wasn't that good a shot even when he took his time, and I believe that nearsighted horse was the only thing he'd ever killed.

Well, the clearing filled with black powder smoke so thick it stung my eyes and my nose. There was a roaring in my ears and when the smoke started clearing it looked like Wayne had cut a few bushes down to size. I was sure them bushes wasn't going to bother us any more, but he still had fire in his eye and was shoving new cartridges into his pistol as fast as he could.

"Hey, Cowboy sumbeech, you done shoot? You got food?"

Wayne jerked his head up and stared at the brush, his mouth working like he had a lot to say if he could just remember what it was. Then he snatched off his hat and threw it at the ground and I was glad to see him finally hit something.

"Roy Lee, you better go get a hold on his mouth, for I swear I'll kill him if he calls me that name again."

"You planning on doing any more shooting while I'm out there?"

"Soon as I get this thing loaded!"

Figuring I'd be safest in front of him, I headed into the brush.

What I found there was an Indian boy, maybe ten years old. He was wearing ragged clothes and had a lot of dirty black hair hanging in his eyes. He looked like he'd missed a few meals, but I guess it hadn't done anything to his spirits because he was sitting on a log and giggling fit to kill.

"Hope you ain't laughin' at Wayne," I said. "He's mad enough as it is. And don't never call a Texan by that name, for we take it hard."

He got his giggling under control and looked up at me. "Okay. You got food, Cowboy sum...Cowboy?"

"Yep. You come on up to the fire and we'll feed you."

"No goddamn beans!"

I stopped short and gave him a look as hard as the one he was giving me, and then decided it wasn't my place to spank him. "Where'd you learn to talk like that?"

"Soldiers teach me. Teach me good."

"More than somewhat," I said. "Come on."

When Wayne saw us, he got kind of red in the face and eased his gun back into his holster. He swallowed hard a time or two and said, "Is that what I shot at?"

"If he hadn't been so quick to sit still, you'd have got him for sure."

"He's short," Wayne said. "And I was just firin' over his head anyways."

I let it go and nudged the kid. "Say howdy to Wayne and tell us your name."

"Someday I get gun, fix you good," he told Wayne.

"Forget that. Just tell us your name."

Well, he told what it was, but it was one of them Indian names like they have. I twisted my tongue on it once or twice, and after that we just called him the Cheyenne Kid.

The way the Kid told it, between mouthfuls of grub, he'd lived most of his life near Fort Riley with a sister for his only kin. She used to take him along with her when she went to the fort to see her soldier friends and it was while he waited for her that other soldiers had taught him his English and a little more besides.

"Dammit!" Wayne said. "It's pitiful!"

"Hey, not pitiful!" The way the Kid stuck his chin out, I could figure his temper was as short as Wayne's. "I talk damn good."

"Sure. Let him tell it, Wayne."

"Well, that ain't no way to raise a kid," Wayne said. "It ain't."

That sister had finally married one of the soldiers and took up doing laundry for the fort, and it gave her so many notions about being white and respectable that she wouldn't have anything more to do with the Kid, nor with any of the other Indians in her tribe. The Kid was left on his own.

"So I leave," the Kid said, rubbing at his full stomach. His hunger had overcome him so that he hadn't minded the beans after all. "I go somewhere and be white, maybe be cowboy sumbeech someday."

Grabbing Wayne's right arm, I held it tight while his fingers twitched at the pistol just out of his reach. "Just hold on now, Wayne. He don't know any way of talkin' except what those soldiers taught him."

"Aw, I'm not gonna shoot him anymore." He jerked his arm away and seemed to relax a bit. "Why do you want to be white, Kid?"

"Hey, no future for being Indian."

"It can't be done," Wayne said. His mouth was firm and he was shaking his head like he'd already given it a lot of thought. "There ain't no way an Indian can ever be white. Now, you better think about that, for winter ain't far off and it'll get cold out on these plains."

"Indians can make out," I said, trying to ease the gloom I saw come over the Kid's face. "They always do."

"Not very good Indian," the Kid said. "Can't find buffalo. Can't catch fish without goddamn fishhooks." He looked up at us, pushing the lank black hair out of his eyes, and when he spoke his voice was low and mournful. "Guess I die if I can't be white."

"Livin' around that fort must have ruined him for bein' an Indian, Roy Lee. You reckon we better take him with us?"

I had a doubtful feeling about the Kid, the same kind of feeling I'd had the last time I played Three Card Monte with a Mexican feller in Waco. But I thought it might be healthy that Wayne was finally thinking about someone besides Rose. "We'd best find him a home and get shut of him, Wayne. I'm bound back to Texas and you got to think about what Rose would say."

"Oh, hell, Rose is a fool for kids. And by now she's probably rich enough to take care of a dozen of 'em."

I still had doubts I was chewing on. "This one's tougher than most."

"Listen, Roy Lee, I feel bad about shooting at him and he ain't wild enough to be an Indian no more."

"You can't make him white. You said so yourself."

"Rose'll take to him."

I could see Wayne was talking himself into trouble but I wouldn't be his partner much longer and wouldn't have to worry about getting him out of it, so I just shrugged.

Wayne grinned his big grin for the first time since we'd set out yesterday. "It's all settled, Kid. You're coming with us."

"Hey! I gone be white? Sumbeech!"

"Watch it," Wayne said.

***

Next morning we got to Newton and used up some of our money buying the Kid an outfit of clothes. It was Wayne had adopted him, but I felt I ought to kick in for half and the Kid did look fine in his new checkered shirt, jeans, and boots. He looked so good to himself that he started figuring he was damned near white already. I didn't tell him different.

After we had him dressed, we started the rounds of beaneries and hash houses looking for Rose. The Kid kind of had his tongue hanging out so I dug a bit deeper into my pocket and started using my spree money to feed him. By the time we hit the last hash house in town he'd ate up most of my money and Wayne still hadn't found Rose.

He came back from talking to the counter man, looking confused and madder than ever. "Well, she ain't slingin' hash no more," he said. "But wherever she is, I know she's getting rich for us. I guess we'd best start hittin' the saloons."

"That's a fine thing, now that most of the spree money is gone!" I said. "Wayne, you can't plan anything right."

"It don't cost money to ask questions. Someone's bound to know if she's still here or if she moved on to Dodge or someplace. Might save us from stompin' all over this damned prairie looking for her."

The Kid had been pushing food around on his plate, looking like he was finally filled up, but now his head jerked up and he grinned. "Goddamn! Now I get whiskey!"

"No, you don't," I said. "What the hell would a kid like you do with whiskey?"

"Learn to get drunk. White man get drunk. Learn to fall down and have good time like white man."

"You think she'd have left, Wayne?"

"It's either that or takin' in laundry. Nothing else for a young girl to do in a belly-up cow town."

There was another line of work I could think of, but it didn't seem the time to mention it.

So we started making the rounds of the bars, asking questions in every one, but because I couldn't afford to buy a drink it was a lot different than being on a spree.

Fact is, I was mournful. The one drink I did pour down only made me a little bit sadder about Wayne getting married and a little bit sadder still that the Kid was going to have to find out how hard life treats us.

As for Wayne, his mad was getting deeper. It wasn't the kind of mad to make him throw his hat on the ground. That's an easy kind to handle and I usually did it by grinning at him until he had to grin back. Now he had his hat set square on his head and a mean hard line for a mouth and I knew that before long he was going to have to hit somebody.

The last saloon we went into was elegant, with big glass windows and a big glass chandelier hanging in the middle of the room, pictures on the walls, a mirror behind the bar, and a staircase with real carpet on it. I was kind of looking the place over, feeling familiar without knowing why, when up come this big bald man with shoulders as wide as a barn.

The man pushed up to where we stood at the bar, tapped

Wayne on the shoulder, and said, "You can't bring no Indian kid in here. Get him out."

Now, I knew those were fighting words and I knew just about how mad Wayne was, but I had to admire what he did. He turned real slow, looked down at the Kid like he was seeing him for the first time and said, "Him? He ain't no kid. He's a Mexican midget."

The big man furrowed his forehead, the look a man gets when he has a hard time thinking about things. "You sure?"

"Hey! I no Mexican! No damn Indian, either. I white man."

Wayne got one hand over the Kid's mouth and his other arm around the Kid's middle and lifted him off the floor. Grinning as big as you please, while the Kid kicked and squirmed, Wayne said, "Listen, you work here? You know of a girl named Rose Reilly?"

"He said he was white," the bald man said, moving his shoulders like a man will do when he's loosening up for a fight. "He ain't white."

"Well, but what about Rose?"

The man gave Wayne a hard and doubtful look. "I know her and she don't want nothing to do with the likes of an Indian lover like you. Now, you take your midget and get out of here."

Well, nobody talks to Wayne like that. I know it and he knows it even better. I backed off a step or two, my hand near my gun and my eyes moving over the other men at the bar, ready to back Wayne however he decided to handle it.

Wayne kind of turned away, set the Kid down easy, and balled up the fist on his off side. Then he turned back quick, putting all his weight behind his swing. His fist caught the bald man square in the mouth and the big man blinked once, blood trickling over his lips, and then the fur began to fly.

Now, I didn't have any doubts about Wayne being able to take care of himself, even though the bald man was mighty big. Wayne was good at rough and tumble fighting for he'd been practicing on me for most of my life and I don't quit easy.

It was a joy to watch them stand toe to toe slugging it out. Then they kind of grappled and took turns tossing one another into tables and chairs and such. That glass chandelier started swinging, things were breaking, and there was an ungodly noise over it all. I was trying to watch the fight and stay ready to threaten anyone who might want a part of it, and the Cheyenne Kid had got himself a glass of whiskey and was kind of hopping around and yelling fit to kill.

Seeing how he was enjoying hisself made me feel so good I let him keep the whiskey. I figured the fight had roused his savage nature and maybe it would make him see he had to go on being what he was born to be.

I also figured the firewater might just put him to sleep so he wouldn't get hungry for a while.

That bald man was big and strong, but Wayne was quick. When it was all over, the saloon was a wreck of busted chairs and tables, the bald man was out cold on the floor, and Wayne was standing over him breathing hard and bloody from head to foot. His shirt was torn off his back and hanging in rags but I could tell he still hadn't worked off his mad.

So, when the pudgy man in the white suit stepped up to Wayne it was the wrong move for him to make. Wayne grabbed his shirt front and lifted him right off the floor, shoving his face close to the frightened face of the pudgy man and growling, "You next?"

"No! Wait!" the man squealed. "I...I want to give you a job. Put me down so we can talk money."

That seemed to get through Wayne's rage. His face brightened and he almost smiled as he set the man back on the floor. "Talk."

The pudgy man looked confused for a minute but then someone handed him the derby hat he'd been wearing before Wayne picked him up, and after he put it on, he seemed better. "That...that bouncer there was the toughest man in Newton," he said. He looked down at the bald man sleeping on the floor and shook his head like he was sad. "You beat him fair and square and I want to give you his job. We'll pay you three hundred a month, flat, and all you have to do is to look mean and throw people out when their money's gone."

"You hear that, Roy Lee?" Wayne was grinning from ear to ear. "That makes me the toughest man in Newton."

"Next to me," I said. While they'd been talking, I'd been taking another look around the place and didn't much like what I saw. It was coming to me why this place looked familiar. A year ago, when me and Wayne were headed home from Abilene, we'd been here. It was where I'd taken up with that tall skinny girl that reminded me of a giraffe. Thinking on that reminded me that the place was somewhat more than a saloon. "I don't think you ought to take the job."

"Now, why not? We need the money and I got to stay here till I find Rose."

"We also got a herd to get to Dodge."

"Well..." Wayne looked kind of hangdog for just a second, and then brightened up. "Hell, you and the Kid can go back and help with the herd and I'll catch up to you in Dodge."

I was shaking my head, my mouth set tight. There wasn't any need to say anything. Wayne knew his obligations as well as I did and I figured he probably just needed a few minutes to come to his senses.

The pudgy man kind of hopped around and in between us until he got Wayne's attention. "Uh...Uh...The proprietor told me I could offer you up to four hundred a month."

"There, Roy Lee. You can't turn up your nose at that."

But I did. I folded my arms over my chest and shook my head slow, feeling about as righteous as Brother Wheeler back home, and trying to look the same. "This ain't no place or no way to bring up a kid. You took him on and you got to bring him up right."

Wayne got a funny kind of look on his face and he worked his mouth around like he had something caught in a tooth. "Now, I hadn't thought about keeping him permanent. I figured me and Rose would get a few square meals in him, that's all."

"You figured on how he's got it figured, Wayne?" I grabbed the Kid from where he was standing moping beside me and eased him forward. "Go on, Kid. Tell Wayne what you think."

The Kid kicked Wayne hard in the shin with those brand-new boots, then put his hands on his hips and stuck his chin out. "You don't push me out, damned Wayne."

"Now, listen, Kid. Maybe..."

The pudgy man had got to hopping around again. "What kid? We can't have any kids around here!"

"It ain't no real kid," Wayne said. "Just a Mexican midget we ride with." He gave me a hard look. "Well, I'll take care of him right here, then. I won't let him get into trouble nor drink more than he can hold."

"Dammit, Wayne! Are you blind?" I pointed to the staircase that had tickled my memories, thinking about where it led. "Don't you remember this place? Don't you remember what's upstairs?"

He looked at the carpeted stairway and his eyes got kind

of wide. "Damn! Have we been here before? Uh...Maybe you're right, Roy Lee. Maybe..."

But it was too late. Satin shoes and black silk stockings were coming down the stairs slow and graceful, and a soft voice said, "Take the job, Wayne, honey."

Every man in the room turned and watched as she came down those stairs. It was Rose Reilly, of course, but Lord, she'd changed. Her hair was a fine sorrel color and was piled on top of her head in soft waves, her lips were bright red, and she was wearing a kind of robe thing that flapped open to show them black stockings all the way up to her fancy garters and gapped open at the top to show most of a wondrous bosom.

I had some swift memories of being with her a year ago and then I quick put my hand over the Kid's eyes. He kicked at me and twisted away and I was too dumbfounded to care much until I felt him tugging at my gun.

"What the hell are you doing, Kid?" I yelped, slapping his hand away.

"Gone shoot damned Wayne." His voice was as mean as the look on his face. "Then I be tough man in town. Can't throw me out then."

"Being an idiot ain't the way to be white, Kid." But I had to admit the two things most times went hand in hand.

"Miss Rosalind," the pudgy man was trying to say, "I...I..."

"I know you tried, Lester. Now I'll try," Rose said. She turned a bright smile on Wayne. "Hello, honey. I see you did come back to me."

There was sawdust on the floor and Wayne kind of moved some of it around with the toe of his boot, his head bent and his ears red like he was embarrassed. "Roy Lee, I think I'm in trouble," he said softly, mournfully. "She ain't takin' in washing and I bet it ain't hash she's been slinging."

I grabbed his arm, all but jumping up and down, I was that glad to see that he'd finally taken a good look at Rose. "Hell, let's get on out of here then and find ourselves a spree!"

"Nope." Looking down, he kind of shuffled his feet the way a man will do when he doesn't know whether to go or to stay. "I guess I got to take the job."

"Wayne Denton, you are seven different kinds of a fool!"

His face got red again and he raised his fists to where I thought he was going to start in on me. I'd had enough of his stubbornness that I welcomed the chance to clean his clock, and I was getting set to whup him good and proper when his face pinched up like he hurt somewhere and he dropped his hands and said, "Dammit, Roy Lee, we made promises."

"I bet she ain't kept none of 'em!"

"No, but I'm bound to keep mine."

"Oh, hell! You made promises to the Kid, too. What about him?"

He got just the confused look I knew he would and said, "What did I promise him?"

"You told him you'd help him learn to be white." I was laying it on thick, of course, counting on Wayne to be too upset to remember all he might have said.

"I'm sorry," Wayne told the Kid. "I guess I can't do it after all."

"You damned Wayne! Someday I shoot you!"

I grabbed the Kid by his collar in time to keep him from attacking Wayne's legs. When I turned him away Rose was at the foot of the stairs, kind of resting her arm on the banister so that robe thing gapped open a bit more at her bosom, and she had the other hand on her hip. She was a sight to admire and it was hard to blame Wayne for being tempted by her, but I did anyway.

"How've you been, Roy Lee?" Rose said.

"You two have met?" Wayne said.

"Come on, Kid," I said, taking his hand. "You and me are through around here."

"You adopt me now, Roy Lee?"

I couldn't find a way to tell him that wasn't on my mind for he was looking up at me with those mournful dark eyes. When he pressed his cheek against my hand, I had again that feeling I'd had about the Mexican Monte dealer who'd cleaned me out, but I reminded myself that the Kid was just a kid and likely not given to wily ways. I covered my feelings for him by giving Wayne a black look and watching him hang his head in shame, and then I said, "I guess I got it to do, Kid."

"Damned Wayne act like my sister," the Kid said. "Nobody want damn Indian."

Rose came over to Wayne. She took hold of his bare arm and kissed him on the ear, I guess because it was one of the few spots without any blood on it, then she rubbed her cheek against his shoulder. He kind of jerked and turned red all the way down to his waist but she kept her hold on him.

It was time for me and the Kid to go, but Wayne and me had been partners for so long it was hard not to look back, hard to leave without finding just one more thing to say.

While I was walking slow, trying to think my way though it, Wayne said, "You won't get far without money."

"I'll worry about that." My voice was harder than I wanted it to be. "You just worry about your fancy lady."

"You got no call to talk to me that way, Roy Lee."

"The hell I ain't! You and your damned promises!"

"Roy Lee..."

Before he could say any more, Rose let go of his arm and kneeled in front of the Cheyenne Kid, holding him by his shoulders and turning him to get a good look at him. "Oh, Wayne, honey, is this little fellow your friend?"

I wondered just who she thought we'd been arguing about.

The Kid twisted and squirmed for a minute, maybe because he didn't like being handled, maybe because of the way Rose's robe gapped open when she kneeled down. To tell the truth, I squirmed some myself at that sight. "Why, he's just the cutest thing," Rose said.

A lot of things happened to the Kid's face then. First his mouth twisted down at being called a cute thing, then he kind of cocked his head to one side like he was studying Rose, or maybe trying to get a better look into that gap in her robe. Then one eyebrow went up and I could just about see the thought crossing his mind that here at last was a person who wasn't throwing him out of anyplace.

When he leaned his forehead on her shoulder I began to have serious doubts that he was the innocent little savage I'd thought him to be.

Wayne opened his mouth twice and bit off his words both times. I knew him well enough to know he was some put out about Rose paying so much attention to the Kid and I thought he was about halfway to throwing his hat at the floor. Then he swung around to Lester, the pudgy man, and said, "I'll take a month's pay in advance, right now."

"Now?" Lester got all nervous and took out a bandanna and started mopping at his forehead. "You ain't done nothing yet."

"I'm about to get rid of this cowboy and his Indian kid."

"My Indian kid?" My fists were balled up and I was ready to whip Wayne to a frazzle if he made one move at me. "Damn you, Wayne..."

"Now if I don't get the pay in advance, I ain't takin' the

job." Wayne thumbed his hat back on his head and grinned a real mean grin. "But I will come in here every day and beat up on whatever bouncer you got."

"You can't do that!"

"I just did it. I'm the toughest man in Newton and you're the one who said so."

"Miss Rosalind..."

"Oh, pay him, Lester," Rose said.

While Wayne was looking about as surprised as I felt, Lester took a fat roll of bills from his pocket, peeled off a bunch, and handed it to Wayne. Wayne didn't even count it; he just turned around and handed it to me.

"You get that kid out of here right now, you hear? Maybe I'll see you again sometime." He grinned and jerked his thumb toward where the ex-bouncer still lay on the floor, curled up and snoring. "I wouldn't want to have to treat you like I treated him."

"Not on the best day you ever saw!"

"Aw, I was just funnin', Roy Lee."

I stood there with the money in my hand, needing to say something to Wayne and not knowing what it might be. There was a big knot in my chest that had got there when I realized he did care about the Kid, but I was still mad as blazes at the fool Wayne was making of himself.

While I was trying to sort it all out, Rose kneeled in front of the Kid, brushing at his hair, fixing his collar, and making little cooing sounds that a mother would make. The Kid, he was grinning now and enjoying every minute of it. They made a hell of a pair, I thought.

"You got to understand," Wayne said, looking a little sad. "I made them promises and maybe I shouldn't have, but I got to keep 'em and get Rose out of here."

"Get her out?" I was ready to throw my own hat at the floor. "Hell, Wayne, I think she owns the place!"

"Well...Maybe..."

"And what about all that goes with it? You know how jealous you get."

"I'll work something out. She ain't a bad person, Roy Lee."

I believed that, though I couldn't work out much reasoning for it. I thought about Velvet and what she'd had to do to get through the war years alone. I thought about Maggie running away from home and how she intended to make her way. I guessed there were times when a woman just didn't have any choices left, though the ones I knew about didn't seem to have gone to it with their heads down or their feet dragging.

And then I thought about Jessie teaching school.

I was scratching at my head, chewing on a bunch of thoughts, knowing good and well that whatever Wayne and Rose thought they had wouldn't last long. The first time Rose went upstairs with another man, Wayne would be pulling his six-gun and slamming bullets all over the place, probably getting himself killed in the process. And I wouldn't be there to help him.

"It ain't the promises holding you here," I said. "It's just your damned bullheadedness."

That made Wayne mad again. "Go on and get the Kid out of here, before I throw you out!"

"You damned Wayne!" The Kid broke away from Rose and kicked Wayne in the shinbone. "You keep throwing me out! Someday I shoot you, Cowboy sumbeech!"

I grabbed the Kid and put him behind me, just in case. But the quick blaze in Wayne's eyes turned to hurt and then I hurt him even more. "You bet I'll get out, Wayne. And don't worry none about me and the Kid. You just stay here and be her fancy man!"

Before Wayne could even think to get mad, I grabbed the Kid by the wrist and dragged him outside, heading for the stable.

Figuring it was my place to be his Pa, at least for a while, I was talking a blue streak as we went, repeating things Pap and my own daddy had told me. The talking helped to cover my own hurt and I was warning the Kid about saloons and cigars and fancy women, trying to get him on a straight path before it was too late. Of course, Wayne's link-up with Rose and my own longings for Velvet meant that neither of us had heeded our dads, but the Kid didn't need to know that.

"Hey, she nice lady," the Kid said, trying to break my grip on him.

"You don't know anything about it, Kid."

"Sure, soldier teach me. She like my sister, get nice when she get marry. Rose be nice if I look out for her. She not throw me out."

Well, I stopped dead in my tracks, standing in the middle of the dusty street while my mind went in circles. "You like Rose, huh?"

"Sure. And she like me, too. But goddamn Wayne throw me out."

"Then there ain't but one thing for you to do, Kid. You got to go back in there and take her away from goddamn Wayne."

He scratched his head like he'd seen me do and it made me wonder how much else we'd taught him without thinking about what we were doing. "How I do that, Roy Lee?"

"Why, you got to do what Wayne does. If you want a woman, you got to fight for her."

"Why not goddamn Wayne just give money, like soldier do?"

"Wayne don't do anything the easy way. Now shut up and listen." I told him a few things he should do, hoping at least one of them would work. When I finished he was nodding and grinning, mostly because I was giving him a chance to shoot Wayne, and I sent him back to Rose's saloon.

It was a good plan and had a fair chance to work. I felt playful about it until I figured that, if it did work out, Wayne would likely kill me.

If my plan was going to work at all, then the Kid was going to have to be as slick as I was beginning to think he was, as slick as that Mexican Monte man and for the same reasons. It was a lot to put on a little fellow like that, but in our own way we'd already put even more on him and he hadn't shied away from any of it. With all the rest he'd learned from us, learning a little conniving wouldn't hurt.

I wandered around looking in store windows, giving the Kid a chance to get set up good, giving Wayne and Rose time to believe the story that I'd thrown the Kid out. Then I got anxious to see if it was working and I went back to that saloon.

They'd found some chairs and a table that wasn't busted and the Kid was sitting on Rose's lap, his head against her bosom while she cuddled him and smoothed his hair and said bad things about me.

Wayne sat across from her, his neck and ears bright red from fuming. He saw me when I came in but he was too mad to do more than give me a black look for sticking him with the Kid.

I found a seat close enough to listen and tried hard not to let Wayne see me chuckling.

"You got a damned nerve, coming back in here," Wayne

told me.

From the look on his face, I figured the Kid was doing just fine at what I'd told him to do. "I thought I might get a drink on credit, now that you're a half-owner in the place."

"Not damned likely!"

"You take care of me, Rose?" the Kid said, his voice small and whiny the way I'd told him it needed to be. "You adopt me now?"

"Why, of course I will, honey. Don't you worry about a thing."

"Dammit, Rose, don't I have something to say about that?"

"There's nothing to say, Wayne honey, he needs me."

"But you can't raise him in a place like this!"

"I was raised in a place like this!" Rose flared.

"Yes, and look what's happened to you!"

Rose's face turned hard. "Don't you say that to me, Wayne Denton! If you cared anything about the boy, you wouldn't bring him to a place like this!"

"But it's your place!"

"That's how I know what kind of place it is." She turned back to the Kid and simpered at him. "Don't you worry about all this, honey. You and me will go someplace. Wayne can tag along if he wants."

"Tag along? Is that the way you see it? You're putting the Kid ahead of me?" Wayne slammed his fist on the table. A little more anger and he'd be throwing his hat at the floor. "What about our promises?"

Rose looked at him with wide and innocent eyes. "What promises?"

Wayne made a noise that sounded like a groan. He leaned his head on his hand like a man grown weary and his fingers worked at the mashed-up brim of his hat.

The Kid looked up at Rose, holding her with his big dark eyes. "I live with you and Cowboy sumbeech?"

"By God, that tears it!" Wayne was on his feet and his hat was on the floor and he was looking plumb wild. "Rose, it's gotta be him or me!"

"Don't let him shoot me!" the Kid yelled. He put enough in it that even I thought he was really scared.

"Kid! Wayne wouldn't do a thing like that!"

"Last night he shoot at me." The Kid was no fool. He buried his face so deep into her bosom that his voice was muffled. "Almost got me," he whimpered.

"Wayne! You didn't!"

Wayne was getting tanglefooted again, moving his feet like he didn't know which way to go. "Well, I did, but...He...Listen, Rose..."

"No more," the Kid yelled. "This time I shoot you!"

Just like he was supposed to do, he jumped off Rose's lap and ran to me. I'd been fiddling with my gun and had it all ready, strapping my gun belt around him. It was far too big and the holster hung down past his knee, but he held the belt up around his waist, stood as tall as a four-foot kid can stand, and yelled, "You come outside, Cowboy sumbeech, and we shoot it out! Winner gets lady!"

Wayne stood with his mouth open, watching the swinging doors flap until they were still, and then he came over to where I was. "Damn you, Roy Lee, you set this up!"

It was hard to do but I tried my best to look put upon, my eyes wide and surprised. "Me? I wouldn't try to make a fool out of you, Wayne. You're the one got the Kid mad."

"Mad?" His eyes rolled around in his head and I knew I had him where I wanted him. And since I'd disarmed myself, he'd have to try me with his fists. "*Me* make *him* mad?"

"Hell yes, he's mad! He's gonna blow your fool head off."

"But you gave him the gun!"

"The Kid's got a right to take care of himself. You shouldn't have been fooling around with his woman."

"Hey, Cowboy sumbeech, you fight now!"

Wayne hitched up his gun belt, picked up his hat and turned away, so confused he forgot to set the hat back to show that lock of hair. When he started for the door, I was some confused myself. The way I'd planned it, he should have been coming at me.

"Wayne, you can't do it!" Rose cried, hanging onto his arm. "He's just a little boy!"

Wayne shook her off and grinned a mean and wolfish grin. "No, by God, I believe he is a midget. And you're welcome to whatever I leave of him."

He went through the batwing doors, Rose pounding her fists against his back until I grabbed her and held her still. What with me having to keep one hand clenched, it wasn't easy but it sure was interesting. Then, when she saw who had grabbed her, she started pounding on me.

"Darn you, Roy Lee! Neither one of you is fit to take care of that little boy."

"I guess you think you are." I waved my clenched hand at the staircase, and then got that arm around her again. "Oh, you'd be a prime mother, Rose!"

"You just bet I would! Lester! Make me an offer for this place!"

The pudgy man quoted a number too high for me to believe in, but when Rose yelled "Sold!" the look on his face made it plain he'd got a bargain, busted chairs and all.

Rose broke free and when I grabbed at her, I unclenched my hand. She stood still for a minute while we both stared at the cartridges I'd dropped, and then she made a funny sound and bolted for the door.

It was quiet in the street, too quiet. People stood on the boardwalks, watching, and I'd swear not one of them was breathing.

Wayne and the Cheyenne Kid were out in the street, walking toward one another mean and slow. The Kid was holding up my gun belt with both hands so he wouldn't trip on it and Wayne was coming on so fierce I was surprised the Kid didn't bolt and run.

In fact, if he'd been thinking of our plan, he'd have known it had gone astray. At this time, Wayne and I were supposed to be in the saloon, beating up on one another. It should never have got to where the Kid was about to fire an empty gun.

But the Kid had that look on his face like he'd had when he kicked Wayne and I figured he was going to make damned sure Wayne never got in his way again.

They stopped with about twenty feet of space between them. The silence somehow got deeper and it had a heavy feel to it. The Cheyenne Kid went for his gun, but when he let go the gun belt it fell to around his ankles and he was leaning sideways and groping for the pistol while he tried to keep his eyes on Wayne.

Wayne drew his own gun and gave it a fancy spin, picked it up and blew the dust off it, then took his own slow time about aiming and cocking it.

"Put it back, Wayne!" I yelled, jumping into the street and putting myself in between them. "You can't kill a little kid!"

"He's fixin' to kill me."

"It ain't the same, Wayne!"

He shook his head like he was trying to clear it of cobwebs. "I'd like to know how the hell it differs."

His gun was pointing at me and I figured I just might have a chance if he decided to fan it. Then Rose flew off the steps and lit into him.

They went down into the dirty street, Wayne's gun went off with a roar, and a dozen or so people dived for cover. Rose and Wayne were rolling around, first him on top and then her. She was working him over with her fists and elbows and Wayne was grinning and getting a kick out of it every now and then.

The Cheyenne Kid had finally got my gun out of the holster, eared back the hammer, and was waiting for a clear shot at Wayne. Before I could grab the gun away from him, he pulled the trigger.

There was an awful look of surprise on his face when nothing happened and I almost felt bad that I'd tricked him into using an empty gun. Then again, he had to learn to quit trusting people.

A gun went off behind me and Wayne yelled, "Watch out! She's crazy!"

Rose had got to her feet and Wayne's smoking gun was in her hand. Her sorrel hair was a mess, hanging down in her eyes so she could barely see to thumb the hammer back. Her stockings were torn and that robe thing was hanging open to show all sorts of wondrous female underthings and I was setting myself to enjoy the show until she yelled, "The Kid's gun wasn't even loaded!"

"Cowboy sumbeech steal bullet!" The Kid kicked me in the shin hard enough that I commenced to hopping around on one foot.

"You set it up for Wayne to murder this boy!" Rose yelled, waving the gun around. "You lied to him, bought him whiskey, brought him into my...my saloon! You showed him fighting! You stole his bullets! What else are you going to do to this poor boy?"

Me, I figured we'd done enough and had done it pretty well. We'd taught him all he needed to know to be white. The rest was up to him.

Wayne got up off the ground and held his hands out in front of him, palms facing her, and saying, "Now, Rose...Now, Rose..."

She didn't much care for it. She put a bullet in the dirt between Wayne's feet and when he backed off, she did the same to me.

"Looks like she means it, Wayne," I said.

"Damned if she don't."

We set out running for the stables. The last I saw of Rose and the Kid, she had her arms around him, he was pressing his face into her bosom, and I was certain sure everything had turned out all right.

We were in the livery and saddling our horses before we quit laughing every time we looked at one another. "Well, you had your spree," he said.

"Yeah." I looked at him close. "You got any hard feelin's?"

"No. She'd forgot our promises and we did find a home for the Kid." He cocked his head and gave me a look like he was considerin' something. "You know, I ain't sorry it happened. Lately I've been doing a lot of thinkin' about that Velvet woman."

My mouth was open in surprise and I couldn't open it any further when I saw the Kid running toward us screaming and Rose running after him with the pistol in her hand.

"My God! Now Rose is trying to kill *him*!" I mounted quick and rode out of the stable, scooping the Kid up and laying him across the saddle in front of me. Wayne was right behind and we put the spurs to our horses, hearing Rose yelling threats at Wayne.

We were a good ways out of Newton and well on our way back to the herd before we dared slow down enough to let the Kid sit in an upright position.

"You want to tell us why Rose was after you, Kid?"

"'Cause I run away."

I figured when it came to dumb answers, him and Wayne would make a good pair.

"Well, then, maybe you can tell us why you ran away."

"Maybe." He looked up at me, craning his head back. "Can I ride with goddamn Wayne?"

Wayne showed his surprise, then grinned and nodded at me. I passed the Kid over and watched him get settled on the saddle in front of Wayne and then said, "So what was it all about?"

"Rather be with you and goddamn Wayne than get a damned bath and haircut."

We joined up with Pap and the herd just a little south of Wichita. It was time to pay off Sim and Tiny, but we were more than a little broke until I recalled I still had Wayne's advance pay in my pocket. I knew he hadn't earned it, but since the money had come from Rose I figured we could treat it as a stake for the Cheyenne Kid, keeping it and borrowing enough to pay off the two road agents.

Sim looked disturbed. "You're just gonna give us money and leave us out here in the middle of nowhere?"

"It ain't exactly nowhere," Pap said. "Them lights you see north of here is Wichita."

"Well, it's still a long way from our rocks," Tiny said. "I liked them rocks."

"There's whores in Wichita," Sim told him. "There wasn't no whores in them rocks."

"What do you think, Pap?" Wayne said. "We ain't got far to go and them horses in our remuda won't bring much cash in Dodge. Want to give 'em a horse?"

"I'd rather go with a whore than a horse," Tiny said.

"Give 'em a horse and let's get shut of 'em," Pap said. As they rode off into the twilight, he said, "You know, I had the damnedest time teaching them to ride. Always takin' off their shirts before they got mounted." Then he looked down at the Kid. "So now we got an Indian for a pet, I reckon."

"Pap," I said. "This here is the Cheyenne Kid."

"Well, he's cute but I hope he ain't simple. I've had enough simple on this drive."

Wayne grinned and patted the Kid on the head. "We're gonna teach him to be a cowboy."

Pap gave him a hard look. "Somebody that stayed around the herd now and then would be a better teacher." He cocked his head. "How'd you happen to go looking for Rose and come back with an Indian kid?"

"It's a long story, Pap." Wayne gave me a look. "And I'm not sure yet that I even understand it."

"It'll all come clear when Rose catches up to you," I said.

The Cheyenne Kid looked up at Pap. "Rose lady gone kill goddamn Wayne."

When Pap looked at me with one eyebrow raised, I shrugged. "I believe he thinks that's Wayne's full name."

"The way things are going, maybe it ought to have been."

Wayne and me spread our bedrolls by the fire and I found a good blanket for the Kid to wrap up in. I got him tucked in and was climbing under my own blanket when Wayne said, "Do you want to hear about me and Rose, Pap?"

"No, I don't," Pap said, getting his blanket situated and squirming around to make a hole for his hip. "I don't believe I'll be able to stand any more nonsense at all for a day or two."

As it turned out, he had a week. That's how long it took us to get to Dodge City and that's how long it took Wayne to get us into trouble again.

Chapter Ten

The End of the Trails

Pap and the Kid took to one another right off. We took a horse out of the remuda for the Kid to ride and Pap said the Kid understood bareback riding better than anyone else he'd met all week.

Rambler seemed to take a liking to the Kid too, and liked to trot along beside him when he wasn't busy making his circles of the herd.

The drive to Dodge was going good and easy and I figured all but two of our problems was solved. We were going to have to find some kind of permanent home for the Cheyenne Kid and I was going to have to decide what to do about Velvet.

I had about decided to do nothing. It was in my mind to go back to Texas with my share from the sale of our herd, buy some land near Waco like I'd promised Jessie I would do, and then brace Jessie's Pa with the fact that I'd managed to become something more than a shiftless cowboy. I reckon I'd have stuck to that plan if Wayne hadn't made it known to me that he had an interest in taking up with Velvet.

Maybe I shouldn't have been surprised about his interest. The way Pap told stories about Velvet was enough to heat up the blood and the imagination of any man who listened. I knew for a fact that Wayne had dreamed about her at least once, and if his dreams were anywhere near what mine were then he was probably damned near on fire to meet her and take up with her.

The Velvet Brand

That sudden interest on Wayne's part made me somewhat jealous. We'd been partners for so long that it was natural to compete with one another, so I put Jessie out of my mind for a while and tried to figure how I could keep Wayne away from Velvet.

In the end, nature took her course and it was Wayne's own hot temper that did him in.

We brought the herd into Dodge on a Wednesday, but held it on grounds outside of town while Wayne and Pap rode in to look for a cattle buyer. Me and the Cheyenne Kid and Rambler kept an eye on the herd, but them cows was so happy to be in that long Kansas grass and not moving that I knew they'd be no trouble to us.

Wayne and Pap came back after an hour or two and looked over the camp me and the Kid had set up. "Why do we always camp under a damned cottonwood tree?" Pap said. "Ever time I wake up, I look like I slept through a snowstorm."

"You boys find a buyer?" I asked.

Wayne nodded. "We'll take 'em in to the holding pens tomorrow and get a count."

"Nine hundred and eighty-two," I said. "Not countin' Rambler."

"We ain't sellin' Rambler," Pap said. "Might need him again next season."

Wayne grinned and thumbed back his hat. "Pap's gettin' to be a regular cowboy."

"Pap not cowboy sumbeech," the Kid said.

We took the herd into Dodge City the next morning, the Kid staying at the camp with Rambler. The cattle buyer had his own man sitting on the fence taking a tally and I sat beside him taking my own. When the last one had been driven through the chute, we walked over to the office and joined

Wayne and Pap.

The cattle agent sat behind his desk, counting out gold pieces and greenbacks. He looked up when me and the wrangler came in and raised his eyebrows like he was asking a question.

"Nine hundred and eighty-two," the wrangler said. "Poor looking things."

"It's been a bad year for Texas cows," Pap said quickly.

"More like a bad ten years," the wrangler said, then left.

"Well, I got to start shipping something back east," the agent said. "But twenty dollars a head is my top offer."

That was about twice as much as I'd thought they would bring, but I wasn't going to argue the point with him.

"How many with the Velvet brand?" Pap asked me.

"Make it an even five hundred."

He nodded and started counting out money in two piles. Velvet's share came to ten thousand dollars and I figured when I caught up with her and told her how I'd made her rich she'd be mighty grateful. Pap put her share in a leather pouch the agent gave him, and put all but four double eagles in another pouch.

"There's your pay, pups," he said.

"Forty dollars each? Hell, Pap, that's our herd."

"And it's your money, but you can wait to get back to Texas to spend it. I figure what you got is enough for you to get into trouble with."

He was right about that. We got into trouble and had change left over.

Wayne tossed his two gold pieces in his hand and grinned at me. "What do you think, Roy Lee? You think this is enough to get drunk and go see about elephants?"

I gave him a hard grin right back. "I don't intend to pay for nothin' but beer."

The Velvet Brand

"You boys go along and celebrate," Pap said. "I'll find you later. I'm going to put Velvet's money in the bank for her."

"Best check your guns with me, boys," the cattle agent said. "There's an ordinance against carrying guns in town."

We took off our gun belts and hung them on a handy rack.

There wasn't any way I could get shut of Wayne, though I tried a few. I walked fast, I turned into saloons and beaneries without warning, crossed the street when I thought he wasn't paying attention. In the end, I gave up and walked along with him and every place we came to we asked about Velvet.

Everyone seemed to know where she lived and most of them pointed out a big three-story house on the other side of the railroad tracks. I began to get a bad feeling and Wayne was looking some troubled himself, but we went to the house.

A little man in a frock coat opened the door long enough to tell us Velvet wasn't there and where she was wasn't any of our business. Wayne popped him in the nose and we went on over to a saloon called the Texas Star to have a beer.

I downed my first one and, while I waited on my second to be drawn, I turned around and hooked my elbows on the bar, looking the place over. It was early afternoon and there wasn't that many people in the place yet, but a table of six men who seemed to already be drunk and rowdy caught my eye.

I watched them long enough to see what they were doing, and when it came clear I nudged Wayne and told him he better take a look. There was a deck of cards and three bottles of whiskey on the table and the six men in black frock coats were taking turns cutting the cards. "Looks like the way they play it is that the high man gets to take a drink out of one of the bottles," I told Wayne.

He was still in a bad mood about not finding Velvet right off and he said, "That ain't all that interesting, Roy Lee."

"It might be when you consider who they are," I said.

"I doubt it."

"Now, those two with badges would be the Earp brothers," I said. "And you remember Wild Bill from a few years ago in Abilene."

"I do recall him," Wayne said. He sounded like his interest was caught. "And that feller with the red beard is old Shanghai Pierce from Texas. We saw him in Abilene, too. Wonder what he's doing with them gunfighters?"

"The feller with the bad cough might be Doc Holliday, though I know I've never seen him."

"That one with the walking stick is wearing a badge, too." He laughed. "Why, hell. With all the law in here getting drunk, we could go rob the bank if we wanted."

The feller with the walking stick took notice of us looking at him and he motioned us to come over.

"What do you reckon he wants?" Wayne said.

"I don't know, but there's an awful lot of law at that table. Maybe they'll know somethin' about Velvet."

So we kind of ambled over to the table and the feller with the walking stick said, "You boys just up from Texas?"

"We are."

"Well, I'm Bat Masterson and I'd like to welcome you to Dodge City. Where's the rest of your crew?"

"We're just about all of it," Wayne said.

Masterson waved his hand at the rest of his group and I thought he was going to introduce us, but instead he said, "You were looking us over kind of serious. You're not thinking of starting trouble in Dodge, are you?"

"Oh, hell no," I said. "We're just looking for a lady named Velvet. You know of her?"

There was some laughter around the table and Masterson

said, "I think some of us may know her. To speak to, anyway."

That got another round of laughter, though I didn't see what was so funny about it. "You'd better speak to her about the money you owe her, Bat," Hickok said.

"An officer of the law has certain privileges," Masterson said.

One of the Earp men said, "Surveying whores is a solemn duty."

It was time for them to cut the cards again, and when they'd done that they laid them on the table face up. The one I knew to be Shanghai Pierce whooped and grabbed a bottle, tapping a finger on the king he'd turned up.

"Well," Wayne said. "Maybe one of you could stop laughing long enough to tell us where we might find her."

Bat raised an eyebrow and looked at the other men.

"Newton," Wild Bill said. "I heard she went over there to pick up a new whore."

I'd been testy before, but that got to me in a deep place. I leaned over, put my knuckles on the table, and said, "I'm gettin' a little tired of someone sayin' 'whore' every time I say 'Velvet'."

"Well, you're just gonna have to stay tired, Cowboy," Shanghai Pierce said. He cut the deck of cards, grinned, and reached for a bottle again.

"Now, why would that be, Pierce?" He was a cattleman, not a lawman, and I was figuring that if I tore into anybody it would have to be him.

"See, boys," he said. "I told you I had me a reputation." Then he half stood and put his own knuckles on the table and yelled into my face, "'Cause she is a whore, dammit!"

There were serious nods of agreement all around, and out the corner of my eye I saw Wayne snatch his hat off and fling it at the ground.

"That tears it! You all are a bunch of lyin' bastards!"

Chairs scooted back all around and hands reached for guns, but then Wild Bill stood up and spread his arms like he was holding people back. "Now, hold on, gents," he said. "These boys ain't armed."

"You get rid of them guns and we'll whup the lot of you right now," Wayne said.

Hickok looked at one of the two we'd taken for Earps. "Wyatt, it's your town. What's your call?"

Earp was shaking his head. "That insult was too serious for a fistfight. If it's up to me, I say pistols." He looked around the table and the other men were nodding agreement. All of them looked like their heads were heavy.

Hickok looked at Wayne and shrugged. "Looks like we have to shoot you, sonny." He half turned back to the table. "Don't be cheating me out of any turns, now."

"Then let's get to it," Wayne said. If he'd had another hat, I believe he'd have thrown it at the ground.

"It may not be that simple," Hickok said. "You insulted all of us and that might take some deliberating." He surveyed the table. "Any of you men got plans for this evening?"

"I have a poker game," Holliday said.

"I was goin' over to the Velvet House to see if that new whore got here yet," Pierce said.

"No, she didn't," Masterson said. "They'll be in on the noon stage tomorrow. And you might want to recall I got first dibs on her anyway, Pierce."

"Gonna be too dark for good shooting pretty soon," Virgil Earp said. Then he put his head on the table like he was fixing to take a nap.

One by one, they all had plans for the evening, so it was

decided by Hickok that the gunfight couldn't take place until tomorrow, not under any circumstances. Again, they all nodded at that.

"Now we got to settle who takes him on first," Hickok said.

"Well, it's my town so I should get to go first," Wyatt Earp said. "Say about 11:00 AM? I should be up by then."

"All right," Hickok said. "Now, who wants to try him on at 11:30? Virgil?"

The other Earp raised his head off the table, looked around and nodded, then put his head back down.

Masterson was figuring something on his fingers and now he held up his hand and said, "Wait a minute, Bill."

"You wantin' to take him on at noon, Bat?"

"No, I've been studying on this."

Wyatt snickered and nudged Pierce in the ribs. "Remember how long it took him to figure out three bottles of whiskey for six men?"

"Now, Wyatt, you know I was just funnin' you all."

"Sure." He winked and nudged Pierce again.

"What's on your mind, Bat?" Hickok said.

"Whores," Wyatt said and him and Shanghai busted out laughing while Holliday went into a coughing fit.

"Can we just settle this?" Wayne said.

Hickok turned and put his hands on Wayne's shoulders, walking him backward until a chair hit Wayne behind the knees and made him sit down. Then Hickok motioned me to another chair. "Gunfighting is a serious business, so you young'uns sit while we work this out. Don't move, now." He went back to the table. "Is it my turn yet?"

"I do believe you were cheated out of a turn, Bill," Holliday said.

"I ain't surprised, considerin' this bunch." He grabbed up a bottle and took a long pull.

Well, I didn't mind a chance to sit and listen to a bunch of drunks. Truth is, I was getting a kick out of it and I figured that before long they'd plumb forget they wanted to kill Wayne.

"Bat, you ready to spit it out?" Wild Bill said.

Masterson crossed his arms over his chest and looked like he was pouting. "Wyatt will just laugh at me again."

"Now, Bat, he was laughin' with you, not at you," Hickok said, patting Masterson's shoulder. "Go on and speak your mind."

"Well...here it is, then. If Wyatt shoots him at 11:00 AM, who's Virgil going to have left to shoot? And who am I going to shoot at noon?"

"By God, that's so!" Pierce whacked his big hand on the table. "You think you could just wound him, Wyatt?"

Earp was shaking his head again. "Tell him, Virgil."

Virgil Earp looked half asleep, but he got his head upright and his eyes focused and said, "Earps always shoot to kill." Then he made a soft belch and lowered his head again.

"Sounds like a damned echo," Masterson said, sounding testy. "Earp, burp."

"Now, I've told you I don't like that joke, Bat," Wyatt said.

Hickok held his hands up, palms out. "That's enough, men." The table got quiet, but Wyatt and Bat was still glaring at one another. "Now, the only way I see to make it fair is for us to all shoot him at the same time. Can everyone agree on that?" There were nods all around the table except for Virgil, but maybe his snoring counted for a vote.

"You're callin' that fair?" I said. "Six against one?"

"We're talking about fair for us, Cowboy. And you don't have a vote anyway, unless you're of a mind to insult us, too."

"I guess not," I said. "Does Wayne get a vote, though?"

"Hell, no."

Hickok looked at the frock-coated men again. "Now, I'd say noon. Can we all agree on that?"

"Now, listen, Bill," Wyatt said. "This is my town and I ought to be the one to say what time."

"Wyatt, you're absolutely right and I apologize. What time would you like us to help you kill this cowboy?"

"Noon," Wyatt said. He nodded like his head was heavy.

Hickok turned to me and Wayne. "You boys can go now. Be on Front Street at noon with your guns loaded, or be on your way back to Texas."

Wayne picked up his hat and put it on. He was shaking his head like he was some confused by the whole thing, but at the same time I could tell he still had his mad on.

When we got to the batwing doors, someone else was coming in and one of the doors bumped Wayne on the shoulder. He grabbed the man by the front of his vest and pulled him close. "Out of my way, you lying bastard!" and then he threw the man ass over teakettle into the Texas Star.

"Damn all!" It was an old man outside who I guess had seen the whole thing. "That man you just threw away was Mysterious Dave Mather."

Wayne looked over his shoulder, then back at the old man. "Wasn't nothing mysterious about him," he argued. "He was right here and I saw him plain as day."

The old man looked a mite confused and then said, "I think he got that name cause he's mysterious in his comin's and goin's."

Wayne wasn't about to be argued down. "He was comin' in the door while I was goin' out. What's mysterious about that?"

The old man scratched his head for a second. "Well...maybe it was somebody else."

***

Wayne and me got our horses and rode on back to our camp, not getting there until after dark. Wayne was still too mad to talk without cussin' a blue streak, so it was up to me to tell Pap what had happened.

"You just got to face it, Wayne," I said, after I'd lined it all out for Pap. "You got just about the whole town mad at you."

"I know." He looked kind of mournful, hunkered down on his heels and poking a stick into the campfire. I knew he was fretting about tomorrow, but I wondered how much of his expression was due to his sitting on his spurs. Wayne always forgets things like that when he's upset.

"Beats me how one man can cause so damned much trouble in so short a time," Pap said. "Though maybe I ought to expect it by now."

"Well, it ain't none of your lookout, Pap," Wayne said. "I got myself into it and I guess I'll get myself out."

"Ha! Get yourself killed, more'n likely. Boy, you got any idea who you're goin' up against?"

Wayne stirred at the fire some more and the wind caught at some of the sparks he raised, causing the Cheyenne Kid to mutter "Goddamn Wayne" and pull his blanket up over his head.

"I know, Pap. I been going over it in my mind most all evening."

Pap Denton wasn't one to shut up when he was on a talking spree. He held his big left hand out in front of him, the fingers splayed, and touched a finger as he called out each of the names of the men who were gunning for Wayne. "Wyatt Earp. Doc Holliday. James Butler Hickok, the one they're callin' Wild Will or some such..."

"Wild Bill," I said helpfully.

"Dammit, Roy Lee, you made me lose count." He moved his lips as he touched his fingers again. "OK, I got it. Bat Masterson. Virgil Earp." His counting finger was on his thumb and he looked a bit lost.

"You got to go to your other hand for the rest," I said.

"Don't I know that!" He made a careful show of bringing his right hand up, then looked at his left like he was not ready to put away the ones he'd named so far. "Dave Mather..."

"That's Mysterious Dave Mather," I said.

"Roy Lee, I'm warnin' you..."

"Why do they call him that?" Wayne said.

"'Cause he is mysterious. No one knows if he's a gunfighter or not, but he's always hangin' around with them who are."

"Oh, all right."

"Now I'm fuddled again," Pap Denton said.

"You was on your right pinky with Mysterious Dave Mather," I told him.

"Thanks. Was there anybody else? Anyone I left out?"

"That's about all Wayne had time for," I said. "Unless you count Shanghai Pierce."

"I'll count him, by God! That's seven against you, Wayne. Seven!"

"Magnificent," Wayne said.

"What?"

"He could call himself Magnificent Dave Mather." Wayne was grinning. "Then he wouldn't be mysterious any more."

I had to laugh at that. Wayne never could keep his mind on one subject long enough to worry it to death like his Pap did, even when the subject was his own dying.

"You boys better start taking this serious," Pap said. "Mornin' ain't that far away."

"It's Wayne got to take it serious," I said. "He's the one they're gunning for."

Wayne gave me kind of a hurt look and I knew what he was thinking. We'd been friends for a long time. I guess he expected me to side him the way I'd always done, but then he kind of nodded and said, "Yeah. It's my fight."

"How you aim to play it, boy?" Pap Denton asked.

"One at a time is the way I'd like to do it. But they'll all be out there together, so I'll just have to shoot the most dangerous one first." He poked at the fire some more and looked thoughtful. "Roy Lee, you're the one reads them dime novels. Who do you think I should start with?"

Well, I'd already been giving that some thought, so my answer was quick. "Wayne, I don't think it makes any difference."

Wayne looked up and grinned. "You think I can take 'em all, in any order?"

Now there had been a time, early on, when Wayne and me had studied to be gunfighters and had even fought against one another. I wasn't as fast on the draw as Wayne, but I did shoot straighter. Wayne was as fast at clearing his holster as any I ever seen or heard about. But then you had to count the time it took for him to pick up his pistol and blow the dust out of it. And if he commenced to fan his pistol, the safest place to be was right in front of him.

Talking kind of low for a change, Pap said, "That ain't what he means, Wayne."

Wayne gave me a look. "Well?"

I'd seen that kind of look before. I'd seen it on a farmer

looking at what locusts had done to his crops, and I'd seen it on my Pa's face when he came back from the war and learned Texas was under Yankee rule. It was kind of bleak. I didn't like seeing that look on Wayne, and it made me mad.

"Dammit, Wayne!" I was so wrought up I threw my cup of coffee into the fire.

Sparks flew up again and the wind caught them again and the Cheyenne Kid was yelling "Goddamn Wayne!" again.

"Go back to sleep, Kid," Pap said soft.

"How I sleep when blanket on fire? Goddamn Wayne."

"It was me did it that time, Kid," I said.

"Goddamn Wayne anyway." He slapped at his blanket for a while, then pulled what was left of it over him and looked like he was asleep.

Wayne gave me that look again. "Well? Who do I start with?"

"Start with any of 'em, dammit! 'Cause the first one you draw on is gonna kill you and the other six will likely carry you to the undertaker."

Things were quiet for a long time. I missed the sounds of the herd we'd brought up the trail. The only one we'd kept was Rambler and he wasn't making any noise at all. Over in the East, the sky was starting to get light. Wayne lost interest in poking at the fire and sat with his arms on his knees, his hands hanging loose.

"That the way you see it, Pap?" He tried to make that cocky grin of his, but it looked a little sickly.

"That's about it, son." Pap was looking bleak, too.

"Well, I can't run away," Wayne said.

"I know that," Pap said.

"Sure wish I'd got to see that Velvet woman."

"They said she'd likely be back in town today, Wayne," I

said.

Wayne smiled kind of sad. "Well, I guess she'll be all yours, Roy Lee."

Pap looked from one of us to the other, and then back again, his mouth kind of hanging open. "If you two don't beat all, then I don't know what does. Y'all been thinkin' about Velvet that way?"

"Reckon we have," Wayne said, soft.

Pap shook his head.

Wayne stood up, dusting off the seat of his pants, and then examining a fresh tear in his jeans. "Damn spurs," he said. "Guess I'd better saddle up and go on into town. No sense puttin' it off any longer."

"Well," I said. "You're probably gonna have to put it off until them fellers wake up."

"Now, I know that, Roy Lee. But I figure on havin' me a good breakfast, somethin' we ain't had much of around this camp."

"Wayne, it ain't my fault Harvey set fire to his wagon," Pap said.

"You're the one complained about his cookin'."

I leaned back on my elbows and took a long and thoughtful look at the stars that were getting pale over in the west. "Guess you might as well saddle my horse, too, Wayne," I said.

Pap Denton jerked his head up. "You gonna back his play, Roy Lee?"

"Hell no." I know my big grin told Wayne different, for he was grinning back at me. "But I ain't gonna miss my last chance to have Wayne buy me breakfast."

"Saddle mine, too, then," Pap said. "Somebody remind me what I did with my scattergun."

"Besides," I said to Wayne's back, not missing a chance to dig at him a little. "I figure on being there to help that Velvet woman get off the stagecoach. Likely she'll need someone to tote her fancies."

"Your scattergun's in your bedroll," Wayne said. "Likely you won't need it the way Roy Lee's shooting off his mouth. Them fellers'll just laugh themselves to death."

Pap Denton was pawing at his bedroll, grumbling about people who couldn't do simple arithmetic.

But I was doing some arithmetic in my head and I knew we were three going against seven. Maybe count Pap's scattergun as two. Maybe figure while they were watching Wayne trying to draw his gun I could draw a bead and get one or two of them. No matter how I figured it, it came up short.

Thinking was making my head hurt so I went over and toed the Cheyenne Kid until he sat up and started looking for more sparks to slap out. When he saw he wasn't on fire again, he grinned up at me. "Hey, Roy Lee."

"Hey, Kid. We're goin' into town. You stay awake and take care of Rambler, you hear?"

He shoved the blanket down to his feet and reached for the boots Wayne had bought him. "I go."

"Not this time, Kid." I fished my last twenty-dollar piece out of my jeans and gave it to him. "If we ain't back by nightfall, you take Rambler and head on back to Texas."

"How I know where Texas is?"

"Just go south. It's big. You can't miss it." I don't know why I told him to go to Texas. I think it was in my mind to give him Pap's ranch, but it wasn't mine to give and I doubted anyone would recognize the claim of a kid. Still, he had to go somewhere.

" I be cowboy sumbeetch in Texas?"

"Yeah, but don't call anyone else that. They get touchy."

The Kid rubbed the sleep out of his eyes and then shook his head. "Hey! Why you maybe not come back?"

I grinned at him. "Wayne's fixin' to get us all killed."

The Kid grinned. "You joke me, huh?"

"Yeah, I'm jokin' you."

Wayne came back close to the fire, leading three horses, and commenced to put our saddles on them. The Kid watched him for a while, and then looked up at me.

"Goddamn Wayne in trouble again?"

"He seems to think so."

"He throw hat on floor?"

"Several times," I said.

"Shit."

"No more soldier talk, Kid." I didn't mind him saying a "Goddamn" or two 'cause he generally only used that word when he was talking about Wayne, but I was kind of blue, thinking I might not have much more time to teach him right from wrong.

"Does anybody know where I keep my shells?" Pap said.

"Pap, they burned up with the grub wagon." He should have remembered it—them shells going off was why we couldn't get close enough to put out the fire.

"Oh." He broke open the shotgun and looked to see if it was loaded. "Well, two'll have to do, I guess."

Wayne finished saddling Pap's horse. The sun was up for fair now, and except for the wind, it was going to be a beautiful day. I checked the loads in my six-shooter and caught the Kid watching me. When I looked at him, he looked away and pretended to be studying the gold piece I'd given him.

Wayne was looking at the sky, watching tiny white clouds hurrying along in front of the wind, and then he set his hat square on his head and swung hisself up on his horse. "Guess I'll go into town and get some breakfast," he said.

"Hey, I like breakfast!"

"Best eat what's left of last night's biscuits, boy," Pap told him. "It's safer."

"Roy Lee...?"

He was tugging at my belt. I couldn't look at him, but I took his small hand away. "Do what Pap says, Kid."

I took the reins Wayne handed me and mounted up. On the other side of Wayne, Pap Denton did the same. The two of them looked serious and determined. Me, I just hoped I'd get to meet that Velvet woman before Wayne got us all killed.

Chapter Eleven

Showdown

We took breakfast in the Hopper House. It wasn't much to look at on the outside, being just a big tent with a sign, but the food inside was good and plentiful. Mrs. Hopper fixed a breakfast of steak, eggs, fried potatoes, and biscuits that couldn't be beat anywhere north of Texas. She also waited on the tables with a cart full of food and when she came to our table she said, "You boys know you're not supposed to bring your guns into town."

"We brought ours in by special invitation of Marshal Earp," Pap said.

Mrs. Hopper kind of frowned. "Hard to think of him needing deputies with all the hardcase gunfighters in town," she said.

"Well, we're kind of hardcases ourselves," Pap said.

"Texas hellbenders," Wayne said.

"Don't start in on that, Wayne," I told him. To Mrs. Hopper I said, "Reckon where I might find Marshal Earp?"

"This time of day? Likely he's still asleep over to his shack on King Street. I don't believe I'd try wakin' him, if I was you."

"Well, I got it to do." It was in my mind to make sure the showdown didn't happen until after the noon stage arrived. I figured if we was all going to be killed, at least the marshal might give us a chance to see Velvet and tell her about the money we'd banked in her name.

Getting up from the table and reaching for my hat, I said, "You fellers wait here whilst I go wake up Earp."

"You in a hurry to get shot?" Wayne said.

"Oh, hell!" Mrs. Hopper said. She looked to be in a fret. "You're the ones caused all that trouble yesterday, aren't you?" She didn't wait for an answer, which was good because me and Wayne was both busy looking sheepish. "Y'all get on out of town now, before any of them gunfighters get woke up good."

Pap patted her hand and she looked at him like she was suddenly fond of him. Pap had a way with women that Wayne and me had been trying to figure out ever since we'd learned about him dallying with Maggie. "Now, don't you worry about it, Missy," he said. "We come to town specially to see them fellers and, besides, Roy Lee's got a plan. Ain't that right, Roy Lee?"

Well, the truth was I didn't have a plan except to hold off the showdown until about one o'clock or so, but I didn't want to tell that to Pap. "I'm workin' on somethin'," I said.

Pap looked up at Mrs. Hopper. He'd quit patting her hand and now was holding it. "There, Missy. It's going to be all right. There won't be any trouble these two boys can't handle." He pulled her hand toward him and kissed her fingertips. They reminded me of my Ma's fingers, made red by lye soap.

By God, I thought, is that the way it's done? It must be, because Mrs. Hopper was all of a sudden looking at him soft as a doe and looking like she might be squirmin' inside.

"I quit serving breakfast at nine and I can have the place cleared out by half-past," she told Pap. She seemed to be having some trouble breathing and, with the hand Pap wasn't holding, she fanned her face.

"Why, if Roy Lee ain't got us killed by half-past nine, I'd

admire to pay a call on you, Missy."

She leaned close and whispered something to him.

Pap shook his head. "That's my bad ear. Did I hear you say you got a cot in the back room?"

Mrs. Hopper turned red, starting with her neck and working up to her ears and then her forehead and she started fanning faster. But she nodded her head quick and then pulled her hand away from Pap and went to busy herself at another table. I thought it was funny that the table was empty but she was laying out breakfast for about six people. Then she put it all back on the cart and took it to a table where men were sitting, looking at us and pointing.

"If that don't beat all," Wayne said. "Dammit, Pap, I thought you was sidin' me."

"I am. I brought my scattergun, didn't I?"

"Well, how you gonna side me if you're pleasurin' with Mrs. Hopper?"

Pap got that angry look he used to get just before he whaled Wayne. Of course, that was years ago, before Wayne got his growth, but I thought Pap was within about an inch of trying him on anyway. "Now, boy, you keep civil about her until you know better. I recollect I learned you to respect women."

"All right, Pap." Wayne put his hands up like a man surrendering. "I'm sorry I misjudged, but..."

"Besides, it don't take me all that long, these days," Pap said. "I don't expect any of those fellers to be awake before ten."

Wayne looked like he was ready to throw his hat at the floor. In fact, he snatched at it and then got a funny look on his face. I guess he forgot it was hanging on a peg behind him.

"Well, I'm fixin' to go over and wake up Wyatt Earp," I

said.

Pap grinned at me. "Is that part of your plan, boy?"

He looked so hopeful that I still didn't have the heart to tell him I didn't have any plan except to hold things off for a while. "I reckon," I said.

There was only one shack on King Street, which really wasn't a street at all. It was just a footpath worn through the prairie grass and at the end of the path was the shack. I banged on the door for a while, and when I heard rumbling and cussing inside I banged some more.

The door flung open and Marshal Earp stuck his head out, and he had that long-barreled pistol pointing right at my brisket. "Who...? What the hell do you want, boy?"

"Who is it?" someone in the shack said.

"Shut up, Virg. I'm tryin' to find that out."

"You might remember me, Marshal. I'm Roy Lee McAllister." He still looked blank and his eyes were bleary. "From yesterday," I said. "I was with Wayne Denton when you said you were going to shoot him."

"That Texas kid that called me a lying bastard? He still around?" Earp shook his head. "I figured he'd be halfway back to Texas by now."

"Wayne ain't that kind and neither am I. He's ready to fight you and your whole bunch. He just wants to do it after one o'clock."

"What whole bunch?" Earp said. I could figure he didn't recall a lot about what happened, since all of them appeared to have been drinkin' pretty heavy.

"You and Virgil, Holliday, Hickok, Masterson, Mather, and Pierce." I took a deep breath and flung down the challenge he seemed to have forgotten about. "Have 'em all on the main street at one PM and tell 'em to bring their guns.

Earp blinked his eyes hard a time or two, then kind of grinned. It was hard to tell for sure about the grin, but I could see that thick mustache twitching. "Did he call all of us fellers lying bastards?"

"Most of you."

Now the grin had some teeth in it. "You tell your friend we'll be there."

"Thanks." I turned and started away.

"Hey, boy!"

I turned back, waiting.

"Is your friend touched?" He tapped his temple with the barrel of that long pistol and I think he tapped harder than he meant to for he kind of winced.

"Some," I said and went on back to Mrs. Hopper's.

When I got back to the restaurant, Wayne and Pap were sitting on a bench outside, picking their teeth. Pap had his watch in his hand and Wayne was fuming mad, his hat already in the dirt between his feet. I didn't have to ask why, for Rambler was tied to the hitching rail and the Cheyenne Kid was sitting on the boardwalk eating out of a pie pan full of biscuits and gravy.

"Don't say a damned thing," Wayne said before I could open my mouth. "He just come ridin' in with Rambler following him and we've been tryin' to argue him into going back to camp."

Mrs. Hopper was shooing people out of the restaurant and there wasn't a man among them that didn't stop and take a good long look at Rambler. He always attracted attention with that one long horn sticking straight out in front, about three feet past his nose, and some of the men were speculating on how easy it would be for Rambler to gore someone.

I grinned at Wayne. "Well, you feed a pup and he's likely

to keep hangin' around."

"Dammit, I ain't the one fed him! Mrs. Hopper took a shine to him."

About that time, Mrs. Hopper came to the tent opening again and wiggled her fingers at Pap. Pap kind of smiled at us, hitching at his belt and sucking in his belly as he stood and then followed her back inside. I guessed it must be half-past nine, and wondered if there was a chance the noon stage might be early.

"I'll tell you what, Wayne," I said. "I'm going down the street to wait for the stagecoach." I knew it was too early to worry about it, but I didn't want to spend my morning sitting in front of a tent and listening to Pap and Mrs. Hopper rutting in the back room. "You take care of the kid and go buy him a gun and a gun belt."

Wayne jumped up. "Now, why the hell would I do that? And what the hell would I do it with?"

"The kid's got a twenty dollar gold piece. And you'll do it because it's part of my plan." It was a plan that was just now forming in my head and it didn't amount to anything that might save our lives, but it was better than all the emptiness that had been there before.

"If it's part of Roy Lee's plan, you do it," Pap called. In a more normal voice he said, "Now I don't know about all these corset laces, Missy. Maybe you could help me some."

I grinned at Wayne. "Unless you'd rather sit here and listen in," I said.

"God, no." Wayne grabbed the Cheyenne Kid by his shirt collar and set him on his feet. "Let's go, Kid."

"Goddamn Wayne! Not finished biscuits!"

"Just wipe the gravy off your mouth and go, Kid," I told him. "We're gonna make a gunfighter out of you."

"I be gunfighter sumbeech?"

"I don't like the way this is shapin' up," Wayne said. "Just what the hell is this plan of yours?"

"It's confusing," I said.

"Well, it's confusing the hell out of me."

"I ain't heard you coming up with any ideas on how to save your hide, Wayne."

"I don't need any fancy ideas. You all go back to camp and I'll just wade into 'em."

"That's exactly the part that scares me," I said. "Go buy the Kid a gun."

Wet, slapping sounds and a few giggles drifted out of the tent and that took all the argument out of Wayne. He clapped his hat on his head, grabbed the Kid by the arm, and hurried off to find a store.

Me, I moseyed around town for a bit but there wasn't anything going on except for the occasional dust devil blowing down the street and whatever was happening in the back of Mrs. Hopper's tent. Finally I went to the stagecoach station. There was a boardwalk in front and a few caneback chairs, so I pulled a chair over to where I could put my feet on a rail and leaned back with my hat over my eyes, trying to imagine how it would be when the stage came in and Velvet gave me her hand to help her down and how she'd go all fluttery when I kissed her fingers.

Then I'd take her carpetbag and walk her to her house and carry it inside for her, telling her about how we'd drove her cattle up the trail, sold them, and put the money in the bank under her name. When we were in the house, she'd take off her hat and then take the pins out of her golden hair and let it all fall loose around her shoulders while she unbuttoned her waistcoat and took it off and flung it at a chair.

The Velvet Brand

Then she'd step close enough that I could look deep into her green eyes and smell her perfume and all the woman smells and she'd kind of tug at her white shirtwaist and say, "Would you like to help me unbutton this, Cowboy?"

Me, I'd drop that carpetbag and start right in on them buttons and she'd laugh, throwing her head back and shaking out that long, wavy blonde hair. When I was through with the buttons, she'd kind of shrug the shirtwaist off her shoulders and let it fall to the floor and then her hands would come up and she'd lift up her breasts, kind of like she was offering them to me. "I'd like to show you how grateful I am for you taking care of my cattle, Cowboy."

Then she'd turn her back to me, giggling. "I'm sorry, Cowboy. More buttons for you to worry at."

And I'd start undoing the buttons at the back of her skirt. When it fell to the floor, she'd give a kind of wiggle and the petticoat would fall free with the skirt and I'd be glad as hell there was no bustle or any of them pantaloon things, just Velvet dressed the way she was the day she was born.

Then she'd turn back around and take me by the hand. "Let's go into the bedroom and get those trail clothes off you."

"No, ma'am," I'd say. "I'm proud to bring your cattle up the trail and proud to help you get out of your travelin' clothes, but I'm promised to a schoolteacher back in Texas."

She'd put her hand on my face and it would be soft and cool. "Won't you let me thank you even a little bit?"

"No ma'am. I finally made up my mind that it's Jessie I want and..."

"Dammit, Roy Lee," Wayne said. "I might've known you'd be taking a nap when the whole town's tryin' to kill me."

I thumbed back my hat and gave him a sideways glance. "I hope your timin's better when the gunplay starts," I said.

The Cheyenne Kid was with him and he looked purely a sight. Being only about ten years old and four feet tall, they hadn't been able to find a gun belt that fit, so he wore it over his shoulder almost like one of them Mexican banditos, but it worked out that the holster was about at hip level so I guessed it would be all right.

"You was dreamin' about Velvet again," Wayne said.

Well, up until now I'd thought it was a secret, but if Wayne knew about it then I'd probably talked in my sleep. "Yep."

It was the last dream I ever had about Velvet.

"Listen, Roy Lee, I been doing some thinkin' about that." He hunkered down next to me, looking kind of pained when he sat on his spurs, then raised hisself a bit. "We come a long way out of curiosity about that woman and I know it's my own fault that I got myself in a fix over her. But there ain't no reason for both of us to end up dead in the street."

I was some surprised because he sounded like he really had been doing some thinking and that just wasn't Wayne's way. Maybe knowing your time is running out makes you thoughtful. "Go on," I said.

"You take the Kid and Pap and go on back to camp. When it's all over, you can come get what's left of me, and then go ahead and take up with that Velvet woman if she'll have you."

I kind of bridled at that, in spite of knowing Wayne was being as generous as he knew how to be and in spite of the fact that I'd already made up my mind I wasn't going to try to take up with her. "Why wouldn't she take up with me, after all we've done to make her rich?"

Wayne kind of grinned. He pulled a splinter of wood off the boardwalk and stuck it in his mouth for a toothpick, then looked up at me and he was grinning for fair. "I've seen you takin' a whiz and I've seen Pap takin' a whiz. Might be she's used to more than you can offer her."

"Now dammit, Wayne, that tears it!" I let my chair thump level and my fists were balled up for a fight before I even got my feet under me good.

But Wayne was shaking so hard, laughing at his own joke, that I couldn't flail him the way I had a mind to, and in a minute I was laughing with him. Then the Cheyenne Kid joined in and we was all of us holding our bellies and laughing in spite of the hurt.

"You're sure as hell a rowdy bunch for people that's lookin' to get killed," Pap said. He was coming along the boardwalk, hitching at his belt, the scattergun tucked under his arm, looking pleased with hisself.

"Button up, Pap," Wayne said.

"By God, don't be tellin' your own Pa to shut up or I'll..."Then he looked down at his fly. "Oh, yeah." He grinned and commenced working at the buttons on his jeans. "Don't want to start no riots."

Before any of us could tell him to shut up, there was a yell from down the street and then the sound of running horses and a cloud of dust that almost hid the stagecoach they were dragging. Even though they were in town, the driver was still snapping the reins against the backs of the horses and it wasn't until he got to within a hundred feet of the station that he leaned back on the reins and put his foot on the brake.

The stage came to a dead stop right in front of the station, and even though it swayed on its thoroughbraces for another five minutes I had to admire the way the driver had done it. The cloud of dust that caught up with the coach and set us all to coughing was impressive.

When the shotgun messenger quit gagging, he yelled, "Damn you, Charley! One of these days you're gonna overshoot the whole damned town!"

Charley kind of snickered. "Well, I ain't done it yet."

They went on about it, back and forth, but I wasn't paying any more attention to them. A slim, bare arm had stuck itself out the window of the coach and was trying to find the door handle. I quick snatched off my hat and made my move, saying, "I'll get that door for you, Miss Velvet."

"Well, thanks, but my name ain't Velvet."

I got the door open and helped her down and before I could say a word Wayne yelled, "By God, it's Rose!"

And sure enough it was.

Well, I was some disappointed, especially when Wayne and Rose kind of wrapped themselves around one another and commenced to kissing and pawing and whatever, so I hadn't noticed the coach wasn't quite empty yet.

"I'm Velvet," a raspy voice said. "Who the hell's callin' my name?"

I looked back at the coach in time to see her crawling out. Her hat was mashed down over one eye, her bright red hair was kind of going off in all directions, and she was trying to spit out what dust she wasn't covered with. Worst of all, I could see she was plump more than somewhat and fairly old enough to be my Ma.

Pap took her by the hand and kissed her fingers, just the way he'd done to that Hopper woman, only Velvet's fingers had never spent any time working with lye soap. "Howdy, Velvet," he said.

She pushed her hat back on her head, skewing it in another direction and looking around wildly until her eyes came to rest on Pap. "Gerald Denton! Is that you under them whiskers?"

"The same," Pap said, grinning like a fool. "I'm surprised you know me after all these years."

"You might want to remember I gave you that scar over your eye." She had a laugh that was somewhere between a screech owl and a coyote. "And you might want to remember why!"

Pap was trying to look sheepish, but I could see the edges of his grin. "Aww, Velvet, I ain't that quick no more."

"Well, good." Her watery green eyes fell to a spot below Pap's waist and then she just fairly reached out and had herself a feel. "And you're still packin', I see. Come on over to the house, Gerald."

Now, if that didn't beat all, I didn't know what did. Wayne and Rose were walking down the boardwalk, arms around one another's waists, telling one another how sorry they both was and just turning in under a hanging sign that said "Hotel." And here was Pap, about to go off and dally with the woman I'd dreamed about over miles of hard trail. And here I was with the Cheyenne Kid, thinking about my lesson in arithmetic.

Somehow, I'd never put it together about how long Velvet had been gone from Waco, though the years on the cattle with her brand should have given me an idea. Nor had I thought about how old she might have been when she left, trustin' Pap's memory of her as a young woman. I guess with the difference in our ages, what looked young to Pap was a mite older to me.

Anyway, I found I was somewhat relieved to just tip my hat to her and watch her as she tugged at Pap's hand.

I will give Pap some credit, though. He didn't just go off with that Velvet woman like she wanted him to do. Not until he got out his pocket watch and checked it, then looked up to see where the sun was and nodded his head. "I got time," he told her.

"You'd better not short-change me again," Velvet said.

Then off they went, arm in arm, Pap carrying the carpetbag I'd dreamed I would carry.

"What we do now, Roy Lee?" the Cheyenne Kid said.

"Kid, I just don't know."

"We shoot gunslinger sumbeech."

"That'll happen soon enough," I said. I looked up at the sun. "And it might be you and me are the only ones standin' out in that street."

"Okay. We Texas hardcases."

"Hellbenders," I said, laughing in spite of myself. "Listen, Kid. Go back and get Rambler. Bring him up here and tie him to this rail."

"Rambler part of plan, Roy Lee?"

"He is now." I wasn't for sure what use I could make of him, except that I knew he'd go wherever the Kid went and it seemed important, especially now that I couldn't count on Wayne or Pap, that I somehow fill our ranks. And there was no doubt that, of the three of us, Rambler looked a lot more dangerous than me or the Kid.

I sat watching the shadow of the hitching rail move, watching the sun move in the sky. The Kid had brought Rambler back and brought him up on the boardwalk in the shade. Just when I got to thinking it was about time, I looked down Front Street and saw six men in black frock coats, and another wearing a tan saddle coat, lined up abreast and walking slowly toward us.

"It's time, Kid," I said. "You remember what I told you?"

"Somebody shoot, I run away, right?"

"Right. Are you going to do it?"

He grinned and shrugged, though the weight of that pistol belt on his shoulder took some of the height off his shrug.

"Dammit, Kid, you got to. You can't be fightin' man fights." I was some vexed at him but it wasn't his fault. It had been a better plan when I thought Wayne and Pap was going to be part of it. "If somebody even looks like they're going for a gun, you run off and hide."

I knew there wasn't nothing else to do but to meet the men who were gunning for Wayne and I guess deep down I thought they might take a look at me and the Kid, decide we weren't any match for their skills, and call the whole thing off.

"Hey, Roy Lee, I know. I get behind and shoot sumbeech gunslingers in back."

"That ain't the way Texans do it, Kid." I stood up and hitched at my gun belt, making sure the holster was in just the right place against my hip, and we moved out into the middle of the street, facing the men who wore black.

"Here come Pap," the Kid said.

I half turned and there he was, buttoning his jeans as he walked, his shirt gone so that his uppers was only covered by his faded red long johns. Behind him, Velvet came bustling along. As Pap got closer I noticed a fresh cut above his eye, but I didn't do more than raise an eyebrow and grin at him.

"It ain't what you think," Pap said, testy. "We got kind of frisky and fell off the bed. I hit my head on her chamber pot."

"Now, I'm glad to know that, Pap. Makes dyin' a whole lot more fun."

He took his place abreast of us and Velvet fell in alongside of him.

"Dammit, Velvet," Pap said. "This ain't your fight."

"The hell it ain't! After what you and them boys did for me?"

"It's just some money in the bank," Pap said. "And you might want to stay alive so you can spend it."

Velvet was checking the loads in her derringer two-shot. "You said your boy got into this defendin' my honor."

"Now, Velvet, he didn't know." Pap's tone was almost pleading. "He thought you had some to defend."

She shot him a mean look and right then I figured that if he lived long enough he'd already earned his next scar.

"Here come Goddam Wayne."

I turned the other way and sure enough, Wayne was buttoning his jeans and fixing to join up with us, whilst Rose was tugging at the shirttail that hung out of his pants. "Rose," I heard him say. "It's my fight. I can't quit on 'em."

"Then I'm fightin', too," she said. She took her place in line. "Who's got a gun I can borry?"

We all kind of looked at one another, shaking our heads 'cause there wasn't a spare gun to be had. "Sorry, Rose," I said. "Looks like you can't be in this fight."

"The hell I can't!" She drew a long pin out of her hat. "Nobody's gonna kill my Wayne without getting by me first."

"Now, Rose, that's a real sweet thing to say," Wayne said, grinning like a fool.

"Well, you just remember this, Wayne." She patted his arm and smiled up at him nice as you please. "As soon as they shoot you, you give me your gun. All right, honey?"

Wayne's grin went away and he looked about the color of the paste we used to eat in school. "I reckon I can remember that."

The gunslingers were close now, still lined abreast and about twenty paces away. I knew them all from yesterday and the way they lined up was that Doc Holliday was facing Wayne, Shanghai Pierce was facing Rose, Wyatt Earp was facing me, and Wild Bill was facing Rambler. On the other side of Rambler, Bat Masterson was facing the Cheyenne Kid,

Virgil Earp was facing Pap, and Dave Mather, who looked more sickly than mysterious, was facing Velvet.

"What the hell is going on here?" Wild Bill said. "Earp, is this your idea of a gunfight?"

"I take 'em the way I find 'em," Earp said. I thought he didn't sound too sure of hisself.

"Well, this ain't gonna do," Pierce said. "I ain't drawin' down on no woman armed with a hatpin."

Wild Bill looked disgusted. "Trade places with me, then. I don't care who I shoot." He grinned beneath his long handlebar mustache. "Hell, when it's all over they'll just be notches on our guns anyway."

"You still doing that?" Bat Masterson asked.

"Yeah, but I got to quit it, I guess. Ain't much left of the grips." When he moved to trade places with Pierce, both of them moving slow and keeping their eyes on us, Bill's coat flapped open enough that I could see the two Navy Colts stuck into a sash around his waist. He was right, the grips were pretty well used up.

Once he got into position across from Rose, he shot his cuffs to loosen them and said, "Everyone ready now?"

"Wait a minute," Bat said. He shifted his cane to his left hand and held up his right, so I relaxed a bit. "I'm gonna move my gun hand quick, but don't nobody draw. All right?"

On our side, we all said okay except for Velvet.

She said, "How you doin', Dave?"

Mather looked sheepish and kind of toed the dirt and mumbled, "I'm doin' all right, Miss Velvet."

"I guess you'll do well today, Dave." She was talking a lot louder than necessary, I thought. "The girls at the Velvet House say you get your gun off pretty quick."

Virgil Earp had a sudden coughing fit and I bet I'm the

only one ever saw Doc Holliday smile.

"Will you all quit that?" Bat said. "I'm serious. Now remember, nobody draws a gun." His right hand flashed down to his holster and then back up with his finger pointing like a pistol.

"That was real good, Bat," Wyatt said. "Can you do that with a gun?"

"Not today," Bat said. "That midget's just too short. My round would go right over his head."

"Christ Almighty," Hickok said. "You could just take time to lower your aim, Bat."

"Oh, sure." Masterson sounded right sassy. "And while I'm doing that he'd be shooting me right in the family jewels."

Hickok took a long look at the Cheyenne Kid. "Yes, he is short and his aim would be low."

"Virg, you're shorter than me. Trade places." Virgil Earp was shaking his head. "I'll let you carry the cane later on," Bat said.

Virgil brightened at that and him and Bat swapped places.

"Can I...can I trade places with someone?" Mather said.

"You can trade places with me," Pierce said. "I'd rather shoot a whore than a dumb animal."

So then him and Mather swapped places and I could see some of us on our side was getting bored with the whole thing.

"What they do?" the Kid said.

"Gunslingers always look for an edge, Kid, " I said.

"Dammit, that ain't true!" Earp yelled.

The other gunslingers all looked at him, but it was Doc Holliday that spoke. "Why, Wyatt, you've got to have an edge." He shook his head. "I don't know how you've stayed alive this long."

"Can I maybe not have to shoot that bull?" Dave Mather

said.

Hickok glared at him. "Now just who do you want to shoot, Dave? Go on, take your pick. We got something for everybody."

Mather kind of shifted his weight from one foot to the other and I thought it might have been a good idea for him to go to the outhouse before commencin' to get hisself in a gunfight. "Well..." He was looking up and down our line, probably trying to see where his edge was, but then he looked us over again and I knew he was having a hard time making a choice.

"What's a whore?" the Kid said.

"That's a word better nobody in this crowd ever use again," Rose said.

Hickok stepped toward us, out of line but holding his right hand up so no one would shoot him. With his other hand, he motioned for Mather to come over to him. Mather kind of dragged his feet, but he did get there and Hickok draped an arm over his shoulders kind of like my Pa used to do me just before he trapped me in a lie and whaled the tar out of me.

"Dave, did you ever shoot a man?" Hickok asked kindly.

"I ain't sayin'."

"You ever been in a gunfight, Dave?"

"I ain't sayin'."

"By God!" Bat said. "That's what's mysterious about him!"

I poked my elbow into Rambler's ribs and heard him snort, thinking that might cause some nervousness among them.

"Leave Dave alone," Hickok said. He patted Mather on the shoulder, and then gave him a kind of squeeze or maybe a fatherly hug. "Go on, Dave. Go on over to the saloon. This ain't your fight no more."

Mather wasn't quite through with us yet. He pointed at Wayne and said, "He called me a lying bastard."

Hickok's voice was still kindly. "Well, Dave, I think maybe he was right. Don't you agree?"

"Well..."

"Sure you do. You just go along now, Dave. We'll see you later and let you buy us some more drinks."

Mysterious Dave Mather hurried out of the line of fire and now the odds were looking a little bit better for us.

"Dammit, Bill," Wyatt said. "Now who's going to shoot the bull?"

"I think you're all shooting a lot of bull," Velvet yelled. "You fellers let us know when you're through with your dancin' around."

"I don't feel real good about this, Bill," Wyatt said. "Ever since that boy mentioned it, I've been looking for an edge and can't seem to find one."

I poked Rambler again and now he snorted and pawed at the ground.

"I don't feel good about it either," Virgil Earp said. "I ain't short enough to shoot no midget."

"You're plenty short, Virg," Velvet called.

Virgil turned red in a second and appealed to Hickok. "Do I have to take that kind of talk from her?"

"Christ Almighty!" The way he looked, Hickok was about ready to throw his hat at the ground.

"Trade places with me, then," Doc Holliday said. "I haven't shot any midgets yet."

Him and Virgil Earp changed places in line.

Now Virg was facing Rose. "She ain't armed with nothin' but a hatpin," Virgil said, kind of snickering.

"That's your edge," Earp told him. "But I still haven't

found mine."

Some little bit of a plan had come to me and I put my hands up shoulder high. "I'm makin' a move. Don't nobody shoot."

"Now, that ain't fair, Bill," Bat said. "Just when we get ourselves about lined out, they go to tradin' places on us."

I moved over to the end of the line, where Rose was facing off against Virgil Earp, sticking her tongue out at him now and then. "I'm drawing my pistol," I called. "But don't nobody shoot."

"Watch him, boys," Hickok said. He sounded like he was tired.

With two fingers, I eased my pistol out of my holster and gave it to Rose.

"Why, Roy Lee, you are the sweetest thing. And here I been thinkin' you didn't like me any more."

Wayne raised an eyebrow at that, but didn't say anything.

"Give me the hatpin, Rose."

I took the pin, seeing how her green eyes were puzzled, and slowly walked back to my place in line.

Virgil Earp didn't seem to feel too good about what had happened. "Now she's got a gun and the cowboy's got the hatpin," he said.

Wyatt Earp smirked. "There's my edge."

"Dammit, Wyatt, that was supposed to be my edge!"

I didn't wait for any more. I stuck that hatpin into Rambler just about where that V was branded on him. He was already upset about my poking him in the ribs and when that hatpin went all the way in he bellered and charged straight ahead, that one horn sticking out in front of him and looking like the most dangerous weapon in the world.

Men in black frock coats were running every which way,

but old Rambler could turn like a cutting horse when he saw the next one he wanted. One time he turned and was wearing most of a frock coat on his horn while Virgil Earp was running away with the rest of his coat flapping and looking like he had a white streak up his back.

Bill Hickok and Shanghai Pierce were jawing about who was going to be first to climb the tree and the argument wasn't settled until Bill whipped out a Navy Colt and pointed it at Shanghai's nose.

We was all laughing fit to kill until I saw Doc Holliday standing his ground and drawing a bead on a place that looked to be right between Rambler's eyes. I quick grabbed the Kid's revolver and flung it at Holliday, trying to throw off his aim, but it was too late. His gun roared, black powder smoke filled the air and got carried away on the wind, and old Rambler was still coming at him.

Doc hadn't lived as long as he did without being smart. He sidestepped real pretty and the next thing I knew he was in our ranks, standing right beside me.

His mustache kind of twitched and he said, "You're the one threw the gun at me."

"I am."

He grinned. "I guess down in Texas they call that a gunfight."

I grinned right back. "There is a tradition."

He shook his head. "Sticking a pin in that bull was smart. We'd probably have killed you all and made fools of ourselves doing it."

"I don't know that it's over, Mr. Holliday. There might be grudges held."

"If any of those idiots give you trouble about this, you send them to me."

Masterson had got the tree between him and Rambler and was flailing out with his walking stick.

"Well, all this is too many for me." Holliday put his pistol in his holster and held out his hand to me. I took it and later I would entertain a lot of people when I told that story and told how soft his hand was. "You boys seem to have won, for whatever it's worth to you."

I looked around at the others, all of them doubled over laughing while they watched Rambler. He'd lost interest in Masterson and was chasing Wyatt down Front Street.

"It was worth it," I said. "None of us had much else to do today."

"I see. Well, I believe I'll stay indoors for a while. I'd appreciate it if you boys would keep that bull outdoors."

"I think we can. He don't seem to be finished with Wyatt yet."

Holliday started away, and then turned back. "What about this short fellow? Is he really a midget?"

Not wanting to give away any secrets, I shrugged. "To us, he's just the Cheyenne Kid."

Holliday put out his hand to the Kid. "You're the first man I ever knew to throw a good scare into Bat Masterson," he said. Then he jerked a thumb toward where a big crowd I'd not noticed before stood on the boardwalk. "Likely there'll be some talk about it, and a lot of people wanting to buy you drinks."

"Kid like whiskey."

***

Some of us went back to Texas and some didn't.

Pap stayed on in Dodge City and became Velvet's fancy man. She bought him a nice suit of clothes and when my Uncle Earl came back from his drive up the trail, he told how

Pap was dressed all fine and shaved clean as a whistle. He'd learned to play the piano somewhat and most nights would be playing it in Velvet's parlor, entertaining the girls. I think he may have took entertaining the girls a mite too serious 'cause Uncle Earl said Pap had a few new scars on his head.

Pap was the one who wrote and told us he'd heard Harvey and Maggie were working for a restaurant in Kansas City.

Rose followed Wayne back to Texas and they set up housekeeping on the farm that Wayne and Pap used to run. It didn't last long, though. Rose got religion and was forever going off to church and all-day camp meetings and sociables and such, talking about what fine sermons Brother Wheeler preached. Wayne finally put his foot down about it and the next news we knew, Rose had run off with the preacher and they was said to be in the Fort Worth jail, where they'd tried to play the badger game on a shirt salesman from St. Louis. It was the preacher's wife told us this, so we had no reason to doubt it.

Me and the Cheyenne Kid took up ranching, living in the big house Velvet had deeded to us, and I got the Kid into the Waco school that Jessie Meacham taught. That didn't last long, either. About the fourth time he raised his hand and asked what a whore was, Jessie came to me and said she really didn't think the Kid was adding anything to her classroom and it might be better if he stayed home and learned about ranching.

The Kid was just doing what I'd told him to do, so I didn't punish him. It was all part of my plan.

When Jessie brought him home, I took the position that he couldn't learn to be a rancher if he couldn't do his sums, so she offered to come over and tutor him on weekends. I made sure the Kid didn't learn any too fast because I wanted time to talk to Jessie and let her know about my new situation. So it wasn't long before I was courting her again. Her Pap went stomping around for a long time with his mouth clamped shut, but he never said anything to either of us until I took him aside and told him I hadn't bought the ranch. When he knew he didn't have to sup with the hogs, he warmed to me.

Rambler came back to Texas with us, of course, and we left a lot of the ranching to him. He'd go out in the brush country and be gone for days at a time, and then he'd come back with twenty or thirty more head of cattle to add to our herd.

That shot Doc Holliday had taken at him didn't do nothing but take out a chunk of his horn about the size of a dollar. I figured it probably gave Rambler a headache, too, the reason he didn't show much patience with them fellers in the black frock coats.

Wayne and me was partners in the herd Rambler was building for us, and when we couldn't agree on whether to use the Rocking D or the Flying M, we settled on just going ahead with using the Velvet brand. Now and then, I'd remind Wayne about the Upside-Down-A-Without-a-Crossbar brand, but I only did it when I wanted to see his hat hit the floor.

One more thing. Rambler did catch up with Wyatt Earp that time in Dodge City, but that's a story Wyatt bid me not to tell.

THE END

Meet the Author:

 A native of Missouri, Mr. Bobo's love of the West began when he was stationed at Ft. Carson, Colorado. Since that time, he has written extensively about the Old West--as well as writing numerous articles on computers and serving as Associate Editor for both Computer Shopper and Computer Monthly magazines. THE VELVET BRAND is not only his first western novel but the first in a series about a group of rowdy frontiersmen--and lusty women--who come to be called the Hellbenders.

Available now

from

Echelon Press Publishing

Redemption

By

Morgan J. Blake

Chapter One

Superstition Mountains, Arizona Territory–late spring, 1873

"Kinson, you don't want to go up there," Lieutenant Sam Skinner called as he hurried after him.

Wylie Kinson barged up the trail, approaching one of Skinner's young underlings who stood in the narrowest part of the path. With trembling hands, the kid attempted to roll a cigarette. Wylie slowed as he drew near, tipping his rifle's barrel up just a little.

"Move," Wylie barked.

The kid's head snapped up, his eyes wide. When he didn't respond, Wylie stopped directly in front of him. The young private stared at him for a second, then glanced at Skinner.

"Don't you look at him. Look at me. I'm the one orderin' you right now." There was no kindness in Wylie's voice.

"Kinson, don't start with him," Skinner said.

Damn you, Skinner…don't you start with me. *Wylie didn't turn, but stepped even closer to the kid before him, bumping the private in the chest with the rifle. The kid backed up a step, then another, much like an animal ready to turn tail and run.*

"It's alright, Portney. Let him through," Skinner said. At his quiet, disarming words, Portney stepped off the path.

Wylie again hurried on, leaving Skinner to tell the young man to find some shade and rest. He then charged after Wylie.

"Kinson, that was uncalled for."

The officer's words barely registered in Wylie's mind, so intent was he on reaching the outcropping of boulders on the hill above them. Trained as a scout, he normally took great care to notice every detail. Now he walked forward, oblivious to everything around him.

One of the settlers had told Wylie the news that morning when he reached the village. At first, he'd been numb. The farther he rode trying to find the soldiers, the more the numbness gave way to rage. Only now, as he walked toward the hill, did he feel the intense ache, and that only served to anger him more. *Why'd you let this happen, God? Huh?*

Wylie felt neither the warmth from the glaring sun nor the occasional breeze, and was only vaguely aware of the trickle of sweat snaking its way between his shoulder blades. Still, he looked past the boot tracks on the desert floor as if there was nothing there.

Wylie slowed his pace when he reached the foot of the hill and looked up at the cactus-speckled boulders. He studied the steep slope ahead of him, squinting against the day's brightness. Skinner now stood beside him, his jaws flapping like a busted gate in a gale wind, but Wylie paid no heed to the officer. Checking the time by the sun's position, he finally turned back to the hill. He closed his eyes.

I don't want to do this. Shifting his feet on the rocky terrain, he opened his eyes again to squint at the place they'd pointed to moments before. He cursed himself silently with a frustrated shake of his head. *Do it and get it over with. You know you'll never forgive yerself if you stay below and let someone else tend to this business. Ya got enough regrets without adding this one to the list.*

Shifting his rifle between hands, Wylie dried one palm, then the other, on his pant legs. With that, he started forward again.

"Kinson, would you stop?" Skinner called in frustration as he again hurried after Wylie.

Ignoring the officer, Wylie walked ahead a few steps before a new sound stopped him. To the right of the path, a good twenty feet out in a small, bare patch among the ocotillo, cholla, and saguaros, he heard the other soldiers' laughter mingled with the sound of shovels biting into the parched desert floor. The laughter started out hesitantly, with one soldier chuckling at some not-so-funny comment to break the tension, the others following suit.

Wylie watched them with a cold expression. How many times had it been him standing there, laughing like a fool? He glanced at the rocky earth between his boots, noticing a dark stain near the edge of the path. As he bent over and touched his fingers to it, he glared again at the bunch of them. Their banter continued, every one of them oblivious to his stare.

His anger exploding, he jacked a shell into the chamber of his rifle, took aim at the ground between the feet of the nearest man, and fired. The gun bucked hard against his shoulder, the concussion echoing against the rocks.

The bullet hit the edge of the hole they were digging, knocking a chunk of the soil loose, and collapsing the ground under the soldier's foot. With a surprised yelp, he started to fall but caught himself. The others looked up, startled, and quickly ducked out of the way. A couple of them even jumped into the shallow hole they'd dug. Two men below scrambled for their rifles, just out of reach. Wylie covered one of the men.

"Next one of you who think this is funny is likely to wind up with an extra hole in his…"

Skinner dashed in front of Kinson, arms up as he hollered out for all to hear.

"Stop this! Now!"

The soldiers below stared up at the two of them, a mix of expressions on their faces. Seething, Wylie glared down at them, his rifle still poised at his shoulder.

Skinner turned on him. "Put the gun away, Kinson. Are you trying to get yourself killed?" he stormed.

His commanding voice lent an air of importance and control to his demeanor. Again, he swung around to face his soldiers.

"Get back to work now."

Like shamefaced children scolded by an angry father, the soldiers set to work without the banter, squirming under Wylie's attention.

Satisfied they would no longer make light of the situation, Wylie lowered the gun and shifted his attention to the stained ground. He couldn't be sure, but it was an easy guess to assume the spot was dried blood. Wylie studied it for only an instant before he started to move again, heading toward the hill. As he reached the base, Skinner hurried around in front of him.

"Kinson, stop," the officer commanded, placing a restraining hand on Wylie's shoulder.

Wylie bristled. He turned on Skinner and brushed his hand away before he stepped around the officer.

"I'll thank you to stay out of my way," he growled.

"Wylie–!" Skinner grabbed his arm.

Wylie stiffened at the contact, then turned to face the lieutenant.

"Who do you think you are, Skinner? Damn you, that's my

mother up there!"

His voice softened when he spoke again. "Kinson, let someone else handle it. You don't want to see her like this."

Wylie prepared to pounce. "What if it was Jaylene up there?" Wylie challenged. "Wouldn't you want to see your *wife*?"

After a moment's hesitation, Skinner responded in a quiet voice.

"I know you're still angry, Kinson...."

"You're damn right I'm angry," Wylie interrupted, taking a step closer to Skinner until he towered over the shorter man. "You cost me the woman I love."

Skinner took a slow step backwards and answered in a gentle tone. "No, friend, you lost her yourself."

Wylie glared at Skinner, wanting very much to plant his fist into that innocent face of his, but the truth of Skinner's statement kept him from it. His own stupidity *had* lost him Jaylene, and getting into a fight with her husband wouldn't change that fact. Besides, there were other, more important things to tend to.

"One thing we're not and never will be is *friends*. Now get out of my way."

Wylie's demeanor dared Skinner to challenge him, but when Skinner didn't move, Wylie shifted his rifle in his hands and started up the slope.

The sound of the shovels slowed, then stopped behind him as he climbed up the rocky steepness. Instinct told him that every man in the camp was watching him. *Is this how it's gotta be, God? Every man down there watchin' what oughta be a private matter? Well, to hell with all of 'em.* He squared his shoulders and continued forward. Yet for all his brash thoughts, he still wished they would mind their own business.

He studied the ground, finding a drop of blood here, a partial boot print a little farther onward. Continuing up the steep hill, he saw a bloody handprint, far too small to belong to a man. He hesitated there, kneeling near the print so he could study it in detail. Wylie touched the stained earth, covering the bloody handprint with his own larger hand. The earth was hot under his touch, so hot he wanted to draw his hand away. He didn't move.

Experience the thrill of
Echelon Press

The Plot
ISBN 1-59080-203-9

Kathleen Lamarche
$13.49

Pattern of Violence
ISBN 1-59080-278-0

C. Hyytinen
$14.99

Missing!
ISBN 1-59080-204-7

Judith R. Parker
$12.99

The Rosary Bride
ISBN 1-59080-227-6

Luisa Buehler
$11.99

Unbinding the Stone
ISBN 1-59080-140-7

Marc Vun Kannon
$14.99

Redemption
ISBN 1-59080-389-0

Morgan J. Blake
$15.99

Crossing the Meadow
ISBN 1-59080-283-7

Kfir Luzzatto
$11.99

Justice Incarnate
ISBN 1-59080-386-8

Regan Black
$13.99

Drums Along the Jacks Fork
ISBN 1-59080-308-6

Henry Hoffman
$11.99

The Last Operation
ISBN 1-59080-163-6

Patrick Astre
$13.49

To order visit
www.echelonpress.com
Or visit your local
Retail bookseller

Printed in the United States
38763LVS00001B/65